The Cutter's Widow

Mary DesJarlais

CALUMET EDITIONS

Minneapolis | London | Nuremberg

CALUMET EDITIONS

Minneapolis | London | Nuremberg

SECOND EDITION 2022
THE CUTTER'S WIDOW. Copyright © 2018 by Mary DesJarlais.
All rights reserved.

This is a work of fiction. All of the characters, names, incidents, organizations, and dialogue are either the products of the author's imagination or are used fictiously.

10 9 8 7 6 5 4 3 2

ISBN: 978-1-959770-57-2

Book design by Gary Lindberg
Cover photo by Mary DesJarlais

Praise for *Dorie LaValle*

DesJarlais…gives her readers a seamless blend of murder, thrills, passion and friendship in a small town, with a pitch-perfect sense of time and place.

An implicit theme of the book is that if people associate the Roaring '20s with flappers and jazz clubs, many women led far less glamorous lives. A friend tells Dorie: "The men in my life never looked at me as something of value. They only saw me as something pretty to touch.

LOVE LOVE LOVE this new writer. Genealogical fiction is a new trend and Mary did a great job. Taking a person in her family history and making up a story surrounding them was genius but the writing and word usage was like having your cake and eating it to. I can't wait to hear more from this writer.

DesJarlais pushes the reader to decide--is Dorie a victim with the intelligence to survive or is she better suited for the Mafia?

I expected to like this book, I didn't expect to LOVE it. The author… kept me turning the pages far into the night.

… took off right from the start. It had everything, mystery, love, heartache and action. I would recommend this book for both women and men. There is a lot of true history…as well.

I simply could not put it down the first time I opened it. Highly recommended.

I couldn't put it down. How difficult to be a woman in the early 20th century when needing to take care of herself and her business were necessary. I would recommend this book to all readers.

Lucille B, Amazon reader

A great first book!

RE Krause, Amazon reader

Great character development, interesting story line, and well told.

Anonymous review

I could not put this book down. My dad was visiting while I was reading it and he picked it up and read it the whole visit. He went home and bought his own copy so he could finish it.

M. Bearce, Amazon review

The characters are compelling and the story unfolds in an almost organic way, much like life.

Jessica Looman, Amazon review

Each chapter is filled with surprise. History, passion, mobsters, forgiveness, morals and a dose of religious references.

Lynn, Amazon review

For my daughters, Grace and Claire

"I wish you to know that you have been the last dream of my soul."

~Charles Dickens, *A Tale of Two Cities*

Also by Mary DesJarlais

Dorie LaValle

The Cutter's Widow

Mary DesJarlais

Chapter 1

Sleet pelted the windows, sounding like the skittering of animal claws on the glass. As the March storm raged on, the world became smaller and lost all color, surrounding Ella in shades of gray and white. Ella shivered, wishing for the warmth of a blazing fire to ease the chill in her bones. She measured time by matching the accumulation of snowflakes that blew into their bedroom through the cracks in the walls to the cadence of her dying husband's breath.

Ella leaned closer to Connor's face, adjusted the cloth on his forehead and spooned a few drops of water between his cracked lips. This was the extent of her nursing care. "He belongs to God now," Dr. Carr had said days earlier. "His blood was poisoned from that dirty knife." He glowered at her as he shook his fist, but she knew his anger was directed against Seeger's Shirtwaist Factory, not her. Connor looked so much older than his twenty-four years. It was as if the dying process made an old man of him before it snatched his last breath.

He was quiet now. The fever-dreams had stopped. Days ago, Connor had shouted out orders about the factory and cursed Aldo, the floor boss. She took Connor by the shoulders, called his name, but he continued to wave his arms. Too bad he would not draw a wage for his dream work. Now, his left hand, swaddled in linen bandages, sticky with pus, remained motionless across his chest. The room smelled putrid and earthy.

Ella moved his hand and unbuttoned his nightshirt to see his chest and shoulders peppered with red dots. She pressed her palm along the familiar curve of his torso, finding the place she had loved to hold each night as they drifted to sleep. Now her fingers could fit between his ribs. She imagined death was more than just his spirit leaving this earth… it involved him dissolving so that one morning, after the snow stopped and the sun appeared to warm the March days, all that would remain was a slight depression in the pillow.

Ella pulled the shawl around her shoulders and rocked. Two weeks ago, in this bed, they had snuggled under heaps of blankets when the winter sky still held the blue-black of night as the remaining embers glowed in the stove. Connor's kisses started just behind her ear, ran along her jaw, down her neck. His beard scratched in a way that both tickled and stung. She ran her fingers along the curve of his cold ears, a contrast to the heat under the covers.

"You have always been my love." This was the thing he said to her each day. His hands slid to her waist, and her fingers grazed the cold metal headboard as he pulled her down deeper into the center of the bed. As he eased himself between her legs, he clutched a handful of her hair and murmured something she couldn't hear.

Ella wiped tears with her palm as the storm grew stronger. The windows rattled, and snowflakes blew onto the quilt. She wadded more newspaper strips, stuffing the gaps between the boards against the determined wind. She startled and turned to see Connor's mouth opened wide as if he intended to scream, but instead he began to gasp, his blue-tinged lips pulled tight across his teeth.

"Da?" he called. Ella turned, half expecting to see Connor's dead father.

She scratched the frosted window and peered through the hole into the white world. All she could see was a lantern glowing and a dark figure pressing forward through the drifts. The streets had lost their distinction to the growing snowdrifts. Ella turned back to Connor and watched him work so hard to pull each breath. She tugged the quilt high over his shoulders and tucked the edges around his body as if he were a small child. The blankets made his form appear indistinct like the world buried under the snow. His breath rattled, wet reedy noises as if he were drowning in the middle of the bed.

The Cutter's Widow

Should she move him to ease his breathing? His stare fixed at the end of the bed, perhaps to see angels, or his Da who died on a shipping boat, or his Ma who perished giving birth. She hoped they were all holding out their hands, clapping him on the back and covering his face with sloppy kisses. Her heart dropped to think that Father McKenna would not be able to brave the storm to perform the holy sacrament of extreme unction to prepare Connor's soul for the next world. Could a blizzard keep a person from entering heaven?

Now his breath came faster. "Connor?" she called out to him, her voice grainy and thin. She realized she hadn't uttered a word aloud for days. She wanted him to say goodbye to her, whisper some last words of love, but he was beyond that now. Each gasp pulled him farther away. She opened the drawer of the table next to the bed. Her fingers found the vial of holy water. She eased out the cork, tipping the neck of the bottle to her finger. She caressed his eyelids and forehead, and said, "Through this holy unction, may the Lord pardon thee whatever sin or faults thou hast committed." She cupped his clammy cheeks. The wind moaned again, the pitch rising, cresting and falling away.

Connor sighed heavily, then remained quiet.

Ella blinked her gritty eyes; her arms and legs felt like sacks of flour. She curled up next to him in their bed that reeked of sweat and the iron smell of old blood, and for the last time cupped her hand around the camber of his ribs, holding him there until the last warmth was gone from his body.

She was eighteen years old and had been married for seven months.

* * *

Connor was only twenty-two years old when he was hired at Seeger's Shirtwaist Factory—the youngest cutter on the crew. He was strong and agile, two traits that helped him secure that coveted position. The older workers accepted him after he demonstrated his skills and bought them pints at O'Toole's after their shifts. If Ella was careful, she could tilt her head in such a way to avoid detection from Aldo and watch Connor from her place on the sewing line. He would position a stack of fabric, often twenty-four layers deep, arranging the pattern pieces to avoid waste, and then wield the sharp knife to follow each curve. He prided himself on both skill and accuracy. He could cut pieces faster than the runners could get them to the machines. In order to dispel boredom, he began to do tricks with the knives, throwing them in the air, spinning around fast enough to catch them before they fell. Of course, this was when Aldo was out for the afternoon selling finished shirts to the shops. She knew Connor was bored even though he admitted the cutting job was far better than the work at the glass factory where he suffered from terrible headaches and burns from the ovens.

He prided himself on the condition of his knives. On the nights when he was nearly too tired to eat, he would spread out a cloth on the kitchen table and squint in the yellow light as he pulled the blades across the whetstone. The rasp of steel against stone was a comfort to Ella as she washed dishes or mended clothes.

They had walked home the night of the accident as they always did, just short of an hour's trek if they moved efficiently. It was after the last light of day, and the glass lamps glowed over the dirty ice. Usually Connor was full of jokes and stories of the day or some stunt they had pulled over Aldo. That night he was more than subdued; the hard clench of his jaw matched his stride. He walked quickly, hands jammed deep into his pockets, so that Ella had to increase her pace to keep up in her thin-soled boots. Had she done something to make him mad? As they passed Schueman's Department Store, her foot slid on a patch of ice, and she fell to her knees on the sidewalk. He turned when he heard her cry out, ran back to her and reached to help her up. In his touch she knew he wasn't angry, but the look on his face upset her more. It was the first time she had seen fear in his eyes.

The last leg of their trek took them across the Wabasha Bridge, the iron link that spanned the Mississippi River, connecting downtown Saint Paul to their lowlands neighborhood. The winds gusted as they walked, feeling like a dangerous shove. Ella was relieved to see the lights in the little rows of houses in their West Side Flats neighborhood that guided them to their door. Ella burst into the kitchen, relieved to be in the place that always felt safe. She was comforted by the simplicity of the two wooden chairs next to the table, the glasses and plates on the shelf, the whittled pegs that held their clothes. She loved the stoutness of the stove and the curtain fashioned from a tablecloth that served as a door to their bedroom. The chair creaked as Connor sat down and leaned his head on the table. Ella lit the kerosene lamp and unbuttoned his coat.

"What is it? What's wrong?" The fear was a live thing thrashing about in her chest.

He pulled his right hand out of his pocket. It was swaddled, fat and clumsy in linen remnants from the cutting floor. The make-shift bandage was soaked with blood. The muscles in Ella's legs felt hot and loose.

"I cut myself. I dunno how it happened. I've never had so much as a nick. Never a drop of blood on the pattern cuts." He stared at the clump as if it didn't belong to him.

"I should heat some water." She moved to the stove and lit a match with shaking fingers.

Ella went to work with her sewing scissors, clipping the knots at his wrist. She imagined him sneaking to a quiet place, ministering to himself, tying the knots with his teeth. Shivering, she picked apart the strips, which were sticky with congealed blood.

Connor ran his good hand through his hair. "I jumped back, Ella. I pulled my hand back so's not to ruin the linen. I stuffed my hand in my apron when I smelled Aldo's cigar. You know what he said to me?" Connor grimaced. "Pale as a Swede's ass, you are," Connor said, mimicking Aldo's accent. "'If I hear one cough from you, I'll toss you out on the streets before you spread any more tuberculosis to the girls.' He waved his cigar at me. The nerve of that bastard to say that to me, his best cutter!" Connor snarled, but Ella heard something broken in his voice. She couldn't look him in the eye, so she concentrated on her task.

"I said a prayer to the Blessed Virgin to get me through to the end of day, I did."

Ella teased up each section of the make-shift bandages with the tip of her scissors.

"Whiskey?" Connor blotted his upper lip on his cuff.

Should they call Dr. Carr, she wondered? How would they pay him? Maybe the cut was not so bad. He had finished the shift after all, walked home. He was just pale, hungry. Maybe he was embarrassed to suffer a gash like all the other cutters routinely experienced. When Ella retrieved the bottle and he grabbed the neck and took a long pull, a dribble of whiskey ran along his jaw like a tear.

Connor sniffed and extended his hand again.

"Are ya in pain?" she asked. She wanted to put her arms around him, press into his chest and find that place where her chin fit against his collarbone.

"Throbs some. You're as white as bride's dress, love."

Ella took a deep breath and began to unwind the last of the linen. Something roiled in her stomach, and she clenched her teeth. Impatient with her stalling, he pulled at the soggy mess.

"No, wait. I'll do it." He would think her weak and witless if she fainted dead-away. She finished unwinding the wrap, and the first thing she saw was the thin gold band—his Da's wedding ring handed down to Connor. As she clipped the last cinched strip, they both watched as the finger tipped to one side like a cut sapling.

"Ella love, you have to sew it back on for me," Conner croaked and guzzled more drink.

"Sew it? Me?"

"Who had the finest stiches in County Meath?"

And so, she proceeded to mend his finger as best she could. Connor growled at the first bite of the needle through skin. The white thread turned red, and the sweat-stained circle grew larger across Connor's back.

When Ella finished, she rinsed the wound and wrapped it in clean linen. Connor drank whiskey until he emitted a chain of ragged snores. Ella lay next to him and stared at the wrapped hand until sleep finally claimed her.

She would always wonder where his mind was when the accident happened. Was he picturing sprinting to a win in a street race, or was he thinking about their last Sunday morning when he nibbled kisses down the length of her spine?

He never did tell her.

She never asked.

Chapter 2

Sunlight blazed through the bedroom window, creating a golden rectangle on the pine floor that stretched toward the bed. Ella's fingers were numb, her mouth dry. When she moved, she remembered Connor's body next to her. She watched each frosty breath trail away.

Someone banged on the door. "*Kotku,* it's Beata." The door rattled with each hearty knock. Her neighbor, Mrs. Pavlak, called Ella by this name, the Polish word for cat, saying Ella's tawny hair reminded her of her favorite tom.

"I shoveled a path to your door. I'm to check on the both of you."

Ella sat up, turning to look at Connor's waxy-white skin. His eyes were opened and clouded. Ella tugged at his arms, but they were stiff as if trying to hide something from her.

"*Kotku,* answer me!" There was more banging on the door.

Ella wanted to cover Connor with blankets, her body, anything to warm him. She stood, legs shaking, and made her way to the door, the quilt trailing along the floor. As she yanked the knob, Mrs. Pavlak pitched forward into the room, and a spray of snow dusted the rug and floor.

Beata's horrified expression told Ella how she must look. She pushed away the red-tangle of curls that hung in front of her eyes, but couldn't hold back tears.

"What happened? It's so cold in here!" Beata's crispy gray hair sprang from under a black wool hat. Her brows furrowed, and her brown eyes followed Ella's helpless shrugging.

"Connor died," Ella croaked.

Crossing herself, Beata lumbered through the front room and pushed aside the curtain to the bedroom. The edges of her shawl were adorned with baubles of ice that clicked together.

"The fevers got worse?" She leaned over Connor's body and grasped his curled fist with her chapped hand. "You have been with him this way for some time now, heh?"

Beata dug into her pocket, found two quarters, and, after pulling Connor's eyelids closed, placed them in his eye sockets. Ella knew enough of Beata's superstitions to understand that the old woman sought to prevent a dead man's stare from cursing the lives of the living.

Ella's nose ran, and she couldn't think of where a handkerchief might be. Even then her arms were too leaden to move. Before Beata pulled the blankets over Connor's head, she touched his brow.

"Here, *kotku*, touch his face, here. This will prevent you from dreaming of him."

Ella stumbled backward, tripping over the quilt. She wanted to dream about him, to close her eyes and feel his arms around her, his fingertips pressed into the small of her back.

"This is not good. We must get you out of here now. Come with me. For warmth, for food." Beata gathered Ella into her arms, and she collapsed against the cushion of breasts into her warm, smoky neck. She felt herself sway, a dance with no music.

"I don't know what to do." Her tears wet Beata's cheek.

"First you eat. I feed you *bigos*. It's not good to do thinking now." Beata tapped her finger against her temple.

Was she hungry? As the first snowflakes had begun to fall, she had dipped some stale bread in milk with sliced potatoes. That was her last meal. The storm, Connor's dying, all these things pressed on her chest making it hard to breathe.

"Go." Beata pushed Ella's arm into a coat, dressing her like one would a child. "Wait, did you open the window when...?" She cocked her head in the direction of the bed.

"It was so cold, I didn't."

"I'll do it now." Beata pounded the heel of her hand against the frame to pry open the window. A frigid breeze shuddered the curtains. Beata looked over her shoulder at Ella. "I think there is still time to let his spirit out."

Ella remembered her first days in the house with Connor. Oh, the first Sunday after they were married, she had stood in this same spot by the window watching her new husband sleep. In the August heat, the sheets had ended up damp and twisted at the foot of the bed, and she thrilled to observe him without censor, the longest glimpse she had ever had of a naked man. Connor slept on his back, head turned in profile. His muscular arms were thrown over his head. One leg dangled off the side of the bed, and his foot touched the floor. Nestled in the delicate cloud of reddish-brown curls lay his sleeping cock, slumped as if exhausted from its activities. Ella had giggled at that thought and put her hand over her lips to stifle the noise. Connor awoke at the sound, those green eyes so like the color of the sky just before a thunderstorm, and he gave her a sly look as he extended his hand.

Beata tugged Ella's sleeve, and the memory bled away.

* * *

The path narrowed and curved through the snow banks as if someone drunk or blind had shoveled it. Ella trudged behind Beata, who rested the shovel over her shoulder. The snow had stopped falling sometime in the night, and howling winds sculpted drifts and rolling curves of glazed icing over the streets. Flat clouds nudged each other against a sky so blue it hurt Ella's eyes, but the air, sharp and clean, was a welcome contrast to the sick smells of her house.

Beata had lived for many years in the biggest house in the West Side Flats, a block from State Street on the south side of the Mississippi River. It was a two-story brown stucco with green shutters. She had moved to the neighborhood as a young bride with her husband Nicodem, and there they had raised three sons and two daughters.

Beata was forthright with all of their stories, even those that made Ella blush. When Nicodem had given her syphilis, she had banished him to live in the cellar for the next seven years. He stayed down there

9

until he died of a weak heart at the age of fifty. "What else could be done with him?" Beata spat. "I didn't want him in my bed. I left him a tray of food. I washed his clothes. He got off easy, if you ask me."

Beata steered Ella into her parlor, fussing over the removal of her coat and mittens before she tucked Ella under a blanket next to the fireplace. The house always smelled of cabbage and onions. Ella closed her eyes for a moment, and when Beata returned from the kitchen, holding a steaming bowl of *bigos*, Ella's mouth watered, and the warmth of the bowl as she received it into her cold hands brought tears to her eyes.

"Here." Beata set a crystal-cut glass of red wine on the table. "It will warm you from the inside out." She stood expectantly in front of Ella, hands on her full-skirted hips, a stained towel flung over her shoulder. At some point after his death, Beata had taken to wearing her husband's rough wool vests with the buttons pulled tight across her bosom. She tucked little things into the pockets... coins, stones, a rosary, candy.

In contrast to Ella's spartan living quarters, Beata's house was stuffed with furniture, chairs, ottomans, side tables and settees. Each piece fought for space with her visiting children who filled the room so that if someone got up to get more drink there would be a great commotion of shuffling bodies and chairs. The heavy drapes kept out the drafts but trapped in the odors of food and tobacco. Ella stared into the flames that hissed and spat in the fireplace like an angry cat.

A pot of simmering *bigos* was one of Connor's favorite meals. He would lick his lips at the mention of the hunter's stew, the broth thick with cabbage, tomatoes and sausage. Ella brought a spoonful to her mouth, and the peppery flavor danced on her tongue. Her vision blurred with grainy tears of fatigue.

The warmth of the fire, the food, the blanket over her legs, made Ella feel heavy and thick. She took a big gulp of wine and sputtered, but then she took another careful sip and began to enjoy the way her tongue curled around the flavors. Beata pulled up a footstool, squatted down and peered into Ella's eyes.

"Better? Another bowl?" Beata's square hand covered Ella's.

Ella looked down, surprised to see she had emptied the bowl. Was she full? It was impossible to tell how her body was feeling.

"Thank you. You have always been so kind to me," she said, remembering the first weekend of their marriage when Beata had arrived at their door wearing her now familiar brown shawl, despite the stifling August heat. She carried a plate of *masurek* in one hand and a batch of daisies in the other. Beata, a perfect stranger, had hugged and kissed them lovingly, as if she were their mother.

"So, can you tell me what happened? Yeegawds, he went fast."

"Connor had fevers. The poison in his blood, it did things to his mind." Was it as fast as Beata claimed? It seemed like forever. Ella shrugged her confusion.

Beata pulled a crumpled handkerchief from her sleeve and wiped her nose. "If I had known, I would have come."

"I should have prayed harder for him. Maybe if I'd said the rosary? He had no priest." Ella burped and covered her mouth. She remembered Beata's attempt to let his soul out of the front room window. Was it floating along the ceiling, wondering where she had gone? Hot tears spilled over her cheeks, and she took another gulp of wine.

Beata took the empty bowl from Ella's lap and studied it, ran her finger over a chip on the lip. "He was a good man, yes? Sweet to you. A hard worker?"

Ella nodded, her lip trembling as she remembered his tender ways. "'The first of everything and the last of everything is always for you,' he would whisper, whether he was talking about kisses, a bite of a shared sweet or a pint of beer."

"Then I say, his suffering and his goodness got him into heaven." Beata nodded and pursed her lips, agreeing with her own proclamation. "If God made the snow that prevented Father from reaching your door, He is not concerned." She poured more wine into Ella's glass and swallowed a slug. "This is the only glass I have left for nice company. I share a bit with you?"

"Beata, how will I have a proper funeral for Connor? How much does it cost?" It didn't matter because she might not have enough for the rent due in a week. "A pauper's funeral?"

"Oh, *kotku*, that is not for your Connor!"

Ella pictured his body flung on a heap with other dead, without coffins—just a hole in the ground and a sprinkling of lime. Ella shuddered.

"We have no money. Connor missed work all week. That's six day's wages." Suddenly her heart hammered. She stood, and the blanket fell to the floor. "It's Monday. I should be at the factory!"

"No one can get to the factories today. Sit, you have been through too much." Beata pressed Ella's shoulders until she sank backward into the chair. She was too warm. Her stomach churned against the wine and stew, and she was aware of her stale-sweaty smell.

Connor was gone.

Beata's hands cupped Ella's cheeks. "There, there, *kotku*. Beata will help. I know the undertaker. We will get your Connor into a proper grave."

Chapter 3

Ella panted in the narrow stairwell on the fifth-floor landing of the Seeger's Shirtwaist Factory, unfolded the damp piece of paper in her hand, and read the name her aunt had written: *Aldo Heininger*. As she climbed higher, the stale July air became thick and hot as the sun smoldered through the grimy window panes. Clusters of men and boys ran up and down the stairs, jostling Ella and causing clumps of white fluff to shift and dance in the air.

She checked the name again and felt for the scissors and spools of thread deep in the pocket of her skirt. Aunt Siobhan had heard there was an opening for a clipping girl, someone, she explained, who would nip the threads on the garments. The factory produced more and more of the white pleated shirts worn by women who went to work in the stores. "In a few years, you will work your way into a seamstress position," Siobhan had promised. Ella had years of practice with handwork and embroidery, and over the last few months she had hemmed garments and sewed buttons for the rich families that lived on Summit Avenue, but she had never had a factory job, even though most girls went to work by the age of fourteen. Her other employment options were rolling cigars at Hart & Murphy or pushing bristles into hair brushes, so this sewing job seemed like the best use of her experience.

"It's time," Siobhan had said, meaning that Ella had been allowed enough time to mourn the passing of her parents the previous year in New York. First her mother had died from typhoid and then, two months later, her father had provoked a fight in a pub and had taken a barstool to the head. Her siblings were scattered to faraway places. The two older boys, Padraig and Rory, worked as hired hands on a farm somewhere in southern Minnesota. Her younger sisters were put on the Orphan Train by the Children's Aid Society. Ella was the only child sent to live in Saint Paul with her mother's favorite sister in a neighborhood named Connemara Patch. So far, she had received only one letter from Aileen and Branna and nothing from the boys. She often wondered, with a painful clutch at her heart, if she would ever see any of them again.

"Can you tell me where I will find Aldo Heininger?" Ella called out to a man who passed her carrying a box of bobbins, each as large as her forearm. When he didn't respond, she asked a barefooted boy, about ten years of age, who balanced four bolts of white fabric over his bony shoulder.

"Through that door, ma'am," he called up to her as he made his way down the stairs. "Look out, he's got a mean one on," he added.

Ella flipped the heavy latch and swung the door open. She found herself standing on a deck that overlooked the main sewing room. In the dim light, she saw three long rows of sewing machines. She wrinkled her nose at the oily hot smell of machines and unwashed bodies and watched the nearly identical bowed heads of the women as their feet worked the pedals in rhythm. A blonde girl on the far-right side looked up quickly, smiled at Ella and immediately tucked her head down. Ella smelled cigar smoke and spun around only to bump squarely into the chest of a burly man with a halo of dark greasy curls.

"I don't know you." He stabbed his thick finger at her breastbone. "What are you doing here?"

"I'm here to see Mr. Aldo Heininger," Ella said, trying to raise her voice over the din of the machines, "…about a job."

"Ya, I am Aldo, and I don't want to see you about nothin'." He mopped his forehead with a handkerchief.

"I was told there was a position for a clipping girl." When he stepped forward, the tips of his shoes bore down on Ella's toes. She knew she should look him in the eye, but all she wanted to do was scamper down the stairs.

Just then, a young man, not much older than Ella, tall and lean, appeared at Aldo's side. He had wavy blondish-red hair and green eyes the color of a summer pond. The front of his shirt lay open to display tanned skin and a delicate spray of freckles across his collarbone. He winked at her.

"Aldo, you are a brilliant man, to be sure!"

"What are you talking about now? You with all the talk, talk, talk all day in my ear like a hornet. It's a good thing you are a fast boy, or I would kick your Mick-ass over the rail." Aldo blew a stream of smoke directly into the boy's face and then turned his attention to the scene below.

"Hiring a girl who's nearly as good a seamstress as I am a cutter! Why, you'll increase your production rate on the first day." The boy swung the sack he was carrying over his shoulder. "Look at me. I'm Aldo with my bags of money."

"But I'm not here for a seamstress job. I was told…" Ella gripped the scissors in her pocket.

"Hey, wait a minute here, young miss. You think you can move up to a cutter position, just like that?" The boy came close enough for Ella to see golden flecks in one eye. "No one is as fast as I am! Really, the nerve, Aldo. Send her back to Minneapolis, back to Bergeron's where she came from."

Aldo stopped chewing on his cigar and turned to face Ella. "You are a seamstress at Bergeron's?"

Ella's heart flipped in her chest. "Well, I…"

"Oh, don't make it worse by lying. Really, Aldo. Should I toss her out on the street for you?" The boy folded his arms across his chest and sniffed.

"Why leave Bergeron's? You get fired? Sick?" Aldo squinted at her.

"I live in Connemara Patch now." This was the only true thing she could utter.

Sweat damped the back of her dress. Ella wanted to forget the whole thing, but under the layer of her confusion she sensed something was happening.

"Come on. Get out of here." The boy took her by the elbow and started to pull her back to the stairwell. She felt his thumb run up and down the underside of her arm, a gentle touch that didn't match his tone. She gasped.

"Wait," Aldo shouted. "I don't have a position for a cutter," he said, narrowing his eyes at the boy, "but I could try you out for a week as a seamstress. One of them, I caught stealing sleeves this morning— stuffed them in her hair, the gypsy thief." He waved his blunt hand at the women working the machines below.

The boy's hand moved to the back of her neck. Ella thought he might pick her up like a cat. She licked her dry lips.

"I pay you four dollars for sixty hours. You buy your own needles and machine oil."

She was accustomed to hours and hours of handwork, but could she run a sewing machine fast enough to keep up? The air was so hot it felt like she was breathing through wet wool. The boy's grip on her neck prevented her from nodding.

"Go back to Bergeron's. We don't want you here," the boy snarled.

"Okay, I pay you four twenty-five. You start tomorrow. What's your name?"

"Ella O'Rourke."

She wanted to thank him, but he had dismissed her and was already heading down the stairs to the main floor. The boy released her.

"I'm Connor Byrne. Pleased to make your acquaintance, Miss O'Rourke," he said as he smiled, raised his eyebrows, and gave a quick bow. Ella looked into the green eyes, those lips red as a vaudeville girl's, and felt her heart hiccup. "Welcome to Seeger Shirtwaist Factory. Can I buy you a pint to celebrate your new employment?"

Chapter 4

It had been a week of tragic deaths. Thomas Harrington had worked harvesting ice for the J. W. Day Company for the past ten years. From mid-November through the end of February, he cut blocks of ice from the Mississippi River, not minding the blustery winds as long as he could stay relatively dry. He prided himself on the fact that each block was identical. Tiny bits of ice flew from the saw blade and clung to his beard as he pulled long strokes. His brother, Michael, waited next to him, holding a large tong poised to catch and heft the blocks from the water to the sled. Back at the warehouse, the ice was coated in sawdust and stored in the deep chilly caves along Shepherd Road. On the same day that Conner cut his finger, Thomas had slipped and plunged into the frigid water. In the last seconds before the strong current took him, Michael pinched his brother's head with the ice tongs and guided him closer to the edge before he heaved him out by the coat collar. It was all the more catastrophic that having escaped death in the river, Thomas succumbed a week later to pneumonia. He was thirty-five years old and left behind a wife and five daughters.

Ella stood next to Beata in Calvary Cemetery, snow spilling over the tops of her boots, as they hid behind a large granite monument etched for the Gavin family. Her eyes watered in the March wind as she watched Thomas Harrington's relatives gather at the gravesite. The pallbearers struggled with the great weight of the coffin and depth of snow. Ella crouched low and peered around the corner of the stone. The two eldest girls, maybe sixteen years of age, held hands, their lower lips trembling as their younger sisters sobbed. The widow held the baby and fixed her stare at some place off in the distance as the priest's voice droned. Thomas Harrington's only bit of luck was that he had secured the last of the graves that had been dug in October. Thanks to Beata's connection to Arthur the gravedigger, Thomas, a man known for his affable ways, now had Connor for a grave-mate. After the final viewing, their last kisses to Thomas's cold cheeks and hands, Arthur had squeezed Connor's corpse into the coffin and nailed the lid shut.

"It's better this way," Beata said. "You'll know for all time where your Connor rests. There will be a headstone and someone to care for the grave. His name won't mark the stone, but you will know in your heart he's safe."

The determined sun rose in the mid-morning sky. "See?" Beata pointed. "His head is pointed to the east so on the day of Resurrection, he will be reunited with the Christ."

"*Dues, cujus miseratine animea fidelium requiscunt, hunc tumulum benedicere digar...*" Father McKenna intoned in a voice clear and strong for his years. He paused to bring a handkerchief to his red nose and a few strands of gray hair lashed at his wrinkled forehead. *Oh God, by your mercy rest is given to the souls of the faithful. Be pleased to bless this grave.*

Ella pictured Connor, arms crossed, nose-to-nose with Thomas, and in that moment she envied Thomas Harrington, wanted to change places with him. Ella was ashamed that she had been unable to prepare Connor's body. She couldn't bring herself to wash his wasted limbs, wrap the damaged finger in a clean bandage, comb his red hair and dress him in his Sunday clothes. Instead, Beata and her daughter, Sophie, stepped in to do what should have been her final duty as a wife. She hoped he would forgive her inadequate nursing skills and the manner of his unusual interment.

"The pallbearers—what if they say the casket is too heavy?" Ella whispered.

Beata shook her head. "No man will admit the weight is too much to bear. That would be a sign of disrespect and weakness. This will be one of the many secrets of this place." Ella waited, expecting more of an explanation, but after a few minutes it was clear that Beata would reveal no more.

"*Eique angelum tuum sanctum deputa custodem: et quarumque corora his sepeliuntur, animas eorum ab omnibus absolve vinculis delictorum.*" The winds carried the priest's voice. Ella sighed, for tomorrow she would have to return to work, back to Aldo, back to the drone of machines and the ache that found its way into her shoulders and back. She would see who Aldo had assigned as the new cutter, and each glance at the table would make her sad. There would be no stolen kisses, no walk home holding hands, no meal together at the end of the day, and then the next day would be the same until Sunday when she could sleep after Mass for the rest of the day.

"*Ut in te semper cum sanctis tuls sine fine laetentur. Per Christum Dominium hostrum.* Amen."

Ella imagined the saints rejoicing as they stood behind the warrior angels. They would host a party with ale and songs as they welcomed both men. A damp chill wrapped around her shoulders. How many times would she stand by a grave as they lowered a casket of someone she loved? First her mother, then her father, and now Connor. The cold numbed her face, and yet her heart beat on, warm in her chest as if it did not know the icy sadness of loss.

She concentrated on Thomas's wife and watched the new widow pass the squirming baby to one of the twins. Father McKenna anointed the casket with holy water as the family recited the Lord's Prayer. They were two women without husbands, but Ella felt a flare of envy for the years Thomas had been able to share with his wife, the children that lived and breathed. She had been cheated from what should have been hers.

"At least she has the children," she said to Beata.

"The two older ones, she can send them out to work. The others? Too young. How will she feed them? Maybe the one in the brown coat, I guess about ten years old? She could watch the other two if the mother found work." Beata nodded as if she had solved their dilemmas.

Ella blushed again. Mrs. Harrington's woes were greater than her own. Even so, she wished she was standing at the graveside with Connor's baby heavy in her belly. It would be a son, she was sure, and she longed to feel the solidness of a baby on her shoulder. His dear baby face and sweet breath on her neck would be some solace for her grief.

The gravediggers, one on each end, worked the ropes to lower the casket into the grave. The widow Harrington did not weep or collapse but stood firm like the granite headstones around them. Instead, it was Ella's legs that gave way as she fell sobbing into Beata's arms.

Chapter 5

Ella smelled onion on Aldo's breath when he leaned in too close and said, "*Sie sind gefert.*" She had no idea what he was saying, but when he ranted in German it was never good. She tried to sidestep him to get to her machine, but he moved as if to dance with her.

"Leave now. I said you're fired."

"But why?" Ella clutched the tin that protected her midday meal from the rats.

"You miss two days' work." He examined the wet end of his cigar and then clamped it between his teeth. Tobacco and crumbs clung to his mustache.

"But I sent word to you! A man named Ambrozy Pavlak, my neighbor's son, came to tell you Connor died. His burial was yesterday." Saying the words aloud, *died, burial*, made her throat ache, and tears gathered even though she was sure she had cried them all into her pillow. "What else was I to do?"

"*Das geht mir am arsch vorbei.*" He spat a gob of mucus at her feet. This phrase she knew because Connor had translated Aldo's favorite saying: *I don't give a shit.*

"I need the job—he's dead. He cut himself here, working for you!" She hated listening to her voice waver and crack as the tears spilled down her cheeks. Aldo despised crying, hated the weakness of women. Connor, if you are listening, please help me be brash like you.

"Last night, I already hire two people to take your place. See?" He gestured to the sewing gallery below. The metallic clattering of machines filled her head.

How would she pay rent without a job?

Up until this moment, Ella had resisted looking at Connor's cutting table, afraid she would see the ghost of his movements that she knew so well, hear the stray melody he was known to hum, or see the way he would press his lips as he completed a cut. Slowly, she turned to see a boy from the pubs laying out pattern pieces. He was slight through the shoulders and arms. Ella wondered how he'd ever be able to cut through the layers.

Ella then turned to look at her position on the sewing line, second from the end in the third row. Next to the grimy window, next to her friend, Amolia, sat a new girl. Her long, blonde hair was braided and wrapped in a crown of curls around her head. Ella watched her thread a needle in a quick motion. She looked to be about fourteen years old.

By now, Aldo had turned away. He examined a piece of paper; one bramble-bush eyebrow dipped over his squinting eye.

"I can sew faster than that girl," Ella yelled, trying to sound like Connor. Her mind went blank to think of a trick or threat to get her job back.

She watched him take a deep breath that swelled his chest. His hands bunched into fists. Aldo bent in a quick motion, and she jumped backward thinking he was going to ram her like a goat. Instead, he picked up an empty spool that was near his feet and hurtled it over the railing toward the work floor. It glanced off a pole, bounced twice and clanked against the base of Amolia's machine. She flinched but didn't look up as she continued her seam.

"Stupid, worthless *schlampe*! Don't you get it? There is always another girl!"

Ella couldn't catch her breath. Suddenly the panic of losing her job, the salty-angry smell of Aldo and last night's wine caused her stomach to clench and rebel, and before she could turn away, she vomited on Aldo's feet. She looked up to see Amolia's tear-stained face. They would not work side-by-side any longer.

"*Geh weg*! If I see you again, I'll kill you."

* * *

Ella walked the streets until her legs ached, and the hem of her skirt hung heavy with slush. The wet leather and wool blistered both heels. Each step was a raw stab of pain, but whenever she slowed her pace, terrible thoughts chased each other around her head. *Connor is dead. He is never coming back. I have no employment. I don't have much money.*

The walking reminded her of Conner's mad claim that he could hoof it back to County Meath if challenged. Ella stepped around the horse droppings, watched older boys selling newspapers as younger ones squatted protectively over their scavenged bounty of chipped pots and rags. She passed the Golden Rule Department Store and wondered if she could get employment there even though they paid less than Seeger's. Her reflection in the window showed her ill-fitting, shabby coat, her wild unkempt hair, and her furrowed brow.

She remembered spending Sunday afternoons looking in department store windows while Connor made lists of the fine dresses, hats, and warm coats and boots he planned to purchase for her. Sometimes they pretended they were guests of the Fredrick Hotel as they walked, sharing a bag of roasted nuts. Now she wandered as if she might be able to find him on the streets.

Ella stopped and steadied herself against a lamppost as the edge of her vision began to blur, and for one terrible moment she wondered if her next calamity was blindness. The sounds of clomping horses and rumbling wagon wheels and men shouting echoed as her vision grew dim, like someone pulling layers of lace over her eyes. What if God had deemed that she would be robbed of Connor and her sight! She would have to make her living begging on street corners.

Her stomach cramped, and she realized her meager breakfast had landed on Aldo's shoes. She smelled grilling meats and brewed coffee and realized she was across the street from V. J. Saul's lunch wagon. Valentine's horses pulled the former railcar from factory to factory serving sandwiches, pig's feet, soups, eggs, wieners and coffee. Connor used to wait in line, shifting from foot to foot, his shoulders and head bobbing with excitement until he received his paper-wrapped sandwich. He'd sink his teeth into the bread with a lusty growl. "Ella, love, you must keep up your strength." She could hear his voice, see him offering to share his meal. She waited for the passing wagons, crossed the street to the service window and ordered fried eggs on rye bread and coffee. She parted with the only dime in her coin purse, leaned against the side of the wagon and tore into the buttery, yolk-soaked bread.

Maybe she should leave Saint Paul and search for her brothers. They must be nearly grown men. Taller than she remembered, arms muscled from work. The only way she could tolerate a life of farm drudgery was to be elbow-to-elbow with them, but the one time Ella had gone to a library and examined a map of Minnesota, it seemed vast and empty. She had no idea how to find them.

Would Aunt Siobhan take her in again? In the months with her Aunt's family, she had slept curled up on a narrow kitchen bench next to the stove. Now there was even less room since the new cousin had been born last fall.

Ella leaned against the side of Val's wagon. The bitter coffee scalded her tongue, but Ella held the cup in her cold hands and savored the warmth. She felt stronger now, and her thoughts were more orderly. She needed to find work. She was shocked when she had looked in the tin where they kept their savings and found it nearly empty. Connor was a good worker, but he also spent money in ways that felt foolish to Ella. Rounds of pints for everyone at the pub happened frequently. She also knew he sent money back home to his younger brothers with the hope they could travel to America, and he gave to the orphan fund at the church. She didn't have the heart to complain about the spending when he was alive, but now she felt hurt to be left like this.

Ella set the coffee cup on Valentine's window, and he pressed his hand over his heart as he gave her a sad smile. Ella nodded her understanding. Word of Connor's death must have traveled.

"For you, Dolly," he said as he offered her a wrapped sandwich. He called all the girls Dolly. Ella held out her hand to receive the brown paper bundle and felt a prickly blush creep up her neck. It had started already—she was a charity case. She remembered her Da scowling and yelling during the months after her mother's death when well-meaning neighbors would deliver meals or clothes.

Ella burst into tears... loud, noisy gasps that surprised and frightened her, and she watched the distress register on Valentine's face as she backed away from the window and ran like a thief from the crime.

"Dolly, Dolly dear," he called.

With the warm bundle settled deep in her coat pocket, Ella rounded the corner, and, with one hand hiking up the wet skirt that threatened to trip her, cut through the alley as fast as she could. She only stopped when her breath stabbed her chest like a handful of darning needles.

She stooped over, wiped her wet face, and then looked up to see a storefront window with gold and black lettering that read "Martine's Millinery." Inside the window sat a mirrored dressing table and a chair with a blue satin gown draped over the back. Ella felt as though she were peering into someone's bedroom. Perfume bottles, a sterling silver hairbrush and a small framed photograph were all arranged on a glass tray. Next to the tray sat a hat with black Chantilly lace and five cornflower-blue ostrich plumes that matched the blue of the gown. Ella's heart pounded when she read a smaller, hand-lettered sign propped in the corner of the display window: "Seeking apprentice milliner."

Chapter 6

This was Connor speaking to her. Ella was sure of it. He had pushed her to find this shop. Under the quilts, wrapped around each other in the warmth of their lovemaking, they would share their dreams. Connor longed to compete in the summer Olympics as a runner.

"Ella, you'll be at the finish line when I win the race! I'll have my picture in the paper!"

Other nights he revealed his plans to own a factory like Seeger's, "...but a better, safer place to work. We will attract the best workers and treat them well. When Aldo comes to me begging for a job, I can kick him in the arse!"

Ella, encouraged by Connor's big ideas, had buried her face in his neck and whispered she longed to own a milliner store where she would make and sell hats. All the rich ladies on Summit Avenue would clamor for her creations. Why, even the wife of J. P. Morgan would send for Ella. They would marvel at her stitching and sense of style. She pictured her three daughters, a set of twins and their younger sister who all resembled their father with his green eyes and ginger curls, working alongside her on Saturdays.

The bell jangled as Ella stepped into the empty shop. She ran her fingers through her hair and hastily removed her coat. The walls were adorned with mirrors, and there were three glass cases containing hats, gloves and lace handkerchiefs and beaded purses. Ella licked her dry lips.

The curtain parted from the back room, and Ella's heart shuddered.

"Bonjour," the woman called. She was thin with dark hair set in waves with a complicated knot at the base of her neck. She wore a black cotton voile dress that was cut to show her slim figure and trimmed with ivory lace at the elbows. She used a cane but still managed to move like silk sliding off a bolt.

The woman circled Ella and hummed a tune. Suddenly, she used her cane to hook the coat Ella held in her hands and toss it over the glass case. Ella shivered.

"Your name?" There was a lilt of French accent in her low voice. The woman tilted her head and smiled. Her dark brown eyes were set at an angle of sadness.

"Ella O'Rourke Byrne, ma'am." Ella watched their reflection in the mirror.

"This garment… you constructed it?" Ella felt the tip of the cane graze her shoulders. How much of the story should she tell? Connor had smuggled out all the pattern cuts of her blouse from Seeger's— the ones with small nicks or flaws deemed unsuitable for use. It took months to collect all the pieces, and then Ella had repaired all the flaws and altered the blouse to fit her frame.

Ella nodded.

"Let me see your hands." The woman held out her hands, palms up, delicate fingers curled.

Ella's hands looked like they had been run over by wagon wheels—chapped, torn nails, bleeding cuticles. Her forefinger was studded with tiny white scars from needle punctures. When her nose started to run, she sniffed and realized she didn't have a handkerchief. Her face burned as she saw herself through the woman's eyes.

"I worked as a seamstress at Seeger's. Before that, I did handwork for some families."

"I am Martine Burreau Carpentier. I apprenticed in Paris under Madame Tore. I moved here for love and set up my little shop." Sunlight, caught in the prisms of the beveled glass window, spilled tiny rainbows of color over the dark rug. Martine continued to hold Ella's hands. "You have left Seeger's?"

27

"My husband died on Sunday, and I attended his burial. For this I was dismissed." Ella clenched her jaw at her anger toward Aldo.

"Do you have family here?"

Ella pressed her lips together to hold back her tears and shook her head.

"You have my condolences, *ma petite*. Schooling?"

"I can read and write, ma'am."

"Good. Come with me."

Ella retrieved her coat as Martine parted the curtain to the back room. They entered a narrow room filled with bolts of fabric, spools of thread and ribbon and precarious stacks of hatboxes. A radiator under the window hissed. Martine switched on a gas lamp, and it bathed the workbench in a yellow glow. In the middle of the table there was a hat perched on a form. Martine hung her cane on the edge of the table.

"I attach the light rice netting first. See? Martine's nimble fingers pleated and pinned the material to the hat. She smelled of citrus and floral mixed with something dark and earthy. "Next, I attach the taffeta along the brim with an overcoat stitch. See the luster? Isn't this the softest shade of green?"

Ella nodded, fascinated with Martine's quick movements.

"Again, I use an overcoat stitch to add a wide bias of binding silk. Ella, what color would you choose?" Martine waved her hand at the dozens of spools of ribbons stacked on pegs on the wall.

"This one." Ella selected a darker hue like that of an evergreen tree. She felt Martine's hand on the small of her back. Her stomach tightened at her touch. Martine gave a slight smile and hummed a one-note tone of agreement.

"To finish this hat, I will use this," Martine said as she unfurled several feet of black velvet ribbon, "to make a series of loops." She pleated the ribbon between each finger. "See? A suitable mounting for the ruby quills." She opened a drawer and pulled out a number of feathers with iridescent red and black tips and inserted the tips of the quills into each pleat until her hand looked like a bird.

Such a contrast from the hazy lighting and thick air at Seeger's! Ella's mind would go numb from the noise of the machines and the sameness of each hour, each day.

"You do beautiful work."

"Of course." Martine picked out a remnant of cream-colored silk from a basket of scraps. "Mend this seam." She produced a needle and black thread from the pincushion and motioned to the stool. "Sit."

Ella swallowed a dry click as Martine stood over her shoulder. She pressed the raw edges together and began to pull the needle back and forth. The needle in her hand, the familiar movement, soothed her for a moment until she remembered the night she had stitched Connor's finger—the bite of the needle into skin and his sticky blood on her fingertips. She blinked hard.

Martine moved to stand in front of Ella, cane in hand. Ella stared at the ring on Martine's forefinger, a heavy, rounded dark stone in a gold setting. She lifted Ella's chin with her thumb, and the tips of her fingers grazed the back of her neck. Martine's touch sent a thousand pin-pricks down her back.

"That's enough. You have a competent technique. I think I should like to try you out here in the backroom as my assistant."

Ella held her gaze and didn't blink.

"You are not presentable for the front room, yet." She boosted the cane in the air and swung it around so that the hook caught and lifted the hem of Ella's skirt. She pressed her skirt down, trying to hide her wet, tattered boots. She expected a piteous look from Martine who had never known what it was like to be hungry or cold or to stand on a factory floor until it felt like metal rods impaled the soles of her boots. Instead of cruelty, Martine's dark eyes crinkled with mischief, her half smile teasing.

Ella exhaled a long breath and felt a thudding in her ears. A job. A good job. No longer surrounded by sick women. Away from the rats that would chew through her coat to steal her food. Oh, Connor would be so proud! She would show Martine she was worthy of instruction.

"I will tell you how you will be paid." Martine patted and smoothed her hair even though not one strand was out of place. "When an order comes in for a hat, you will assist me and get a percentage of the sale. I will also pay you to make deliveries. *Est-ce que c'est agre'able?*"

Ella had no idea how to calculate how much money she would earn from this arrangement. Still, it had more promise than begging on the streets or asking the Benevolent Society for a loan.

"Come, let's drink to celebrate!" Martine opened a cupboard and produced a tray with a green bottle, a pitcher of water, a small cut-glass bowl of sugar cubes and two glasses. "Don't you just love absinthe?"

Ella nodded in agreement even though she hadn't tasted it. "Is it dangerous?" Beata once told a story of a woman who jumped from the bridge after a single drink.

"That's ridiculous. People here are afraid of its beauty—that's why they make it hard to come by, but in France we drink it all the time." Martine placed sugar cubes on a slotted spoon and strained the green-tinged liquid over the cubes. She added a splash of water to each glass and handed one to Ella.

"To you. To making beautiful hats, yes?" Martine clinked her glass against Ella's and took a delicate swallow.

The liquid glowed in the glass. She sipped, surprised by the sweet yet bitter taste rolling on her tongue. Her heart pounded... Martine, the job, the absinthe.

"Welcome, may you be my greatest creation," Martine said as she leaned in and kissed Ella on the cheek. Ella startled, unsure of the correct response. Martine lifted a strand of Ella's hair and studied it. "Tomorrow then?"

Chapter 7

Connor sips a glass of whiskey as he sits at the kitchen table. Ella frowns as she struggles to fasten the dove to the crown of the hat. She wraps a length of copper wire around the twig-leg of the bird and feeds the end through a loop on the hat. Just as she gives the wire a final twist, the bird begins to flap its wings. When Ella presses the brim of the hat to the table to keep it from moving, the dove splatters droppings over her wrist.

"Damn," Ella mutters and wonders how to keep the dove stationary.

"I'm flummoxed," Connor says after he drains the glass. "Why the bird?"

"You don't understand… this is what Martine wants. It's high fashion in Paris." She pronounces it like Martine would… parr-eee.

"Maybe I'm off my nut, but whoever'd wear this hat will get covered in bird-wick." Connor's shoulders shake as he wipes the tears that flow down his cheeks.

Ella stands back to survey her creation. Sewn to the curved brim are several white sleeves from Seeger's, draped to veil a woman's face. Connor is right. It's ugly. Absurd. She doesn't know how to tell Martine. Could it be she doesn't have the skill to follow Martine's vision? Will she sneer and scoff and declare that Ella is hopelessly unsuited to fashion design? Poor Irish girl who will never understand the ways of the French! Ella starts to cry. The dove calls coo-OOo-

ooo, blinks its black eyes and slumps over dead. "Oh no, Connor! I'm going to get sacked!"

* * *

Ella startled awake as a glass shattered. She stared at the kitchen table where Connor had appeared. Oh, to have control over her dreams! Each night she willed herself to dream of him, planting memories like seeds in the garden. The sly look as they turned down the lamp, the way he would take her hand and kiss her palm and then her wrist. So why did she dream of making that awful hat when she should have wrapped her arms around his neck and kissed him?

Streaks of yellow and pink light smeared the early-morning sky. Ella looked down to see the shards of glass glistening in a puddle of wine. Her neck and foot were cramped from her position in the chair. She couldn't bring herself to sleep in Connor's deathbed, so she sat in a chair in front of the stove drinking Beata's homemade wine to make her drowsy.

Today, like most mornings, a blunt and deep pain thrummed behind her eyes. Her tongue felt sour and thick, and she vowed to stop this. But she knew that as the dusky shadows of evening seeped into her house, she would find herself pouring a glass and settling into the chair again. She often slept in his coat.

Ella fed coal into the stove to heat water for washing and tea. She touched the cuffs and collar of her shirtwaist hanging near the stove, pleased to find them dry, and then set the iron to heat on the stove. For the past two weeks, she had spent most of her time at Martine's shop, dusting and organizing. It surprised Ella that the business of selling hats wasn't brisk. Thus far, she had helped make two of Martine's creations and completed one delivery. Her wages, combined with the money in the tea tin, were barely enough to make rent. When Ella worked up the nerve to ask about sales, Martine waved her hand and said blooming lilacs and warm breezes would inspire ladies to buy hats.

While the front of Martine's shop appeared to be orderly, the workroom was not. Ella found Martine was prone to stuffing things into crates and hiding them under curtained tables. Ella untangled a box of ribbons, ironing them flat, bundling and pinning the raw ends together, only to have Martine say, "Oh, throw those scraps away." She didn't complain, however, when Ella boxed and labeled jumbles of feather, tulle, buttons, pins, beads and hat pins. Ella wasn't getting paid for this work but keeping her hands busy meant she wasn't spending the long days alone in her house. She also wanted to impress Martine before she figured out she didn't need an apprentice at all.

Ella slathered a slice of stale bread with Beata's stew. There was no money for coffee beans. Ella surveyed the house, once a place of such happiness. As the morning sun flared through the smudged glass, she could see the fine layer of dust that had settled over everything, the grit on the floors, crumbs on the tables, and yet she had no energy to keep house as she had when Connor was alive.

As Ella chewed the bread and stew, she continued to mull over the mystery of Martine. Most days, Martine drifted around the shop and hummed sad French tunes. Ella noticed that Martine's limp was more pronounced on some days than others. Twice Ella witnessed a tremor in Martine's hand. Her boss gave no mention of any maladies, so Ella didn't pry, especially since Martine continued to post the apprentice position on the card in the window. On a few occasions, Martine would disappear for hours without explanation.

Ella licked her finger and touched it to the iron with a quick hiss. Satisfied, she sprinkled a bit of water over the bodice of her blouse and nudged the blunt tip of the iron into the wrinkles. Maybe she could take in some mending and ironing for the rich families. She would have to boil tubs of starch and water and construct some kind of rack to hold the inventory. And then there would be the problem of delivery. How would she keep the garments clean as she delivered them? She pictured burns and blisters, aching sore wrists from the heavy iron. She hurried to finish the press and then set the iron on the stove to cool and slipped on her skirt. Ella was lacing up her boots when she heard a knock on the door.

"Coming, Beata!" she called as she buttoned the cuffs of her shirt.

Beata checked on her every day, dropping off food wrapped in towels, sometimes a bottle of wine. Once she left a set of mother-of-pearl hair combs nestled in a velvet bag. When Ella protested her generosity, Beata waved her off explaining she no longer needed pretty hair combs for her graying nest of curls. On Saturday night, Beata had brought a deck of Tarot cards. "To show you there are good things coming to you."

Another rap on the door. "I'm here, Beata!" Ella plucked her coat from the peg and stuffed the last bite of bread into her mouth. There would be no time to talk today if she wanted to get to the shop on time. Ella opened the door.

It was not Beata. Instead, standing on the front walk was Amolia, her only friend from Seeger's. They had worked side-by-side for months, sharing spools of thread, lunches, and trying to avoid trouble from Aldo.

Amolia flung herself into Ella's arms, and they were both crying, wiping each other's tears. Foreheads pressed together, they squealed, and their words stumbled over each other until they laughed.

"I'm so sorry about Connor! A blessing on his soul!"

"What are you doing here? I've missed you." Ella realized in a rush how much she did miss Amolia's large brown eyes and thick brows and that one dimple, like a tiny crescent moon.

Ella heard a mewing sound and moved to close the door so that the stray cats wouldn't sneak into the house. She spun around but didn't see a tabby winding around her legs. Amolia burst into tears and opened up the front of her coat to reveal a bundled blanket she had cinched to her middle with a length of rope. When she peeled back the edge, Ella saw the round, serene, sleeping face of a newborn baby.

A baby. She looked at Amolia's face, so full of misery, and then studied the baby's face as its mouth moved to the memory of its suckling.

"Ella, I need your help. Can you mind my baby so's I don't get fired?"

Chapter 8

Ella stood with Amolia on Beata's doorstep in the damp April air. Wrens trilled sharp kit-kit calls in the dense hedge along the side of the house. The baby slept in her arms. Ella knocked and tried to figure out how to ask Beata to take care of a stranger's baby. The door opened. Without a word, Beata pulled the baby from Ella's arms and positioned him on her shoulder. She cooed to him in Polish as she turned her back to them. Amolia shrugged as they followed Beata into her kitchen, which smelled of tobacco and cinnamon.

"This is Amolia —me friend from Seeger's."

"The singer?" Beata had heard Ella tell of the songs Amolia sang all day to pass the long work hours.

Spread on the kitchen table were the remnants of a gray wool coat, a rabbit fur pelt, a measuring tape, spools of thread, scissors and a large pile of black buttons.

"Amolia here is in a bad way. Her shift is starting soon—she's afraid of losin' her job, like I did. She says Aldo is in a terrible fit of tempers these days."

Beata kissed the top of the baby's head. "*Maly jeden*, what's your name?"

"Ma'am, he doesn't have a name just yet." Amolia twisted a length of hair around her finger.

"When was he born?"

"Friday night," Amolia said softly.

Beata continued to sway. "You birthed him alone, yes?"

Amolia nodded, holding back tears. "My family, they can't know."

"Where did you have him?"

"In the bathroom at Seeger's. After my shift."

Ella gasped, picturing the two toilets that were always splattered, and the filthy rust-stained sink, the faucet that trickled cold water. Pigeons congregated on the sill of the broken window, leaving their droppings down the wall on the floor.

Beata pulled Amolia into her arms and said, "Do you have some cloths for the blood?"

"I sewed some from cotton scraps at work."

Ella gave a wry smile and wondered how many of the seamstresses followed the same practice. Why, if Aldo knew of this he could start another business more profitable than the shirtwaist garments.

"Good. You go now. Don't give that bastard Aldo a reason to hurt you." Amolia flinched.

"Mrs. Pavlak, this is to feed the baby." Amolia dug into her apron and pulled out a bottle with a brown nipple and a can featuring a baby's face that read: "Farine Lactee Nestle."

"What's this?" Twin lines appeared between Beata's brows.

"Cow's milk, wheat, flour and sugar."

"Hmmmmf," Beata responded. She caressed the dark hair on the baby's head with her thumb. "I care for him, you go. But I give him a name for the day!"

"Oh, thank you so much!"

Amolia clung to Ella for a moment and hurried out the door to get to Seeger's before the second whistle sounded. Ella pulled back the curtain and watched her hurry down the street. Was she strong enough to work for ten hours under Aldo's cruel direction?

"Did you see that?" Beata moved behind Ella and watched Amolia disappear around the corner. The baby's cheek was squashed against Beata's shoulder. "She didn't kiss little Ozor goodbye."

Chapter 9

Martine caressed Ella's cheek and pressed a few coins into her hand to pay for the streetcar ride.

"The address is 89 Western Street," Martine said, smiling. It wasn't a fake smile but Ella noted dark circles under Martine's eyes.

From the looks of the worktable, she must have stayed up all night finishing the hat for Thomas Cochran's wife. The stubs of Martine's hand-rolled cigarettes filled the tea saucer, and snippets of lace and ribbon littered the table and floor. Martine stretched her shoulders and neck. Ella noted the nearly empty bottle of absinthe.

"Who doesn't need a little madness and muse in the night?" Martine gestured at the glass, smiled again and handed the hatbox with a crepe bow to Ella. Her skin was sallow and pulled tight across her sharp cheekbones.

"I wanted to see it first," Ella said.

"Then you should arrive on time. I promised the delivery this morning. Mr. Cochran ordered this for his wife because the pregnancy has been difficult, and he wants to raise her spirits."

"I'm sorry. A friend from Seeger's—she is in trouble and I—"

Martine cut off her explanation with a wave of her hand. "You will see the hat when you help her try it on. She is the former Martha Andrew Grifter." Martine announced this fact as if Ella would recognize the name. "Mr. Cochran will pay for the hat if it pleases his wife. Present this bill." Martine shifted her weight and leaned on the cane; with one hand she folded a piece of paper and handed it to Ella.

When she saw the look on Ella's face, she added, "No worries, *mon tout-petite*. Who doesn't love my creations?"

Ella flushed and fidgeted with the bow on the hatbox. She didn't want to display her chapped hands and shabby coat to a woman worthy of one of Martine's creations, but she needed to be paid for the delivery.

"I have something for you." Martine snapped her fingers and pulled a box from under the curtained table and placed it on top of the worktable mess. "The spring air graces us now, and your winter coat will be too warm."

Tears burned, and Ella brushed them away with her knuckle but couldn't move to raise the lid.

"Open it." Martine nudged the box with the tip of her cane, waited a moment, and then removed the cover.

The box held a bed of carefully pleated lavender paper that made crisp noises as Martine shoved the box toward Ella. "It's a present! People give them to each other, and when they open them up they say, Oh, *por moi*?"

Connor's last present had been a chemise he had placed as a surprise on her pillow. She immediately protested the cost and argued he should spend money on practical needs. When she was done, he presented a pair of woolen stockings he had hidden behind his back. "It's in honor of the Patron Saint of Love, St. Valentine. His bones were exhumed from their resting place in Rome and are now in a church in Dublin. I've seen them with my own eyes! So, really, the church requires us to honor him in this way." He fell to the bed laughing, so Ella had modeled both of the gifts at the same time.

Ella reached out and parted the tissue to find a light-green velvet material.

"I made you a cape!" Martine couldn't wait any longer. She shook the cape free from the box and tissue.

It landed with a light rustle on Ella's shoulders.

The lining was a lemon silk embroidered with so many twisting vines and leaves that Ella felt enveloped in a garden. Martine had embroidered her signature under a slim pocket.

"See, I knew the green would be perfect for your eyes and hair. Oh, why the tears, *mon cherie?"*

"Thank you. It's so beautiful. I've never owned anything so fine."

"Scraps, a little of this or that. You have been very good to me, helping me here." She waved around the workroom. "This is how I repay you."

All of Ella's feelings sloshed against her heart and throat—her sadness over Connor and how this had led to a moment of kindness from Martine. Amolia's baby and the child of Connor's that would never live in this world.

"Go now, he is expecting the hat this morning." Martine brushed a light kiss on her cheek and pushed her out the door.

* * *

Ella got off the streetcar at Selby Avenue and walked down Western Avenue past the wrought iron fences and gates that divided the grand brick houses from the street. The buds on the branches waved like tight green fists. She walked past a garden full of yellow tulips and crocus and watched men rake wet leaves and prune bushes into squared-off shapes.

She walked faster, watching the numbers over the door as her head pounded with questions. How much money could Connor's knives fetch? Each scuff of her heel prompted a new question. Why hadn't Amolia confided in her? There were no answers to her questions, and the hatbox began to feel heavy and awkward in her hands.

Ella turned up the cobblestone drive at 89 Western Avenue and made her way to the stables past an empty black carriage with gold handles. A crest on the side depicted a tiny horse and a headpiece of armor all surrounded by red and silver foliage. The phrase, *Virtute et labore,* in fancy script, was printed on a scroll above the Cochran name. She saw a groomsman heft a saddle in the gloom of the stable. A solemn young boy struggled to lift a shovel heavy with manure.

Ella walked to the back of the house. A maid, about her age, sat on the top step with her face buried in her apron, weeping. Her fine golden hair was plaited and pinned to resemble a crown. The wind shifted and swirled around them, billowing Ella's cape. The bare tree branches thrashed.

"I have a delivery from Martine Burreau Carpentier. It's a hat Mr. Cochran ordered for the missus." Ella held out the box.

At this announcement, the maid wailed into her apron. Ella stood there, unsure of what to do next. She had the urge to leave the hat with the weeping maid, but Martine would expect a report and payment. If Martine didn't get paid, Ella wouldn't either.

"Is Mr. Cochran home?"

The maid looked up at Ella, her red face crimped. "Mr. Cochran just got home from a business trip to Duluth. He is in his study."

"Can I see the lady of the house?"

The girl motioned Ella to come closer. "Mrs. Cochran—her baby was born dead early today. She suffered a terrible long labor. The doctor gave her medicine to sleep." The maid brushed at her tears, and Ella saw that her brows and lashes were the same pale gold as her hair.

Ella pictured Amolia's delivery in the bathroom at Seeger's.

"There's more." Her robin's-egg-blue eyes darted around, and when she pulled Ella's cape to whisper in her ear, her breath stank of whiskey. "The lady's maid, Britta, helped the doctor, you see. She said the head of the babe, it was missing, so it was just a face, really. Have you ever heard of anything so dreadful?"

Ella shook her head. She had heard of babies born without limbs or fingers, but she couldn't picture a face without a forehead.

"The missus—she doesn't know."

Dark clouds rolled across the sky, and fat rain drops began to fall. The girl stood and grabbed Ella's hand. "Come into the kitchen. I'll ask Mrs. Whitely what to do with the hat."

The rain crashed in sheets behind them as they burst into the kitchen. Panting, Ella looked outside and saw the blurred form of the groomsman as he ran to pick up the boy. He darted back into the stable. The maroon crepe bow on the box was limp and stained her palm.

The girl put her finger to her lips and motioned for Ella to stay on the braided rug by the door. No other maids moved about, and the sounds of thunder and rain filled the room.

Ella heard muffled sounds coming from the hallway. A man's voice. Thomas Cochran? She pictured his jowls wobbling, fat from juicy meat pies, sweet cakes and whiskey. He would have a bushy mustache and mean eyes. Men who lived in houses like this, in Ella's experience, all looked the same.

She followed the rise and pitch of the voice. Ella walked down a long hallway, passing portraits of men and women with erect postures and stern expressions. She peeked into a room and saw Thomas Cochran speaking into a telephone device. She pressed herself along the wall and sniffed tobacco smoke.

"I can't keep my mind on business. Father, you must understand, I cannot go back to Duluth tomorrow."

Ella heard footsteps.

"I'm not sure if her mind is strong enough to bear this news." His next words were lost in the clap of thunder that pounded through Ella's chest.

"...the farthest the pregnancy has ever gone. There were others we lost, you see. She didn't want it known." Ella heard the sounds of ice clinking in a glass.

Ella leaned over to peer into the room. Mr. Cochran pressed a handkerchief hard against his mouth. His looks were far different than she'd imagined. He was slight of frame, clean shaven with a shank of sandy brown hair that fell over one eye.

"Our doctor who attended the birth had a name for the deformity. He said it was called anencephaly. The brain is absent—it never grew properly." He said this as a whisper.

He paced behind the desk. "Annulment? I would never think to do something so cruel. Don't you see this is my fault?" He was shouting now. "I urged her to try again..." A strangled noise escaped him. "I wanted a son so badly."

He cried openly now. "She is the dearest thing to me." He leaned his forehead against the window behind the desk.

"What's that? Well, I have had a drink. Wait—hello? Operator?"

He looked up and locked eyes with Ella.

"Margaret, is that you?" He squinted and gestured to her with his tumbler. "What is it?"

He patted the top of the desk until he found his spectacles, and he pulled the curved bows around his ears.

"You're not Margaret! Who are you? What are you doing skulking in the hallway?"

Ella's words were stuck on her tongue. She thrust the hatbox out in front of her as an answer.

"Are you mute?"

"Delivery, sir. The hat you ordered from Martine Carpentier."

Mr. Cochran righted the chair and sat down slowly.

"Ah, the hat. It was meant to be a surprise." He poured more whiskey into the glass. "I pictured we would push the baby in a pram together, and she would wear this hat." He gulped the amber whiskey and wiped his mouth with his hand. "Excuse me, I'm not myself. Put it there, on the chair. Can you see yourself to the door?" He pushed his hair back from his forehead.

Ella's loss and sadness bubbled in her chest. To see a man who clearly loved his wife so much driven to tears and drink at the death of his deformed baby. This was surely a kind man, and she had the urge to pat him on the shoulder because they shared the great pain of loss.

She looked down at the invoice in her hand, damp and stained. "Sir, beg pardon, but there is the matter of the invoice? I was told you would pay upon inspection of the hat." The tree outside the window stilled, raindrops clung to the swollen tree buds.

"What? Oh, yes. Of course." He squinted at Ella as she wiped her tears. "It's been an upsetting day for us all." He sighed and pulled a leather ledger from the front desk drawer. "Hand it to me, please. What is the amount?"

Ella placed the hat on the straight-back chair and smoothed the invoice before she set it on the desk. He dipped a pen in the ink well and started writing.

"Sir, I'm sorry to have troubled you today." Her throat ached against the misery.

"I imagine you got an earful. What's your name?" He blew on the ink.

"Ella O'Rourke Byrne, sir."

"Well, Miss Byrne, I will ask you as a gentleman, if you have any decency about you, please keep my family's troubles to yourself."

"Sir?" There was a roar in Ella's head, louder than the thunder that had ripped through the April sky. Ella didn't know that a powerful idea could be so loud.

Thomas Cochran held out the check. "You must be expecting some sort of tip for your troubles." His words slurred as he pulled out a money clip.

"No, it's not that." Ella swallowed hard. She wanted her voice to be strong, persuasive, like Connor's. "Maybe there is a way to spare your wife, sir. Maybe she never has to know her child died."

Chapter 10

As the last of day's sun flared across the evening sky, Thomas Cochran's carriage arrived to pick up Ella, Amolia and the baby. All the excitement of babies and mothers made Ella recall a day when she was a young girl, still living in Ireland, and the teacher sent her home sick from school. Her throat had burned as she walked the gravel road. She longed to be in her bed, quilt pulled up to her chin, waiting for her mother to apply a poultice across her chest and prepare a cup of tea, sweetened with honey.

Her heart had beat a little faster when her house came into view. Ella was comforted by the sight of the vines that clambered over the lime plaster and thatched roof. The house was quiet. No wash hung on line, the shutters were closed. Ella pushed open the door and found her mother slumped over the kitchen table, her head resting on her arm next to an empty tin cup. Beads of sweat dotted her forehead, and her hair, a faded shade of Ella's, lay plastered to her temples. Did they share the same sickness? Her mother didn't stir.

"Ma?" Her heart flopped in her chest. The pot her mother used to boil herbs contained a dark, oily mixture. Ella's eyes roamed the counter, recognizing dried clumps of marjoram and thyme bound with string and a knobby root ball that looked like witch's hair. Her mother's herb book was lying open next to the pestle and mortar. A picture of a fern and root, rendered in a drawing by her mother's careful hand was labeled *worm fern root*, also known as prostitute's root.

She had witnessed her mother's use of this root on two different occasions. Once she made a tisane for a local farmer named Tommy McCarthy, who had shrunk to skin and bones no matter how much food he consumed. Her mother said he had a particular kind of worm living in his gut, and this tea mixture would kill it. Another time, a woman came to their house late at night, her face hidden in the shadow of her hooded cape. Her mother didn't invite her into the house but slipped her a small muslin bag. As they touched foreheads, her mother whispered something. Ella had watched the woman walk down the drive, pushing hard against the wind and sleet.

When Ella asked why the woman was out in such dreadful weather, her mother said, "Ah, Ella, it is too much for you to understand now, but there are times when a baby has to be sent back to God, and I help with that sometimes."

Her mother's eyes flickered now, and she slowly raised herself to a sitting position, but she held the edges of the table as if she were in a rowboat on the sea. "Ella, me darlin', what are you doing home from school?" Her fingers pressed to her lips.

"Where's Aileen?"

"She's with Seanmhathair."

"Are you ill?" Ella pointed to the book and the herbs.

"Come closer," her mother ordered. Ella trembled, her head pounding from the fever and the feeling that something in her world had tilted and was starting to topple and slide.

Her mother cupped her cheek. "You're burnin' with fever!"

Ella pointed to the wormwood illustration. Her mother's eyes registered that long-ago conversation.

Her mother's fingers, strong from chopping wood and hefting kettles and wet baskets of laundry, dug into the undersides of Ella's arm until she winced.

"Someday, when you have a family of your own, you will understand that it is sometimes impossible to accept all of the children that God sees fit to send your way."

* * *

Ella remembered her mother's angry stare, the bitter tea, and the fate of unwanted babies. She realized Amolia might have drunk her mother's bitter tea if given the chance. When Ella presented the adoption plan to Amolia, she had giggled and burst into tears, babbling, "Yes, yes, yes," even before Ella added all of the details. Amolia was happy to be relieved of motherhood.

Now Amolia was giddy to be riding in a rich man's carriage. Her eyes were bright as she caressed the blue satin upholstery; her fingers followed the curves of the button tufting and the lines of the nail-head trim. She hummed and looked out the windows, waving to strangers in other carriages. She acted as if she were going to a dance instead of to be releasing her baby. Ella kissed Ozor's temple and smiled to catch Beata's hearty scent of onions and garlic. Amolia told Ella she had cut the cord that joined her to the baby with her sewing scissors, and Ella wondered if this action had also severed the connection to her heart.

"Amolia, Mr. Cochran wants to talk to you to make sure you are serious about giving up the baby."

"I'm serious. That's why I'm here." The light from the gas lamps flickered over her face.

Ella fingered the worn blanket wrapped around the baby. "He may ask some hard questions."

"He is a teacher, is he?"

"Not a teacher." Ella clenched her teeth against Amolia's dull-witted question. "He doesn't want anyone to know his baby died. He can't have you changing your mind."

"Ella, I can't take care of him. If my family knew, they would be so ashamed! I'd be put out on the streets." The baby mewed and squirmed in Ella's arms.

"So's there no chance you would get married? Were you sweet on one of the cutters?" Harry O'Dell came to mind, and Ella's throat ached to think of another couple at Seeger's finding love.

Amolia snorted. "A crush on a boy? I work six days a week. I come home, eat, wash my dress and sleep like the dead until it starts all over again." Amolia turned to look out the window. They were both quiet. The horse's hooves clattered against the cobblestone. Amolia offered no hints as to the father's identity.

"You know I would have helped you—"

"First Connor is sick. Then he dies, and you are fired. I thought that was enough for you."

The carriage turned and lurched up the drive. The horse's head lifted as the groomsman tugged the reins.

"We're here," Ella whispered. She wiped her damp hands on her skirt as they waited for the door to open. The baby slept, warm against Ella's chest. He curled himself tight.

As they stepped from the carriage, Ella breathed the clean April air. The groomsman moved to wrap a blanket that reeked of horse sweat around her shoulders. At first, she thought he was protecting her but then realized he was trying to disguise their arrival as they made their way into the house. How would he keep the gossiping maids quiet?

The groomsman bunched his hat in his hands and wiped his boots on the rug, but didn't cross the threshold into the kitchen. His hands were mapped with ropey veins. "Miss, you are to wait in the study."

Ella bit her lip and adjusted the baby higher on her shoulder.

"Don't worry, Miss. All will be well." He winked at her, and deep dimples sliced his cheeks when he smiled.

The smell of boiled fish followed them down the hallway. There were no servants in sight. Amolia's eyes were wide, and she pressed herself to Ella's back.

The study was dim save an electric lamp on the desk. When Ella looked around the room she couldn't believe she had failed to see the stuffed animals. There were two deer, a bit different from the red deer of Ireland in size and color, and an enormous elk with a spread of antlers that reached out over the fireplace like giant claws. On the shelf sat a fox with a mouse held in his mouth, his narrow snout raised in the air. She swore his plush tail might start to switch back and forth. A bear skin rug lay on the floor near the fireplace. His mouth and eyes were opened wide as if he were poised to bite their feet.

Amolia sucked in a breath. "I hate their eyes a lookin' at me. What if the baby is afeared to live here?"

"They're dead. They can't bother you at all. It's what the rich do—shoot and stuff things rather than eat them." She wanted to distract Amolia before she changed her mind. "Ol' Brownie, here…" Ella raised a finger pistol at the bear's head and fired. "See? I killed him. He's no trouble to anyone."

Amolia giggled and covered her mouth. "Shoot another one, will ya?"

Ella pretended to pull a pistol from under her cape. She narrowed her eyes and fired at the elk. "Watch out! He'll crush you if he goes down."

Amolia shrieked and eyed the cut-glass decanters. "Oh look, brandy. Do you think I can boost a nip?"

Ella looked up to see Thomas Cochran standing in the doorway.

"Sir?" Her heart pounded, and she pictured he would pinch their ears and toss them into the street like common thieves. His eyes were bloodshot, and she saw deep creases frame his mouth.

"Miss, I am Thomas Cochran."

Amolia pressed her nose into Ella's shoulder.

"Sir, this is me friend, Amolia." She patted the baby's back and swayed.

"You are the mother of this infant?" The spectacles magnified his eyes.

Ella elbowed Amolia, prompting a nod from her.

"If you two are up for stealing my brandy, maybe you steal babies too."

Ella licked her dry lips. The interview had gotten off to a poor start. "No, Mr. Cochran, the story is as I told you this morning."

"I can't afford to have the police knocking at my door upsetting my wife." He walked to the window behind the desk and stared out into the darkness.

Amolia's fingers dug into Ella's arm. "Is this proof enough?" She stepped out from behind Ella and untied her shawl to reveal dark stains on the front of her dress. Her milk had come in, and her full breasts strained against the buttons. She raised her chin.

The baby began to stir, and Ella's arm was wet under his bottom. She sucked in a breath at the turn in Amolia's behavior. First she was a mute mouse, and now she seemed angry and brash.

Mr. Cochran spun around and quickly averted his eyes as if she had shown herself to be without garments.

Baby Ozor fussed, rubbing his face back and forth against Ella's shoulder. Her arms ached from holding him for so long, but Amolia made no move to comfort him. Ella said a prayer that Mr. Cochran would see them for the truth—two young girls without enough sense to bring supplies for the baby.

Hands clasped behind his back, Mr. Cochran paced back and forth and stared at his shoes. His shirt sleeves were rolled to the elbows, and his braces dangled below his hips.

"The father of this child?" Ella noticed his teeth were pointed and sharp, reminding her of the wild animals surrounding them.

"There is no father."

Mr. Cochran stopped pacing and looked at Amolia.

Her chin quivered. "He will never know."

"And you, the mother... your claims to this child?"

"After tonight, sir, I have no claims." Amolia's dark eyes held his gaze, but no tears appeared.

As if in answer to his mother's declaration, the baby started to squawk as if he too wanted a say in the discussion.

"His health? He is free from disease? Defects?"

Ella pictured the headless baby that had been removed from the house that morning.

"Other than hungry and wet, he is well," Ella answered, raising her voice over the baby's cries. "Do you want to examine him yourself?"

A maid entered the room, her gray, limp dress stained with sweat. A dark braid ran the length of her spine. "Sir, excuse me, but Missus Martha heard the crying and wants to see her baby. I didn't know what to say." Her eyes were red-rimmed, and she dabbed her nose with a handkerchief.

"Margaret, tell me, is she well?" He stood next to Ella.

Margaret raised her eyebrows at Ella but turned her attention back to her boss. "As well as can be expected."

Thomas placed his hand on top of Ozor's head. His fingers were long and delicate without scars or grime, each nail a shiny and perfect oval. The baby calmed for a moment at his touch but then renewed his cries.

Ella held her breath.

"Thomas, darling, where is the baby?" They all turned at the sound of the voice coming from the upper floor of the house. The air in the study was a heavy mix of damp, sweat and soiled diaper.

"Margaret..." Mr. Cochran sniffed and bit his lip.

"Sir?"

Ella saw twin lines appear between his pale brows. His breath came in hard bursts as if he had run a race like Connor. The decision that would change everything was poised to burst from him. His thumb moved back and forth over the baby's temple.

"Take the baby to the nursery, change him and then bring him to my wife. I'll be up shortly."

Margaret looked at Ella and Amolia and then back to Thomas Cochran. She gave a fast nod, hesitated for a heartbeat and then gathered the baby. Ella caught sight of his bare feet drawn up tight to his body. Amolia did not reach out for one last caress or kiss to his brow but turned as Margaret headed out of the room.

"I don't expect to see either of you again, and you will speak to no one about the deal we have brokered." He reached into his pocket and withdrew a money clip and began to peel out a series of bills.

Ella was embarrassed and stunned. Of course, this was a man accustomed to paying for things, and in his mind he had just purchased a baby.

Chapter 11

Inez Laudenbach adjusted the belt of her uniform. The brass buttons felt warm. She squinted into the afternoon sun and pushed her glasses up. The spring air was warmer than usual, and the collar of the woolen coat scratched the skin along her jaw. Despite the discomfort, Inez thought the coat looked smart and did wonders to disguise her large shoulders. It was her father's police coat. She wore it partly as a nod to his memory and partly because the police did not issue proper uniforms to females.

She carried a small memo book and a pencil in her pocket. Today she had recorded two things.

Mrs. Violet Hentges living at 124 Avon Street, sixty-one years old. She lives with her son, Monte, his wife Ellen and their infant son. Mrs. Hentges reported a mad dog slinking near the back porch. Upon inspection, no dog was sighted. John Carroll, at 600 Arlington Street, reported his horse as stolen. The horse is a five-year-old mare, stands fourteen hands tall and is chestnut in color with white markings on the nose and throat. The horse was last seen in the stable behind the house yesterday evening.

Inez's tongue had curled into a piece of burlap. She longed to release the top button of her coat and sip a glass of cool lemonade on a porch swing, but she pressed on with her walk around her assigned area. Her instructions were to "be observant, avoid loitering and get to know the residents and businesses in the neighborhood." Inez was the third woman to be hired by the Saint Paul Police Department. Her duties were far less rigorous than those of the men in the department. Women didn't have the right to vote or to hold public office, therefore they had no authority to make an arrest. Minnie Hession and Mary Smith, her predecessors in the department, had been tasked with monitoring proper behavior in dance halls, reporting on a theater that featured scandalous movies, and investigating the general welfare of women and children at schools and factories.

Inez longed to be a policeman in the brave tradition of her father, Joseph, who had been shot after he surprised a burglar who was attempting to blow up a safe. She wanted to solve real crimes and change the reputation of Saint Paul as a "dead-tough town." At her father's funeral, amidst the heavy sweet scent of dianthus, a dry-eyed Inez told a surprised Police Chief Tim Murphy that she wanted to join the department. At the age of thirty, with a college degree in classics and no prospects for a husband (her large hands, feet, and shoulders were viewed as unladylike), and with no living parents or siblings, she was deemed suitable for duty.

A carriage passed by, kicking up the dust from the street. The driver tipped his hat while clucking commands to the horse. Tender new grass blades sprouted through patches of brown thatch. A cat, thin and missing one ear, slunk under a low hedge. The air was still, and the neighborhood seemed unusually quiet as Inez strained for cries of distress or a whiff of a smoldering fire. Instead of danger, she smelled baking bread. Her stomach clenched, but she was unsure if she was allowed to eat a noonday meal. She listened for the sergeant's call—a nightstick banging on metal. Two strikes if he wanted to locate you. Would she appear to be impertinent to ask such a question?

She heard the laughter of two young boys and looked up to see a metal wheel rim rolling on course to trip her. Inez grabbed the wheel and held it aloft on the tip of her nightstick. The boys skidded in the gravel, stopping at her feet. Twins, like their Greek counterparts Castor and Pollux, with pink faces and dark hair. Beads of sweat gathered on the layer of grime on their upper lips. Inez faced them.

"Are you going to arrest us?"

"Should I?" Inez rose up on her toes to loom over them.

"Are you a lady?" They wrinkled their identical noses.

"What do you think?" She wished desperately for a police badge, silver and menacing, pinned to her coat.

"Whadda ya think?" They mimicked her when they snatched the wheel from her and ran down the alley, their stick-thin legs pumping and kicking up dust. They ducked into the first backyard. So much for her ability to influence future criminal behavior with her authority!

"Be virtuous," she called after them.

Inez shook her head and headed down the street to the din and bustle of businesses on West Seventh Avenue, swinging her arms in a way she hoped looked police-like. Her face felt hot and greasy. By the end of the day, her nose would blaze red with sunburn. She heard the clip-clop of iron-shod feet, the call of the street vendor with his pushcart selling ribbons, needles, hot peanuts and pickles in salty brine.

She turned the corner to see a man with a droopy mustache and a thin shirt, open at the neck, sitting against the cool of the brick building, turning the crank on a hurdy-gurdy. He hummed and bobbed his head with the off-beat tune. Inez closed her eyes and tried to commit all of his physical details to memory as practice for identifying real criminals. The color of his hair, his nationality, a guess at his weight or estimated height (from a seated position), and any moles or scars. Once, at the station, she stole a look at the book of pictures of known criminals. If she could memorize their faces, she reasoned, she could be on the lookout for crime before it happened.

Inez nodded in his direction and continued her walk past the meat market and then crossed over to Jueneman's Hotel and Saloon. She knew spirits could incite tempers and loosen tongues. Her father, a man of all things modest, would have a glass of sherry only on a holiday. After she graduated from college, he offered her a glass and a toast to her successful conclusion of studies at the University of Minnesota.

"To my daughter, the scholar and companion. May you enjoy many years of intellectual pursuit." He had held the glass in the air and beamed at her. Joseph Laudenbach's lips were full, and his teeth were strong and white, for he had abstained from tobacco products. His eyes were dark blue, and his blonde eyebrows looked soft as downy feathers. At first, Inez thrilled at the camaraderie of this moment with her father—to feel more his equal than just a child, but then she winced as the sherry seared its way down her throat. Then, to her horror, what followed was a sloppy disconnect of her brain to her body. Why would anyone seek out such a state?

"Hey, you there, lady."

Inez turned to see a large man in a suit coat shoving a woman out of the door of Jueneman's. He grabbed the back of her dress with a meaty hand as if she were a cat he was tossing into the street. "I found her in the room of one of my guests. I'm sure she's a stealing whore. Arrest her!" He was breathing hard, red-faced and snarling though his clenched jaw.

Inez lifted her chin and wondered how to tell him she had no authority to arrest anyone. "Sir, is she in possession of stolen property?"

They both looked at the woman whose shoulders were pulled up to her ears. She was perhaps in her mid-twenties. Her black hair hung in tangled waves to the middle of her back. Standing at full height, she was nearly five feet tall. One eyebrow arched over her wide-set eyes, and her upper lip curled as if she had heard the best joke in the world.

"Check my pockets, if you like," she challenged. Her voice was low and cool. "I wasn't stealin' anything. I was visiting a friend."

"The room I found you in is currently inhabited by Mr. and Mrs. Pilon. I'm sure you are not acquainted with either of them." Beads of sweat ran down his cheeks and soaked his collar.

"Sir, what is your name?" Inez pulled out her pencil and notes, flipping to an empty page.

"Reger." A crowd had gathered behind him. They stood on their toes and craned their necks.

"And your name, Miss?"

"Lettie."

"Surname, Miss Lettie?"

"Why don't you ask Mr. Pilon? He invited me."

Mr. Reger snorted and shook the fist that held the back of Lettie's dress, jostling her like a puppet. "What would a fine man like Mr. Pilon have to do with the likes of you?"

Inez blushed, recalling the stories her father told of men who needed an outlet for their passions.

"Sir, you can release your hold for the moment. I'm sure she intends to help clear up this matter, correct?"

Mr. Reger exhaled. He smelled of onions and hair tonic. He released his hold.

Lettie smoothed her dress, checking her décolletage, then suddenly turned around and lunged at the crowd, fists raised like a boxer. She watched them flinch, and she sneered in a way that was part laugh, part disgust.

Inez had never encountered such a brash woman before. To be accused of theft, dangled in the street and exposed but not at all embarrassed or concerned! Inez realized Lettie was staring at her.

"You have pretty white hair, Missy Police," Lettie whispered.

"Turn out your pockets."

Lettie made slow exaggerated movements, her eyes wide open like a vaudevillian performing a trick. She reached into her skirt and pulled out the linings of her pocket and began to hand things to Inez—a key, a fifty-cent piece, and a brown stone the size of a thumb.

Inez considered that it might be possible to conceal jewelry or other baubles in the deep cleft of her bosoms, but she didn't want to broach that subject on the sidewalk in front of the hotel.

"Satisfied? You got the wrong girl," Lettie spat.

"Can you hold her until my guests come back? That way they can check to see if they are missing any of their belongings."

What were the rules here? Even if she were able to arrest Lettie, there had to be a reason. Would the three of them stand there all day in the sun?

Inez heard the crowd muttering, "Take her away. Lock 'er up. Why ya waiting?" If only she had a pair of handcuffs or had access to the Black Maria, as the other patrolmen called it, to haul her off to jail.

"If you want to get out of here before things get ugly, I suggest you give your rightful name and address," Mr. Reger growled.

"Before your guests get more upset, why don't we move this discourse elsewhere. I've nothing to arrest her for." Inez saw a pulse ticking near his temple.

"You'd think for the money I pay, I could get some rightful assistance." He licked his lips and turned to the crowd. "Come on back in and have a drink on Jueneman's!"

The crowd clapped and whistled.

"And," he pointed a thick finger at Lettie and Inez. "I don't want to see either of you here again." Lettie didn't flinch when a drop of spittle landed on her cheek.

"Let's go." Inez pulled at Lettie's arm. They strolled off looking like companions, Inez realized, so she picked up the pace until she was dragging Lettie behind her. She was stunned to be the object of Mr. Reger's wrath when she thought she had handled the situation well.

"So, because you're a woman, he doesn't see you any better than a pickpocket, even in that fancy uniform of yours."

"He's angry. He wanted an arrest."

"Men are nothin' but over-grown children. And that one," Lettie sniffed, "he's not worth throwing a leg over."

As they moved away from the din and noise of Jueneman's, Inez heard the clink-clonk of metal. She looked down and saw bulky shapes in the bottom of Lettie's hem.

"You didn't tell me your last name." Inez knew by the time she had secured help from her sergeant, Lettie would have stashed her stolen valuables.

"Name's Kokinos. My ma says my father was a Greek sailor. I never met him. Anyway, I don't really have a place to live just now, but sometimes you can find me at Bucket of Blood. I write letters for some of the men that don't know how."

Inez held her expression still. She had identified a thief but was powerless to arrest her.

Lettie gave a little wave and swung her hips as she sauntered down the street.

Chapter 12

Inez stirred the porridge and cream. This had been her standard breakfast fare for as long as she could remember. She lived in the stately home in Saint Paul near Como Lake with Louise Moore, a woman who had been employed by the family for the last twenty-seven years, beginning just after Inez's mother died of typhoid. Inez was three years old at the time of her mother's death and had no tangible memories of her. Not even the photograph of her mother seated on a low stool and Inez standing next to her, both in white linen dresses and identical long looping curls, could spark a memory. She couldn't conjure up her smell or the sound of her voice. So in that void, Louise had filled the mother role. She tried briefly to interest Inez in feminine pursuits of dolls, cross-stitching or baking, but learned that when Inez wasn't reading, her interests were more aligned with archery practice or croquet games. Louise proved to be a loyal companion when Inez was ignored by the other girls at school because of her lanky physique and curious ways. Louise, with deep dimples and white curls, had simply always been there. Ares, her parakeet, squawked and ruffled his feathers as he sat on his perch. Inez whistled, and he bobbed his head.

Another day of rain. Inez welcomed the gray skies and cool breezes. Drops on the window panes merged into rivulets like curving rivers. She blew into her teacup and ran a hand over the large leather-bound book. She held her father's pocket watch, enjoying its heft. She had been awake for hours, yet it was only 7:30 in the morning. She awoke most days when it was still dark but willed herself to stay in bed until she heard the clock strike six. She closed the watch and slipped it into the front pocket of her skirt. Inez thought of these things as her father's property, but in truth, it was all hers now—the house, some stocks, the parrot, a roomful of books and one of her favorite things, the Book of Crime.

At some point in his career with the Saint Paul force, her father had begun to compile his thoughts and memories of certain cases that had plagued the city. As time went on, he illustrated the accounts with detailed pen-and-ink drawings. He rendered portraits of suspects, items of stolen jewelry, crime scenes and wounds left by knives, guns, or blunt weapons.

Inez let the book fall open to a random page. She leaned over the drawing and inhaled, trying to find his familiar scent of saddle soap and tack, but the pages smelled like the rest of the musty books in the study. For this drawing, he had used a red ink with a wash to render a portrait of a woman, no longer youthful, but the angle of her cheekbones, and the lift of her brow showed a woman of timeless beauty. She had a sleepy look and a mouth that looked like a bow. Her father had written:

> Molly Harrington was 45 years old when she married a man 20 years her junior and then set off for her honeymoon. No one saw her alive again. When her new husband, Jack Veach, showed up in Saint Paul, alone, he reported to the neighbors that Molly had gone off on an adventure to South America for several months, and he was in town to look after her interests. Molly's nephews called the station when they realized Mr. Veach was spending their aunt's money at an alarming rate. Upon investigation, records revealed that the suspect had a previous arrest record for assault and robbery. We also learned that he had several large trunks shipped to a cottage on White Bear Lake. Acting on a hunch, divers searched the bottom of the lake. After several weeks, they recovered the trunks, and when they were opened, they found a dismembered

body, although the head was not recovered. Veach
protested that the body was not that of his new wife,
but he was found guilty and hanged in 1905.

At the bottom of this account was a portrait of Veach, rendered on the day of his conviction, his eyes downcast and his shoulders sloped over his handcuffed wrists.

Inez touched the drawing and wished she had a chance to sit down with her father and inquire about each case. How did they hear about the suitcase delivery? What was his demeanor when they questioned him? At the very end, as the noose was pulled over his neck, did he confess?

Inez wanted to write her own Book of Crime, a supplement to his life's work, but all she had done thus far in the three weeks of her career was return a lost child to its mother's care. She had heard him crying, found him crouched and mud splattered next to a shed at the back of the property. Inez had no experience with small children, so it was hard for her to determine his age. He didn't seem capable of speech, but she was unsure if this was due to age or a detriment of sorts. As they walked the streets, he was finally able to identify his house. When Inez rang the bell, his mother opened the door, and the boy entwined himself around Inez's leg and pushed his face into her coat. Inez looked down and saw bruises and old welts on the backs of his skinny legs and then the angry brow of the mother. She instantly regretted having returned the boy to the flare of bright, hot anger.

Inez sipped her bitter tea, the precise temperature no longer scalding her tongue, and considered her other police-duty experiences of rousing drunks. They were everywhere—in alleys, in front of businesses, in saloons, on streetcars, and on the banks of the Mississippi River. One was even laid out on the front steps of the Church of the Assumption. As it turned out, Inez had no more experience with drunks than she did with children, and while she had enjoyed a life of books and reading, she realized that many practical approaches to life could not be found in the classics.

At first, she had tried to speak firmly to the inebriated, pleading with them to honor the law against public intoxication, but most of the time they were nearly dead to the world, smelling of vomit and urine and the sour tang that reminded her of chicken soup. She tried to get them to sit up, bending over to grasp both wrists and pulling hard as her corset gouged her ribs. They immediately slumped over, their limbs like cooked noodles. All of her life she had considered her corporeal form to be more reflective of a man's physique. Her father recognized her unusual attributes and always handed her Mason jars to open or asked her to move pieces of furniture. She performed these tasks as he requested even if she was uncomfortable with the bulky awkwardness of her movements. However, when struggling against the leaden bulk of a drunk, she felt like a dainty girl.

Frustrated with these experiences, Inez had consulted the Book of Crime and found a notation describing the use of knuckles applied with force to the sternum to create a reaction. The next day, a white-haired woman waving a cane called to her as she walked her route and pointed to a man, snoring and drooling on the gray-planked boards of her porch. "He's half-seas-over," she cried. "You've got to get him out of here before my husband finds him. This is the second time this week, and he's apt to take a shovel to his head if he finds him here again."

Inez turned him over on his back, breathing through her clenched teeth at the foul smell of him, gathered a fist and began to agitate her knuckles in the middle of his stained vest. In an instant, he was bucking and swinging his arms, and an open palm smashed her nose. Inez fell against the porch rail, and the shock of the crisp stabbing pain made her eyes water. It took more than a week for the bruises to fade from under her eyes, but after that day she made certain to first kneel on the wrists of the drunk.

Inez was surprised to find the men at the station took notice of her periorbital hematoma and a few inquired after her injury. Usually she felt like a shadow walking though the station. Sometimes the older policemen, the ones that had worked with her father, would touch the brims of their caps and nod in her direction, but she knew that was in honor of her father's legacy rather than her own contributions. The first day when her nose was swollen, and the bruises were the same dramatic blue-black of her uniform, one of the younger men, David

Gabrielli, shared his preferred way to awaken a drunk. "Press a pencil hard against the white part of the thumbnail—that way you only have to dodge one fist!" He smiled, showing an alarming array of white teeth and pretended to cuff her on the chin. Inez was so shocked to be included, she could only nod her head in thanks.

Inez stood at the sink to wash her bowl, cup and spoon in the steamy water even though Louise remarked there were never enough chores to keep her occupied. It was time to get dressed and go to the station. Inez inhaled deeply and hoped she would find a crime to solve and the fortitude to do the best job.

Chapter 13

Inez wrote a note to Louise, gave Ares a crust of stale bread, and slipped on her coat and hat, pulling the brim low over her eyes, partly against the rain and partly as a way to disguise herself. As she stepped off the back stoop, raindrops caused the heads of the tulips to bob and sway. Fat earthworms inched along the walkway. The wet smells of dirt and leaves mingled with the green scent of rain. Inez steered the bicycle to the end of the walk, stepped through the frame, and hopped up on the seat. She hiked her skirt to her knees and pushed the pedals as hard as she could. She followed the road around the west side of Como Lake, past the boathouse and docks that led toward Calvary Cemetery. The red and green rowboats bobbed against the dock as the breeze pushed the waves through the tall reeds.

Inez considered her plan to investigate the cemetery. As the swelling around her nose receded and the bruises took on a turmeric hue, David Gabrielli had begun to seek her out at the station to give her updates on his patrol activities.

"I've been working on another big case," he told her. "Absinthe, you know what that is?" He didn't wait for her response, but Inez wanted to tell him that the French gave it to their troops in the mid-1800s as a malaria treatment. It's made with artemisia absinthium, a green herb known more commonly as wormwood.

"It's liquor, but it's been illegal since '12. It makes people crazy. One guy drank it and killed his whole family. My partner, you know, Tim Gorman? We were close to catchin' the guy that's been smuggling it into the city. He was making a delivery, but when we stopped him, he shot Gorman in the neck and got away. Anyway, I'm going to find out who that sonofabitch is. Oh, pardon me for the language."

At first, she interpreted the rants as bragging but then considered he was trying to teach her aspects of the job. He told her how he had interrupted a house robbery and gave chase to a suspect who leaped out of a second-story bedroom window and fled into Calvary Cemetery. Inez thought there must be a reason for a criminal to take refuge in such a place and decided to investigate.

The clouds thinned, and the gray skies brightened to patches of clear blue. She steered to avoid the puddles. Inez smiled, enjoying the freedom of exertion without her corset. Police work was not suited to such restrictive clothing! She had directed Louise to construct an undergarment without any boning. The satin material fit her torso and clung to her back when she started to perspire, but she marveled at her ability to breathe freely and bend and pedal the bicycle. As she coasted under the iron archway of the entrance gate, she vowed to never subject herself to another corset ever again.

She coasted to a stop and leaned the bicycle against a granite mausoleum. Inez liked the quiet of this place, the sameness, this town of the dead. Her favorite statue was that of a woman leaning against a pillar, her head cradled in her forearm. The draping of her marble garment made Inez think of Hera, the wife of Zeus. Inez liked that this was a woman of strength and muscle. Her hands were large, capable, perhaps rendered by the artist in an unrealistic scale, but Inez felt as if they were kindred souls. How odd that this stone-mother was her most frequent confidant. In the northeast corner, two grave-diggers were preparing a site for service.

Inez spotted a young girl, dressed in a green cape, kneeling next to the mound of a new grave. Her back was to Inez, so she stopped to observe the girl's wild mass of red curls that lifted and waved in the breeze. She heard an off-pitch melody. Inez watched the girl's bowed head as her shoulders began to shake. Suddenly, she keened a long sad note, a sound that chased down Inez's spine, and then she collapsed on her side in the wet grass. Inez remembered her task of assuring the welfare of women and children, so she kept watch, listening to the twittering call of the goldfinches and the wind rustling the new leaves of the poplar trees. Inez was nothing but patient.

Finally, the girl stood up, adjusted her cape and brushed something from her skirt. She wiped her cheeks and bent low to pick up a stone from the grave and settled something under it before she headed down the path. Inez watched the girl depart out the south gate and then headed over to the grave not yet marked with a headstone.

Inez retrieved a paper, folded many times into a tiny square, hidden under the rock. It was a note written in a careful and deliberate hand.

> My Darling Connor,
> May the sun shine upon you. All love surrounds you
> and the pure light within you guides your way over.
> All My Love, Ella.

Inez blushed to read such a declaration of love. Brother? Father? Was she old enough to have been married? What would it be like to have feelings of love for another person? She loved her father and missed his stories and the way his eyes squeezed shut when he smiled. She was grateful to have been born and raised by a smart man who accepted her for all of her quirks and oddities and encouraged her studies, but in the months after his death his void felt like a healing bruise. It was sweetly tender, but fading and bearable.

Inez's shoes crunched the gravel path that led back to her bicycle, and she wondered why the sadness of the young girl draped over her shoulders like a caul. She squinted as the sun arched higher in the sky. Something glittered in the grass. Inez raised the hem of her skirt and walked through the headstones to the mausoleum that was built into the side of a hill. The surname Sullivan was carved in the architrave, and twin Doric columns framed the tall copper door. The grave-diggers were gone, and there were no other mourners about. She squatted down in front of the door and picked up a heavy silver spoon engraved with a letter "D." Could this be loot dropped by the thief? She looked around but didn't see anything else in the grass. Now she was unsure of the procedure. Should she leave it and alert David Gabrielli? What if someone else happened upon it? In the end, she slipped the spoon into her pocket and wondered why she felt like a thief.

Chapter 14

Ella was able to pay her rent on the first of May. She also bought a pair of shoes to replace the ones lined with cardboard, along with a ration of lamb and coffee beans. She made a batch of *Ballymaloe* stew and had Beata over for dinner. Amolia hadn't wanted any of the money that Mr. Cochran had offered. She told Ella she wanted to forget all about the baby and said anything she purchased would be a reminder of what happened. Ella wasn't sure if she was referring to the baby's conception, birth, or the final act of giving her baby to the Cochran family. In any case, Amolia never revealed the name of the baby's father, and the number of her visits started to wane as the temperatures grew warmer. Finally, she stopped coming by altogether. Ella waited outside of Seeger's at the shift's end a few times but failed to find her.

Business at the hat shop failed to pick up at the rate Martine had predicted. Ella couldn't see how making two hats a month was going to feed either of them for very long. Ella had suggested creating a line of elegant baby bonnets, thinking of Mr. Cochran and baby Ozor, but Martine had just shrugged indifferently at the idea. She also proposed creating a still life in the window—she would wear one of Martine's hats and sit in the window to attract customers. Martine said she would rather starve than adopt the business practices of street walkers.

Some days, Martine grew listless and depended more on her cane. Often, she smelled strongly of alcohol. By the time Ella had completed organizing the supplies, Martine sometimes asked Ella to mind the store for a few hours. Ella was never sure where Martine went or when she would return, so she kept busy polishing glass cabinets and windows. In the afternoons, the sun beat through the windows, and the air became thick, making her drunk with sleep. If she sat on the chair behind the display cabinet, her head would bob. The tilted transom provided only a breath of air. Martine ordered the shop door to be kept closed to prevent the grime of the streets from settling on the hats. While Ella didn't miss the grind of Seeger's, she did appreciate being busy.

In those dreamy afternoons, she revisited her best memories of Connor but panicked one day when it became hard to recall the exact tone of his voice or a specific word he had used. Could a memory wear out like things in the real world? The sharp edges of memory had grown rounded and soft, melding into one another until the distinctions were gone. She returned to their bed and hoped to dream of him or soak in what was left of his essence, but now the bed just smelled musty.

As the clock struck six times, she hung her apron on the hook, flipped over the closed sign, and locked the door. The streets resembled a muddy swamp. As she prepared to walk across the Wabasha Bridge back to the West Side Flats, she remembered how Connor would tease her once he learned she was afraid of the churning waters of the Mississippi River. Once he had pretended to hurl himself over the railings as Ella shrieked, and her legs quivered as if her bones had dissolved. Connor laughed until he sank to his knees and then apologized when he saw her tears.

Now, she tried to notice the things in nature that Connor would have pointed out. He always remarked on the smells of cut grass and blooming lilacs. Overnight, tree buds had burst, and new leaves, some as big as her hand, rustled in the wind as the sky relaxed. She decided these colorful skies would make a beautiful hat, and she memorized the way the pink seeped into the edge of dusky violet. She was excited to see the world as an inspiration to create lovely things. The lapping river waves translated to fabric pleats. A pheasant sprinting across the golden sand became the color palette for a fall hat. These distractions pulled her away from her sadness and worries about money.

After she crossed the bridge, the air became heavier, and she longed to shrug it off her shoulders like a woolen blanket. She headed up the hill, counting her steps to distract from the pain of blisters, courtesy of her stiff new shoes. She wanted to shed her damp blouse and skirt and lie on her back in the grass. "Hotter than the hinges on the gates of hell," was Connor's favorite hot weather saying.

Oh, her little house was in sight now! She spotted movement on the front steps. A woman stood, looking in Ella's direction. Too slight for Beata. Too tall to be Amolia. Suddenly the figure leapt from the stoop, stumbled, and disappeared between the houses.

"Wait. What do you want?" Two of Mrs. McCarthy's barefooted boys ran past, raising their faces to the wind. They waved switches from the willow tree at each other. The sky roiled a greenish yellow, and a wind hummed. Ella ran as raindrops pelted the dirt. A wooden crate sat on her steps covered with burlap bags. The streets were deserted now, the windows and doors closed. Lightning flashed, and when the thunder cracked the sound shot through her chest. Was a stranger trying to steal the food or wine left by Beata? She reached the steps as a curtain of rain crashed down. Ella pulled the burlap bags from the crate and gasped.

Three tiny, naked babies. Two boys and a girl. They were wrapped in a dirty coat, the lining torn and smelling of sour dirt. Pinned to the front of the coat was a five-dollar bill and a folded piece of paper.

Ella unpinned the note and read:

> Mrs. Byrne, please take my babies and find them a home.
> I will bring you more money when I can.

Chapter 15

"These boys, their heads are no bigger than an orange." Beata nestled the boys on either side of her neck. Her thick forearms were broader than the backs of the infants. "I've never seen babies this size. Not ones that lived." Beata's lips pressed into a line of seriousness.

Beata walked back and forth between the houses several times that night, holding candles in Mason jars to light her path. The candles softened and slumped against the teal-colored glass, the ocher tongues flickering all around them as the rain fell all evening. The illumination softened Beata's wrinkles, and Ella glimpsed what she might have looked like as a young woman. Ella ached with love for this woman who always rescued her from all her problems, always appearing by some summons of the heart.

Ella leaned against the back of the chair as the baby girl, wrapped in blankets from Beata's attic, slept on her lap. Rain pelted the windows. The sister was smaller than her brothers. Her skin bunched and hung in loose folds at the knees and elbows, and the set of her mouth reminded Ella of an old man's grimace.

Beata's steady hand dribbled a mixture of cow's milk, water and honey into their flower-bud mouths. "You don't know the mother?"

"The note wasn't signed, but it must be someone Amolia knew." Ella moved the girl to the crook of her arm and dribbled the milk mixture on the baby's lips, but unlike the boys, her mouth remained sealed, and the milk ran down her cheek.

"And what will you do with three little runts?"

"Runts? You sound like you don't like them." Ella smiled knowing this wasn't true as she watched Beata plant a chain of kisses on their heads. "Do you think I can find them a home?"

Baby Ozor had a new family, but what if it was just a stroke of Irish luck?

"They are babies. Of course I like them—although they are not as fine as baby Ozor. And who do you know that wants a sick baby with a head the size of a fruit?"

Ella looked at the trio as Beata circled the table. "So you think they're diseased?" She flashed to Thomas Cochran's questions about the health of Amolia's baby.

"I think they were not-done babies—like bread taken out of the oven too early." A breeze, delicious as ice on the tongue, rippled through the room, lifting curtains. A spray of rain wet the sills. "See, my Ella, tonight this storm brings good things—cool air but not so much water to flood our neighborhood again." Beata winked. "I like feeling like I am in the middle of all that power! I think I can bring it all inside of me, you know?" She inhaled until her nostrils pinched shut. "Ack, don't listen to a crazy old lady when you have these problems at your door."

Ella wished she could glean the storm's power and use it to make her strong. Could this force take away the feeling of leaden limbs and an aching head each time she realized Connor was gone? Every morning in their bed, a crushing weight sat on her chest, a crouching beast with hot breath that mocked her, reminding her of the curse to those who dared to grab a bit of happiness.

"They're all sleeping. It's after midnight. Go home and get some rest," Ella whispered to disguise the wet in her voice. Beata nestled the boys in the crate, and Ella situated the girl between them.

"*Kotku*? You will be all right with these little ones?"

Ella nodded. There were piles of flannels and plenty of milk.

Beata peered into the crate and cooed. "I think I should stay here. I sleep in the chair in case you need me."

Ella imagined Beata's rumbling snores as her chin met her breastbone. "No, go home. If I need you, I'll come over. Sleep. This heat has been hard on all of us."

Beata patted the babies with a hearty rhythm. "I'll come back in the morning with more clothes from the attic." Beata kissed Ella on the forehead. "Maybe tonight, you forget about the wine?"

Ella studied the infants in the crate. Her eyes burned, and she had a clawing ache in her lower belly that predicted her monthlies. Once again, a reminder there would be no babies coming. "As soon as the door swings shut, my head will be on the pillow. Promise." Ella crossed her heart and turned away to wipe a tear.

"Good dreams to you and the little ones." Beata opened the front door and stuck her hand out. "The storm has passed." She picked up one of the Mason jars, kissed her palm and flung a kiss. Ella watched the painful hitch of Beata's hips.

Despite her vow to Beata, Ella washed out her shirt and chemise and hung them over the sink. She lathered soap on a cloth and scrubbed her face and teeth. Just as she climbed into bed, she heard the bleat of a baby.

Ella picked up one of the boys and changed his flannel. The pins looked cock-eyed on the enormous diaper. He opened his dark eyes, and she held him against her bare skin, marveling at his sweet smell. She walked to the table, stirred the milk mixture, and stroked his cheek the way she had seen Beata do earlier. His head craned to the side, and when she touched the spoon to his lips, he opened his tiny mouth.

He gulped but didn't choke. Ella felt a swell of hope, tight and high in her chest, a confidence that she could take care of this baby, make him hearty enough to find him a new home. He moved his silky head against her bare breast, and she stroked the delicate web of blue veins at his temple. Oh, the feel of him, skin-to-skin, and the way he curled against her as if he had always been a part of her.

How she longed to be touched! Was it a sin this reminded her of how Connor would rest his head between her breasts when she wrapped her arms around his shoulders? She remembered counting his kisses and the salty smell of his hair. Tears fell now as she ached for his warmth, the glimpse of his golden lashes, and the spray of freckles at his throat. How odd that this baby's touch soothed the pinching pain yet sliced new scores in her heart.

It rushed at her, the moment of perfect knowing. She could take care of these lost children! She closed her eyes and took in the wet smell of earth mixed with dying flowers, listening to serene rain and feeling a silky breeze. Years from now, people would whisper her name as a saint. Ella would tell the story of these babies left at her door during a storm and how she fed them with a spoon until they gained strength. She swayed and rocked with the little boy in her arms. One day, he would appear at her door as a grown man. She would wipe her hands on her apron as she opened the door, uncertain of his identity. He would bend down to embrace her, his back and arms strong, roped with hard muscles. He would smile at her as if they shared a joke, and she would know she had held him as a tiny baby. "We healed each other," she would tell him.

Ella's knees buckled, a treacherous fatigue pressed on her shoulders. She arranged the baby in the crate, blew out the candles and climbed into bed. She laid her arm across the three babes. There were no other sounds or smells, and sleep felt like tumbling off the Wabasha Bridge.

Chapter 16

Ella lost track of the days. Nights stumbled into rose-streaked early mornings, and before she knew it the somnolent afternoon heat pounded in her head. Sometimes she would doze in the chair on the front stoop only to wake with a start, one or two babies still in her arms, to the sound of crickets and plaintive wails. The sturdy smells of ammonia and spoiled milk hung in the air. Often, they all bawled at the same time, chins trembling with red-faced anger, and Ella sobbed along with them.

She had never been so tired, not even after working a shift at Seeger's and then walking home to cook, mend, and wash laundry. She forgot which baby she had fed last and sometimes couldn't tell who was crying. Ella forgot to eat. There was always one baby in her arms, sticky and damp, as she boiled more milk or washed diapers on the stove. The clothesline in the backyard sagged to the ground with the weight of wet diapers.

Beata had not been over to help since the night of the storm. "An illness of the bowels," Beata's son, Ambrozy, reported with downcast eyes. At his mother's direction, he had delivered supplies—sets of cotton suits with arms and a sack-like section at the bottom for their legs that cinched with a string, more flannels, India rubber nipples for the bottles, and today, a baby carriage.

"From the State Street dump!" Ambrozy had proclaimed proudly. The body of the wicker carriage bore a few holes, suggesting a family of mice had been the previous occupants, and one wheel was bent, but all three babies could fit, an improvement from the peach crate.

Ambrozy pulled a note from his pocket. "My mother says to prevent bad luck the babies need names." He unfolded the list and read, "She says the names are Janna, Gerick and Lujan."

Ella laughed for the first time in many days. "Did she say which boy is which, or can I decide that?"

Ambrozy shrugged and blushed. Ella swayed as Janna fussed in her arms, and she knew he noticed her stained blouse and the mess of her hair that was plastered to her neck in wet waves. Her feet were dirty, but she was too tired to care.

"Mrs. Byrne, what are your plans for all of these infants?"

"Ambrozy, I'm Ella. Just plain Ella. I want to find homes for them. A family that provides food and clothing and education."

"And there are people that wish to take care of a baby, um, not of their own issue?"

She wanted to tell him the story of baby Ozor, but her oath to Mr. Cochran held her tongue. Instead she nodded, and Ambrozy frowned, trying to make sense of the information.

"Thank you for the carriage. I will use it to walk to the hat shop. I have a delivery to make on Friday." Her hand flew to her mouth. Had she missed the delivery day? "When is Friday?" A panic pounded hard in her chest. She needed this delivery job to find more rich families.

"Tomorrow is Friday, Mrs. Byrne."

Ella let out a big breath. She waved her hand to shoo away the flies that crawled on the leg of one of the boys. He had a little red mark between his brows shaped like a leaf. The boy would be named Lujan.

Ambrozy's wavy hair was the same color as a German chocolate cake. He was always so formal, bowing when he entered or left the room, even though he was only a year younger. He twisted his cap, his broad knuckles white with effort.

"They are bigger. Growing, to be sure."

"Really, do you think so? They are all drinking from the bottle now—even the little girl. Janna," she added. This brought tears to her eyes. Maybe all this tending was doing good after all?

He nodded. "Most definitely so. If you'd like, I could weigh the mites on the meat scale." Last month, Ambrozy had secured a job at Cohen's Grocery Store on South Robert Street. He stood a little straighter as he said this. His broad arms and shoulders were the masculine reflection of his mother, and she could picture him maneuvering carcasses and wielding cleavers to slice the meat from the bone.

"How do you like working for Louis Cohen?"

"I am learning the trade. It is more difficult than I imagined. See? I've cut myself again!" He offered his upturned palm as evidence.

The cut located at the base of his thumb had crusted and resembled a purple smile about an inch long. Ambrozy's wide palm disappeared in a fog of memory, and she was recalling Connor's hand and the wad of blood-soaked linen. She gasped.

Ambrozy shoved his hands into his pocket, backed off the porch and ran to his mother's house. A cloud of brown dust plumed behind him. Janna wailed and stiffened, as if she was distressed to see him go. Suddenly, Ella heard a rumbling gurgle in Janna's belly and then felt a hot rush of diarrhea soak the front of her blouse and skirt. Ella stood, stock still, stunned that one tiny infant could produce such volume.

Chapter 17

Janna was ill. Within hours she had soiled a pile of diapers with watery loose stool, the color of a lake in August. When she fussed, beads of sweat, like tiny blisters, formed across her forehead. She arched and whimpered whenever Ella tried to hold her. There was no amount of rocking, patting or singing to console her. Perhaps if she had borne children of her own, she might have a better understanding of the wisdom and patience of mothers.

Gerick and Lujan had taken bottles an hour ago and slept, unaware of the state of their distressed sister. Ambrozy was right—they were thriving. Their cheeks had filled out, and their color had improved from yellow-tinged to a golden sweet olive. Ella marveled how they always managed to find each other in their slumber. Often times they ended up nose-to-nose, arms flung around each other's necks. It seemed unnatural to break this bond, and she would insist they be placed together.

Ella closed her eyes, swayed even though her arms were empty and marveled at the feeling of quiet. Her body hummed as the evening sun surged through the west windows, glowing pink behind her eyelids. She listened to the branches scratching against the window and smelled the first bloom of shrub roses that hung from the trellis near the porch. Is this what pink smells like? She felt happy in this pink world. She giggled at her crazy thoughts and then worried she might be fit for the asylum. A terrible thirst made her weak all over, her tongue thick and stale. Her lips were dry. She went to the kitchen and chugged a glass of water. Her heart pounded, and she wiped her mouth with the back of her hand as she leaned against the table. She needed to rest, close her eyes for a minute to gather her strength before attending to the washing duties.

Janna gave a screechy-hoarse cry. Ella ran to the front room before her cries woke the boys. Sulfur filled her nose. Watery stool stained the length of the sleep suit. Was it possible she seemed lighter than when she had put her down? When Ella removed the flannel, it was tinged with bright blood.

Ella felt numb all over, and the baby's spindly, limp legs blurred from her tears. Janna was getting worse! The skin across her bottom was red, and hot-looking sores had erupted. She stopped crying, and her hands lay limp at her sides. A pair of flies chased each other over her small belly. Each breath stretched the skin across the delicate fan of ribs.

What to do but gently dab the cracked skin and pin on another diaper? Ella put Janna next to her in bed, curled around her and stroked the dark wisps of hair at the crown of her head. There was no time for despair as she joined the slumbering trio.

* * *

Ella is searching for something. She wanders throughout Seeger's shifting bolts of linen, peering under the cutting tables. She shoves open the door to the toilets, but the room is empty. The toilet has overflowed, and in the corner near the sink is a pool of blood, dried to a dark sheen. She hears weeping and turns to see Amolia rush toward her, dressed only in her underclothes. Tendrils of blood twine down her legs like bright red ivy. She shoves a cigar box in Ella's hand and flees. *Wait, come back.* Ella calls, but all she hears is the slap of bare feet echoing in the hallway. The wooden lid of the cigar box is adorned with a drawing of a woman wearing a flowing white robe, holding a sword and shield. A red cape billows behind her shoulders. The word "RELIANCE" arches in gold block letters over her head. Ella raises the lid of the box and sees an infant. The skin is a dusky purple hue, and the arms and legs look like twigs pulled tight against the body. The mouth is set in a grim line. When Ella nudges the baby with her finger, it rolls to its side revealing a jagged cut across the neck.

* * *

Ella's eyes popped open in the dark bedroom. Her heart kicked in her chest, and she strained to hear the weak cries of a baby. Was that part of the dream? She rolled off the bed and felt on the table for the kerosene lamp and lit a match. Both boys were squawking in the stroller, their arms flailing. Ella scooped them up and changed their wet flannels. She carried them to the kitchen and settled them in the crate while she set some milk mixture to warm on the stove. She pulled Connor's pocket watch from her apron. It was just after three in the morning. She had slept for four hours! The dream shimmered—the dead baby, Amolia crying.

The boys began to whimper again as Ella tested the warmth of the milk and filled two bottles, tugging the rubber nipples over the necks. She discovered she could feed two babies at the same time if she arranged the both of them across a pillow on her lap. She went to the bedroom to retrieve a pillow and watched the shadows bounce off the walls in the tangle of sheets. Gooseflesh rose on her arms.

Janna.

She moved closer and put her hand on the baby's chest and felt no movement, heard no sound save for the pounding in her ears. Her fingers scrambled to move the night dress and feel her legs and face. Ella gasped. The death chill.

Ella sank to the floor and leaned her head against the straw bed. Janna had died as she slept.

Another death in this bed. Had Connor been there to cuddle the baby and whisk her away in his arms? The boys raised the pitch of their demands in the kitchen, and Ella sobbed with them, pressing her face to the mattress and screaming until she choked.

She scrambled to her knees. Surely the neighbors next door heard the wails of the babies. How would she explain a dead baby that didn't belong to her? She rolled Janna over and saw her back and buttocks were a dusky purple hue.

In the amber glow of the lamp, Ella knew she had to get rid of the body… before the sun came up.

Chapter 18

What Ella remembered about the family's trip across the ocean was that the churning waves matched the churning of her stomach. Her mother had stroked her forehead with a cool, dry hand, even though at fourteen years of age she was much too grown for such attention. Weak tears ran in the comfort of this touch. When she leaned over the wooden bucket to vomit stringy, yellow bile, she shivered under the burlap bag that served as a blanket.

The steerage area where her family slept smelled of wet wood, vomit, and sweat. During the squall, they had been forced to stay below deck for more hours than she could count. Since the illness started, she had moved to the lowest bunk with Aileen, her youngest sister. Her brothers were bedded in the top bunk, and her sister Branna and their mother slept alone in the top sleeping area. Ella was too sick to care where her Da spent the night.

"Ya see what your witchery has brought to this family?" Her Da braced his hand on the upper bunk and leaned in close enough for Ella to feel the spray of spittle on her cheek. His gingered hair hung in lank waves around his face, and one eye was swollen shut. Fighting with the crew, her brother had whispered yesterday.

Her mother continued to stroke Ella's forehead, her voice calm, but Ella could feel the tensing of her mother's thigh against her cheek. "I was doing what was needed." Ella closed her eyes, feigning sleep but wanting more of the story to be revealed.

"We need ya more! What would have happened to us if I had let them take you to prison?" Ella saw the muscle in his jawbone jump.

"How many times do I have to tell you? I am innocent."

"A woman is dead." Her father spat the bitter words out.

"Only because of her husband's cruelty—Maura's death was not by my hand."

"But you gave her those potions of yours!" His finger stabbed her mother's shoulder. Ella pictured her mother walking to the edge of the woods, the late summer sun warming the waves of her long hair. She would lift the branch that led to her hidden path and then disappear to collect the secrets that grew above and below the ground.

"Yes, she came to me."

"And Patrick found out what those poisons were for." He swayed with the movement of the ship. The sickness clutched Ella as his rum-sweat smell poured around them.

"Someone must have told him." Mother's calm voice soothed Ella. She pictured her face looking like a saint, sweet and holy despite persecution.

"Told him ya murdered the babe in her womb."

Ella heard his anger and knew how he clenched his jaw to reveal his broken eye-tooth.

"She couldn't care for any more children. The youngest of her seven was still a babe. Shouldn't she have the right to control that?"

"It's not your business."

Her mother's fingers clutched Ella's shoulder. "If I've the ability, 'tis my business."

"Your ability almost got you thrown in Kilmainham Gaol."

"I have apologized to you more times than I can count, but I would prefer to face the courts than to flee. It should be me that suffers, not you and the children."

"Is it sainthood you're seeking?"

A tear landed on Ella's temple. "No, but..."

"You know what happens to prisoners? You'd have died from disease or starvation before the court heard you. What about your children?"

As an answer, Branna wailed.

"So I'm an arse for savin' ya, then? For leavin' me job and sellin' off our things to buy us passage?" He limped back and forth.

"No, you're a loyal man, to be sure. I hope we can go home one day." Her mother sniffed and dabbed her eyes.

"I imagine you'd stop one of my babes if the mood was in ya, if you haven't already." He left them all there and went up to the deck to greet the storm.

* * *

Ella pushed the carriage across the Wabasha Bridge. A full moon lit her way. The breeze carried the smells of the river and decaying wood. She shivered under the green cape and pulled up the hood. She followed the wink of the gas lanterns across the bridge as the wheels rumbled over the slats. Far below, the waves crashed against the stone pilings. The boys, fed and diapered, slept peacefully next to the gray-striped hatbox from Martine's store.

Ella was alone on the bridge.

She planned to leave Janna's body at the cathedral's steps. Connor had told her the grand church was fashioned after St. Peter's in Rome. The sheer size of the church made it feel trustworthy. She had prepared a note of explanation. *Please bury this baby in sacred ground,* she wrote. She hoped the Sisters of the church would look upon this innocent with kind hearts. She walked briskly, hoping to reach the church before daybreak, but the bent wheel caused the carriage to stutter and pitch to the right.

Crossing the bridge always reminded her of Connor. She tried to push these memories aside because something new had erupted in her heart and filled her with shame. Sometimes she was mad at him. The anger fought with the tender part that loved him. Connor had told her he didn't know how he cut his finger, but now she believed that was a lie. She pictured him showing off, flipping the knife in the air as he spun on his heels before catching it. Or maybe he egged on another cutter in a speed contest. This thought stabbed her. Connor's carelessness and prideful ways had caused all of this hardship. Now she was alone, pushing a dead baby across the bridge in the wee hours of the morning.

She stopped, breathing hard. The guardrail felt splintered and gritty against her palms. She planted both feet on the lower rail and leaned over. Now that she had let out the first dark thought, more of them swirled like spirits and whispered in her ear. Maybe she should just take the boys, one in each arm, and pitch forward into the dark, roiling currents. The fall would break her neck, and all of the ache and grief, the worry, would be over. Maybe Connor would come for her holding baby Janna, and they would have the family they'd missed. The wind picked up, cool against her tears, but she felt calm. The liquid hot fear she always felt on the bridge had drained away to an airy peace.

She held out both arms in supplication. Would the departed turn their backs on her for the sins of murder and suicide? As an answer to her question, she recognized Gerick's cry. He had already known such loss, his birth mother, his sister. She owed it to the boys to find a good home. A life. She stepped down from the rail and resumed her walk as the sky lightened to a gauzy pink at its far edge.

It would be daylight soon, and she needed to hurry or risk discovery. Northbound Wabasha Avenue was muddy, and the wheels bogged down in the muck. She pushed and shoved the carriage, breathing hard as mud splattered her skirt. By the time she reached Kellogg, sweat was pouring down her back, and she mopped her forehead and upper lip with a handkerchief.

A horse and wagon carrying blocks of ice from J. W. Day Company rumbled past her. The driver kept his head low as he passed the switch over the horse's haunches. Other delivery men appeared now, and Ella held the hood with one hand to hide her face. Was she too late? Should she turn around and wait for nightfall? Her throat clenched to think of spending the day in the house with Janna's body. Two scrawny brown dogs, one missing patches of fur, the other with a rusty scab across his nose, began to follow her. She walked faster, and one of them bared his teeth and snapped at her skirt. When she kicked him in the nose, he yelped, and then they both ran off.

As Ella approached the notorious Bucket of Blood bar, she looked up to see the cathedral glowing in the morning light. The copper cross pulsed with warmth. She imagined a patron stumbling out of the bar, gazing westward to see the church shimmering with God's first light.

The thought of the bar both thrilled and repulsed her. Connor had always cautioned her to give this place a wide berth. He said it was a haven for pickpockets so swift you wouldn't know you had been robbed. They played cards at all hours that led to brawls with knives and guns. Ella knew women frequented this place, but she didn't know how they could stand those greasy-faced men with groping hands… the type of men who brandished their tongues and cocks like weapons and greedily pushed their hands over women's breasts and thighs.

Just then, two women pushed the doors open, and a cloud of smoke billowed behind them as if they were on fire. Their hips rolled as they sauntered down the hill. One welcomed the cool of the morning by piling her hair to the top of her head and dabbing her neck with a kerchief. The other said something, and they both bent over laughing and hooting. The taller blonde slung her arm around her friend as they headed down the hill to Madame Nina's house. Ella pictured the women lounging about in fancy underthings, sleeping the day away until the dusky hours called them back to work. Ella stopped pushing the stroller. They were just like her, it seemed. With no decent way to make money, they did what they could to survive.

A man propped open the door of the bar with a broom handle and pitched out a bucket of water in a wide splattering arch. The cobblestones glistened.

"Ma'am, did you drop your handkerchief?"

Ella turned to see a man spill out of the shadows next to the bar. His long fingers pinched a flash of white fabric. He looked briefly behind him, causing Ella to look too, but there was no one there. He wore a morning coat with long tails, frayed in places at the cuffs and collar. In this light, his eyes appeared gray. She blushed to notice his lips were very red as if he had spent the long night kissing someone. As he waved the lace-trimmed handkerchief, she saw it was monogramed with the letter "M," and Ella moved closer and reached out to touch his smooth fingertips even though the handkerchief wasn't hers. His look made her feel as if she already knew what it was like to press against him and feel his bottom lip graze the corner of her mouth.

"It's not mine."

He held out his palm. "Dance with me?" Sad harmonica notes drifted out from the darkness of the bar. "What's your name, Green-Eyes?" He leaned his shoulders against the brick wall.

"Ella."

He moved closer when she answered.

"Nice to meet you, Miss Ella. I'm Richard Gale." The sound of his voice soothed her, and for some reason he smelled of fresh bread. She closed her eyes, hoping he would say more, but then heard a plaintive wail.

"Wait, the children! I must—" She turned and ran back to the carriage. How had she managed to get so far away? When she looked up, Richard Gale had disappeared. Gerick punched his fists in the air and cried. The sun was up now, burning through the wispy clouds. She had failed to get to the church in time to hide the body.

It turned out not to matter. When she bent to pick up Gerick, she realized the hatbox was gone.

Chapter 19

Workers trudged to the factories. Heads down, bundles or satchels on their backs, they moved like a sad army, resigned to the heaviness of the new day.

She spun around, looking for someone scurrying away with her hatbox, but how could she risk calling out "Stop thief!" No one else emerged from the bar; no one was looking at her. Breathing hard, Ella turned and headed to Martine's. Trembling, she gripped the handle of the carriage until her knuckles ached. Who was the thief? Surely the box was heavier than if it contained a hat. The pounding in her ears muffled the morning sounds of the city as she walked. Was this Connor helping her out in some strange way? Had her problem just been solved? It wasn't funny, but at some time in the future she realized that it might be. She could imagine Connor laughing.

The spring air, so clean as she had crossed the bridge in the early morning was now layered with smells of rotten garbage, hot oil and manure. Both boys were awake. Their dark eyes squinted and searched the sky above them. The dirty bottoms of the clouds scuttled across the sky, low enough to brush the tall tops of the buildings. The babies didn't fuss, but regarded Ella with solemn matching frowns, as if they knew she had failed their sister.

Ella's legs burned as she rounded the corner to Martine's store. Dark spots danced in front of her eyes, and she was breathless and dizzy from hunger. She dug into her pocket to retrieve the shop key and propped the door open while she struggled to maneuver the stroller.

Martine would not be at the shop at this early hour. Ella went to the workroom and located a tin of biscuits hidden under the table and gobbled the stale cookies. She was always hungry and tired. Would it ever end?

The room brightened as she diapered and fed the boys with a bottle she had wrapped in their blanket. She realized she missed spending time at the shop watching Martine fuss over a new hat.

Ella looked around. The new hat to be delivered sat on top of the glass cabinet, packaged and ready to go. The pale, gray-striped box was festooned with Martine's exaggerated bows, her initial in a gilded letter M. The invoice was tucked inside the lavender envelope. Maybe she should just complete the delivery instead of waiting for Martine. She pulled the tail of the ribbon through her fingers.

She couldn't stop thinking about the hatbox. What if someone called the police after they found the box and Janna's body? Would the police think Martine had something to do with the dead infant? Ella pressed her clammy hands to her face.

The door jangled open. Martine. No time to dash out now.

"Ella! So early to see you!" Martine's eyes glittered with energy. She wore a cream-colored dress with a lace overlay. Her fingers fluttered over the bodice and circled a large brooch pinned near her throat.

"It's been too long since you minded the store for me. What's this?" She moved to the carriage and pulled back the blanket.

"*Bebes*? Ella? *Mon Dieu, l'odeur!*" Martine pinched her thin nose between her fingers.

"I'm taking care of the wee ones. I will..." Ella faltered and then went on. "I will find them a home—for a business, you see. I'll get paid."

Martine circled the carriage, picked at the broken wicker and ran the tip of her cane over the bent wheel. "Hmmm, a business. I thought you wanted to apprentice with me. To learn the art of hat making, not the care of smelly infants."

"I do, Martine, want to learn from you, but there hasn't been enough—"

"Been enough what?" She held a handkerchief over her nose.

"Enough work. To pay for rent, food."

"Getting paid to find them a home? How is this possible?"

Ella sniffed and wondered if she was so accustomed to the smell of sickness that it no longer roiled her stomach. "The mother left five dollars."

"And how long have you been caring for these two urchins?"

How long had it been? The days were sewn together in one long strip. "More than a week."

"So you are getting paid twenty-five cents each day for one baby. And you think my little hat business is slow?"

"But the new family. The ones that will take them. They will pay me too."

"Pffft. People pay you for a child that is not their own? I don't believe it."

Ella wanted to tell her about baby Ozor and Mr. Cochran but held her pledge of secrecy. "It could happen."

"This business, how do you get babies? Where did these two come from? An ad in the paper?"

Ella considered that this might be a better method and was embarrassed she hadn't thought of it herself. "They were left on my doorstep."

"What nonsense! You can't just open your door every morning to discover you have new items to sell!" Martine paced back and forth, waving her arms as if she were shooing away pigeons. She wasn't using her cane and looked thinner than usual. Ella noticed the hard edges of her elbows and hips. Even her nose seemed sharp and precise like a blade. "What if people left me ugly hats and asked me to sell them? They would sit on the shelf, and people would laugh. All my customers—gone!"

Martine gestured around as if there were a shop full of women waving fistfuls of dollars. Ella was hurt and annoyed at the same time. Gerick started to fuss, and Martine's eyes widened in disbelief.

Ella picked him up and put him on her shoulder, and when he burped a string of milk ran down the back of her cape.

"Euew, the velvet. It will be ruined!" Martine hid her face in her hands as if Ella had slapped her.

"Martine, why do you dislike babies so much?" Ella had to raise her voice over Gerick's cries. "Don't you want a child of your own?" Ella realized this wasn't the time to make a case for Gerick's brown eyes and dimples. Not now, when he smelled of soiled diapers and sour milk.

All of Martine's fluttering movements halted. She looked Ella in the eye. The energy seeped from her, and Ella pictured water gushing from a hole in a bucket. The sun angled into the shop windows, and Martine pressed her forearm to her brow as she grimaced.

"You are so young, Ella. Years from now, when you think about this question, you may have a different heart."

Tears rolled down Ella's cheeks. She was tired, and her throat ached. Martine's disapproval stung. Was she done with her? She continued to sway even though Gerick had gone to sleep.

"I'm sorry." Her voice faltered. "I would like to apprentice with you, if you'll have me."

Martine moved behind the display case and slumped over, resting her head on crossed arms. Her voice sounded flat and muffled. "I need to sleep. Deliver the hat, please."

Ella tucked Gerick into the stroller and wedged the hatbox at their feet, thinking of the theft of Janna's body and the need to be vigilant during the delivery.

"Go out the back way. I don't wish for a customer to see that awful carriage."

As Ella parted the curtain to the back room and shoved the stroller through the narrow opening, tears ran down her face, and she bit her lip to keep from sobbing. When she wiped her tears with the palm of her hand, the smell of ammonia made her cry harder. The right wheel caught the leg of the work table, and the babies started to cry. The harder she worked to push the stroller to the back door, the more obstinately it behaved and the louder the babies wailed. The air was thick and hot, and Ella flung the cape into the carriage. She slid the bolt to the door and burst into the dank, narrow alley where downspouts filled oily puddles. She saw a man walking in the alley. He glanced over his shoulder and then darted around the corner.

Richard Gale.

Had her eyes played tricks? Had he followed her here? She remembered his green eyes and the way her heart pounded at the touch of his hand. She turned the stroller and headed in the opposite direction.

Chapter 20

After the delivery, she walked home in a hot wind that swirled around her, twisting the leaves on the trees. The noon sun beat down, and sweat ran between her shoulder blades, soaking the band of her skirt. Muddy streets dried and cracked. She fed Lujan as she sat on a wrought iron bench and watched as he greedily sucked the nipple.

When she reached home, Beata was there, pale and smiling. She hugged Ella. When she asked after Janna, Ella could only shake her head, her tongue thick and useless. Ella drank water until she choked. Janna's pinched face, her pale legs pulled tight to her body loomed behind her closed eyes. Beata, wiping tears with her forearm, took Ella by the hand and put her to bed, untying her shoes and pulling the sheet over her shoulders. Ella sobbed into the pillow because Beata had changed the soiled sheets on this death-bed and replaced them with the smells of sun and borax.

She slept.

There were no dreams or muffled cries of infants, dancing strangers, or hats. There was nothing at all. As she blinked her eyes in the low shadows, she realized it was early evening. The day had cooled on its own without a storm, and the curtain rose with a breeze that felt like an exhalation. A mourning dove cooed lonely notes. She should get up and eat something, launder diapers and tidy the kitchen, but she found herself staring at a crack in the ceiling that looked like the profile of a man with a hooked nose.

Were the babies sleeping?

She gasped and sat up, heart pounding, until she remembered Beata's promise to look after the boys. Martine was right. This business was a failure. She lacked Connor's sure knowledge of the working world. Alone, she couldn't make sense of any of it.

A knock at the door. Her mind tripped through the faces that might be on her doorstep. Another weepy mother and baby? The police? Two of them, Irish brothers with no sympathy for one of their own, eager to drag her off to jail. And for some reason, she pictured Richard Gale leaning against the door frame, a bottle of champagne in hand. He would grin, one eyebrow arched. Ella shivered and pulled the sheet over her eyes to block out the thoughts that pelted her like sharp rocks.

The rap became more insistent and a voice called, "Answer your door, will ya? I know you're in there."

Ella pushed herself off the bed and ran to the door, the grit on the floor sticking to her bare feet. She opened the door just wide enough to reveal a woman standing with one hand on her hip, the other fist poised to beat on the door. Ella panted. The woman twisted a heavy gold necklace around her forefinger. A medallion dangled over the swell of her breasts.

"Can I come in?" Her dark hair sprang away from her face in dark waves. Her skin was a warm olive tone.

"Who are you?"

"Someone who knows you. Knows what you've been up to." A wren darted toward its muddy nest under the eaves. Ella flinched. The woman didn't move.

Ella's thighs quivered. "Me children are asleep. Can you come back tomorrow?"

"I'm here now. What I have to say won't be any different tomorrow. I won't be loud, if that's what you're fussin' about." Her teeth were square and strong, with a generous space between the two uppers. Her tongue pushed at the gap when she smiled.

"What do you want of me? I don't know you." The grin confused Ella. It felt warm and friendly.

"Talk is all."

"Talk?" Ella repeated and gripped the door knob.

"I've seen ya pushing those babies around town." The woman's eyes were wide-set and a curious color of amber with brown flecks like loose tea leaves. There was a roar in Ella's ears.

"Earlier today, it was."

Ella swallowed a bitterness at the back of her throat.

"I think I should come in. Maybe you can give me a drink."

"Me husband's not home. Anyway, I was doing errands today. What of it?"

The woman bent over, laughed, and slapped her thigh. It was a raucous noise that ended in a raspy whoop. "That's a good joke. I s'pose next thing you'll be pissin' in my ear and tellin' me it's rainin'." She was shouting now, and Ella pushed open the door to see Mrs. O'Malley standing on the street watching the exchange. The blue velvet sky was streaked with muted pinks.

"First of all, there's no a husband here. You've no children of your own. I asked around."

"Come in," Ella hissed.

The woman sauntered past Ella, her solid hips swinging like a bell. Ella opened the window. The smells of old milk, wet diapers and sour sweat crawled to the back of her throat.

The woman produced a paper fan from her sleeve and snapped it open. The fan was from some faraway place with a complicated drawing of a green and gold dragon with a coiled tail. She turned a chair around and propped both elbows against the back.

"Whiskey?"

Ella shook her head. "I can warm some coffee is all."

The woman nibbled at the skin above the nail of her forefinger, paused, examined the spot and gnawed at it again.

"I don't think so. Have ya something to eat?"

"I asked your name before."

The woman plucked something from her tongue. "Lettie is all you need to know."

"How did you know where I lived?"

"I followed you."

Ella's mouth went dry. "Since when? Why?"

Lettie shrugged. "Say, it's awful quiet here. What did you do with the other two? Ya put 'em in hatboxes again? Or flour sacks this time?"

Dark spots welled in Ella's vision, and she gulped air.

"Better sit before ya go down like a boxer." Lettie pointed to the floor. She didn't offer her chair.

Ella squatted, out of breath. "They aren't—the babies are with a neighbor."

"I'm right then. They ain't yours."

Ella pressed her temples hard and shook her head.

"Ya stole 'em?"

"Someone left them at door."

"Why ever with the likes of you?" Lettie licked her lip.

"Once, I helped me friend find a home for a baby she couldn't keep. I think she told someone."

"So you were plannin' on selling 'em." Lettie propped her chin on her stacked fists.

"No, I'll find them homes. Good places to live with rich folks!"

"Like charity work, then?"

"Well, no, I would be paid. I've been paid in that other case."

"That sounds like selling babies to me." Lettie toyed with the pendant again, pressing it between her lips as if she might take a bite.

"That sounds awful!"

"So one of these free babies, the one in the hat-box, what happened?"

"You stole the hatbox?"

"Whoa! Don't jump to conclusions. It was just some talk I heard at Bucket of Blood."

"Are you going tell the police?" Ella's throat tightened. She had heard about the criminals that visited Bucket of Blood.

"Do you think I should? I bet they might be interested in this sort of thing!"

Ella sobbed. Her nose ran, and the sadness gushed from her. She pictured Janna's cold legs, sticky with diarrhea and the dusky blue of her lips. She cried until her stomach ached and she was out of breath. She lay curled on her side, not caring if the dirt bit into her cheek.

A dog yipped somewhere on the street. Ella's nose was clogged. "I was taking care of them, and they were sickly, the little girl especially. She had runny bowels, something awful and then… she just died."

"Sure you don't have any whiskey?"

There had been no whiskey since Connor. Oh, Connor. Her heart felt like a smashed plum, juices running from the pulpy meat.

She opened her eyes to see a handkerchief land on the floor. She picked it up, dingy and wrinkled, and dabbed her eyes and nose. The sharp scent of flowers from a foreign place filled her nose. A small kindness made the tears start again.

"Wine. I have wine." Ella walked to the kitchen using her hands to steady herself against the walls of the hallways as if she had already had several glasses. She welcomed the numbing of all her tender edges.

Ella tucked the jug under her arm and grabbed two glasses. Did she want money? *Oh, Connor, please tell me what to do.*

She returned to Lettie and sat on the floor at her feet. They drank the warm wine without talking. Ella's tongue curled from the bitterness of the drink. Everything sounded loud—crickets chirping, the screams of a cat fight, each gulp of wine. Lettie watched Ella, at times smiling, twirling her medallion. Finally, the wine loosened Ella's tongue, and she found herself talking about Connor's death, her position with Martine, baby Ozor and the triplets. Her chest ached, and she cried into Lettie's handkerchief until the room dimmed. Ella stood, her legs loose and wobbly, and she lit the candles in the jars and set them on the window sills. The shadows exaggerated Lettie's features, darkened her eyes.

Lettie changed position and poured the last of the wine into her glass. "I'm thinkin' this over. Your business with all these babies, you've been doing it wrong."

"Wrong?" Ella hiccupped.

"You can't do it alone."

"Then you think it's a good idea?" Martine's harsh criticism echoed in her mind.

"You need a partner." Lettie tilted her glass and held out her tongue to receive the last drops of wine. "You need me."

Chapter 21

In the late afternoon, the thick air in the Central Police Station smelled of tobacco and sweat. Inez sat on the long bench taking care to write her report as concisely as possible. Many desks were unoccupied, but she hadn't been assigned to use one, so at the end of the day her shoulders ached from hunching over her notes. She took great care with her reports to prove her work was vital to the well-being of the citizens of Saint Paul. Sometimes she wondered if anyone really read them, for no one ever made a comment. She had the urge to write a fictional account of a murder or a dramatic tale of foiling a robbery just to see if anyone would acknowledge it. In the end, all Inez could write was the truth of her day.

Another officer burst through the door, dragging a handcuffed man. His charge was small in stature with a bushy dark mustache and dark curls. He had a cut over one eyebrow and smears of dried blood on his cheek. When the officer shoved him toward the bench, he had to spin and skip like he was doing a jig to land without injury. He looked at Inez and then scooted closer. At first it appeared he was winking at her, but then she realized his eyelashes were matted with dried blood.

"So's you can read and write, eh?"

Inez ignored him.

"I've never seen the like of you at Nina's. I'd remember them white brows and hair. You work on your own?" He looked her over from head to toe.

Inez realized he thought she was a prostitute. She gave him her best stern look and twisted her nightstick into his side which only caused him to giggle.

"If you'd be wantin' to take a night off, you can go to Bucket of Blood and do some writin' for some of the fellers." Inez recalled her conversation with Lettie, the thief.

"I'm a police matron. I work here."

"A girlee! I never heard a such a thing. You can lock me up in the workhouse anytime. I'd go gladly if you'd put the cuffs on me." She considered a knuckle to the breastbone, but he was too lively to attempt that move.

Suddenly, David Gabrielli lifted the man by the ear and tossed him on the floor. The cut over his eye opened again, sending fresh blood dripping across the bridge of his nose.

"Are you harmed?" David's sable eyes crimped.

"I'm bleedin' again!"

"Shut your bone box, Dickie. I'm not talkin' to you." David pressed his knee to the man's shoulder, forcing a groan out of him.

"Don't mind him—Dickie's another Admiral of the Red." David pantomimed taking a drink.

"He wasn't a bother." Inez was embarrassed that David thought her to be a helpless ninny. "Listen, I wanted to show you something. I was at Calvary today—remember you told me about the burglary suspect that escaped though the fence?" Inez pulled the spoon from her pocket. "I found this and wondered if the burglar dropped it."

David examined the spoon. "The Dolan family reported the theft. I'll show this to them—seems likely it could be theirs." The front of David's shirt was unbuttoned and stained dark with sweat. From her angle she could see a nest of dark curly hairs sprouting from the V-shape. It felt strange to have him kneeling before her.

"Then you think this is important to the case?"

"We know he escaped that way. Doesn't tell me where he is now."

"Maybe he lives nearby? It's the fastest route to his house."

"So are you an Edgar Allen Poe reader?"

"What?"

"You know, Poe—cemetery stories and all. He writes about that sort of thing." He wiped his forehead on his rolled cuff.

"Oh, no. I just thought I would follow up on your story about the burglar."

"Well, don't go there alone at night."

"I was there early this morning."

"Anyway, you should be careful, is what I'm sayin'." He narrowed his eyes at her, and she felt like a scolded child.

"Will ya let me up then? I can't breathe!" Dickie wheezed, his cheek still pressed to the floor.

"If you don't behave, I'll give you a bunch of fives!" David smirked and showed him his fist.

"I'll be good, promise." As David hoisted him to his feet, there was a smear of blood on the floor.

"Come on, let's go."

"I'd love to kiss those luscious lips," Dickie said as David pulled him down the hall.

Inez watched them walk away and thought it was the first time any man had ever expressed an interest in kissing her.

Chapter 22

The damp night air licks her skin. Inez looks down and realizes she is naked. Her bare feet, wet from dew in the grass, flex in the mud; the cool clay oozes between her toes. Inez searches for stars in the sooty sky, but the moon is the only celestial navigational sign; thin and sharply curved. She blinks hard at the shifting sable shadows. Granite headstones.

The cemetery.

Her heart flutters as she tries to remember how she arrived here. This place is dangerous, David had warned her, especially at night. Scratching sounds, the sighing and rustling of trees, build to a din. She covers her ears with clammy palms.

A shape suddenly appears before her. Her breath hitches, and she feels something drape over her in a gauzy whisper. She presses her back to the cool headstone and smells earth and salt on her skin.

The shape envelops her, pressing against her legs, torso and breasts. The caress is tentative. She has no urge to run or fight. Her eyes close as she waits for a kiss she has never had. Her mouth opens, her arms try to capture the edges of the shape, but her fingers close on air. What a curious thing to have weight without density! The pressure intensifies until she can no longer draw a breath, and she welcomes this feeling. Suddenly, the pressure breaks through her skin, muscle and bone, and then it is gone. Inez slumps against the headstone, trembling, her face wet with tears.

* * *

Inez woke in her narrow bed, the damp sheets tangled between her legs. She fumbled for her spectacles on the bedside table and squinted in the dusk of her room to orient her desk, chair, lamp and her stack of books. The lace curtain billowed like a yawn and then relaxed on the sill.

Inez couldn't explain her fascination with the cemetery. Her new nightly diet of Edgar Allen Poe poems before bed was certainly part of it (*My love, she sleeps! Oh, may her sleep as it is lasting, so be deep, soft may the worms about her creep*). The poems make her think of the girl of sorrow who curled on her side and left the love poem on the grave.

Inez had begun patrolling the cemetery in the evenings as the last hours of May daylight burnt to a warm carmine hue over the oldest graves. All the walking and biking of the past weeks had strengthened her legs and arms. Her lungs filled with night air, and she was confident she could walk the entire city without tiring. She was a courageous Athena in armor. On these patrols, she left her hair unpinned and flowing over her shoulders.

Inez believed the cemetery was the clue to catching the robber she nicknamed the Tombstone Thief. Whatever his name, he had been striking more frequently, more blatantly. He pilfered jewelry, silver, stashes of money and even food. One family reported that he feasted on a plate of cold roast beef and potatoes and helped himself to several glasses of port. After that it appeared he slept for a time in the bedroom of one of the children. The citizens were on alert, and reports of robberies were featured in the *Saint Paul Dispatch*. Today, Inez learned that the Tombstone Thief was shot by an elderly woman sitting in a wheelchair. She had been at the watch with a Civil War Colt revolver hidden in her lap blanket. Despite her significant palsy and the age of the war relic, she managed to fire two shots, at least one of which found its mark before he fled out the backdoor. David and another officer followed the trail of blood, but lost track of him.

As dusk relaxed over the landscape of headstones, Inez pushed up her spectacles and looked for anything that seemed out-of-place. She walked past a freshly dug grave that gave off a smell that was both tart and sweet under the last of the lilac blooms. There was a shovel propped against a neighboring headstone.

As she neared the place where she had found the stolen serving spoon, Inez turned when she heard muffled thumping sounds. She stopped, closed her eyes, and tracked the noise to a white marble mausoleum. She left the gravel path and circled around to see one of the large doors propped open. She drew her nightstick from her belt, the leather handle dampened with sweat. Inez imagined this was the lair of a crouching Cerberus, the giant dog with three heads and a writhing mane of serpents. He would be waiting to escort the next doomed soul to the Underworld. She heard a low moan and clenched her teeth.

There was a smear of blood on the door handle. Inez peered into the gloom. She heard the striking of a match, and the bright flare illuminated a bloodless face with a mouth set in a painful grimace.

The man screamed and swore. "Tarnation seize me! Are you a spirit?" He stooped low, his eyes darting back and forth. One bloody hand clutched his shoulder. They stared at each other, and Inez saw he was perched in a clutter of candlesticks, silver trays, loose silverware. Just as the match burnt to his pinched fingers, she saw him raise a knife.

Inez backed out the door and pushed it closed. She ran over to the new grave, grabbed the shovel, and threaded it through the round brass handles just as the man heaved his weight against the doors. The shovel-head clanked, and she wondered if the handle would snap. He screamed.

Inez backed up, her heart thudding. "If you try to escape, the spirits are all out here waiting for you." In the absence of a gun and handcuffs, a spiritual haunting was her only weapon. She ran to her bicycle, hiked up her skirt and peddled as hard as she could, sweat running down her back.

It wasn't fear that caused her heart to ram against her ribs. It was excitement. She had captured the Tombstone Thief. She was a policewoman. She repeated this as she pumped her bike pedals the length of Fifth Street to the station house. She hopped off her bike and dashed toward the station door, running headlong into David.

"The thief, your suspect," she gasped, struggling for breath. "He's trapped in the big mausoleum at Calvary Cemetery." She leaned forward, hands on her knees and pulled deep, ragged breaths. David opened the door and called to two other policemen. They clamored out the door like a pack of feral dogs, jumped into the Black Maria, and drove off, leaving her standing alone with trembling legs and a sweat-soaked blouse.

Chapter 23

The front page of the *Saint Paul Dispatch* displayed a picture of President Wilson. The accompanying story recounted a plea to the president from the Armenian citizens of Minneapolis and Saint Paul on behalf of their fellow citizens in the Ottoman Empire, who were said to be in immediate danger at the hands of the Turks.

The lead local story gave the account of the Tombstone Thief.

> Police officers, acting on an anonymous tip, captured Arnold Arseneau, the suspected burglar who has been invading private homes in St. Paul for at least six months. Arseneau was captured Tuesday evening in the Calvary Cemetery. Police theorize that Arseneau, a former grave-digger, broke into the mausoleum belonging to the Sullivan family and used it to stash his purloined loot. Arseneau is currently being treated at St. Joseph's hospital for a gunshot wound he suffered at the hand of Adeline Conahan when he broke into the home she shares with her two spinster daughters. Through excellent police work demonstrated by St. Paul police officer, David Gabrielle," Chief Tim Murphy commented, "our city is once against a safe place for its fine citizens. Families can sleep peacefully in their beds tonight knowing a cold criminal is now where he belongs—behind bars!

When Inez asked David what happened, why she was referred to as an anonymous source, he cast his eyes downward and mumbled something about how the chief had thumped the desk and yelled he would be goddamned before he would admit a girl had solved the problem that had befuddled his officers for months.

"You're doing good work," David said to Inez. "You followed the clues and kept after it. You and I know what really happened." He bobbed his head and grabbed her hand and then looked surprised to be holding it.

"Yes, but no one else is aware. The other officers, they don't even see me." Inez pulled back from him and clenched her teeth. Her face felt hot and prickly.

"They're embarrassed. We should have sent someone to patrol the area after you found the stolen silverware. Hell, I'm ashamed I didn't go there." He pulled on the limp collar of his shirt and then looked at his pocket watch. "Listen, we'll talk soon, yeah?" She realized she was staring at the damp curls that sprang up around his temples and cheeks.

Inez didn't answer but watched as he walked out the front door of the precinct. Her jaw ached. "The next time I solve a crime, you can bet everyone will know it was me." Her voice echoed in the long hallway, but as usual, she was alone.

Chapter 24

Streaks of pink smeared across the honeyed firmament as the sun hung low over the jagged, dark trees at the west side of the lake. Ella squinted at the thousands of sparking waves until they danced behind her eyelids. She linked arms with Lettie and flexed her bare toes in the cold, damp sand.

She was a bit drunk.

They were celebrating. Tomorrow they would go the Saint Paul Depot to meet a couple from Fairbault, Minnesota, who would take the boys back to their farm. Lettie had brought home a map and traced the line from St. Paul to their new home. Ella rolled the name of the pretty town on her tongue. Ella pressed the musty map to her nose and considered marking the towns with sewing pins to track the whereabouts of all her babies. She pictured, years from now, hundreds of silver heads shimmering her success.

After they sealed their partnership, Lettie had convinced her to place some ads in the papers, not only in Saint Paul and Minneapolis, but also in other cities in northern and southern Minnesota.

Pregnant With A Bastard Child?
If you are unable to give proper care for a newborn, consider putting the child in care of a competent woman who will find a loving home for your child. Discreet transactions assured for a nominal fee.

The second ad read:

> **Are You Barren?**
> Consider adopting a baby, free of disease or physical malady. All babies are well-nourished and have been cared for by a competent woman. Rates are reasonable.

In less than two weeks, Lettie showed her stacks of letters that filled the post office box. It was better to use the mail service, she declared, than to be at the mercy of strangers who would drop babies at her door. She recalled Martine's scolding of her activities, but somehow through Lettie's eyes the advice seemed sound and wise. Ella leaned into Lettie's confidence as if it were her own.

They sipped spicy whiskey from a shared flask as they walked to the end of the long dock at the east end of Lake Phalen. Waves slapped against the pilings of the dock, and she giggled to feel her body sway, loose and warm, to the same rhythm.

Beata had agreed to watch the boys but only if Ella and Lettie promised to stay away from Bucket of Blood. Beata believed Lettie to be a bad influence and did little to conceal her feelings.

"She doesn't trust me," Lettie surmised. "It's no bother. Most people don't. Must be something about my look? Hmm?"

Ella trusted Lettie. The boys would have a home, and a small bubble of contentment rose to the surface. However, at night, the vision of Janna's body curled in the hatbox haunted her. In one dream, a customer brought the hatbox with Janna's body to Martine's, slamming it on the glass countertop as she demanded a refund. Ella pushed her fingers hard against her eyeballs to push the images from her head. It bothered her that the baby had not been laid to rest in a proper grave. Where was she now?

The sun tipped over the edge of the lake, a slash of deep purple across the murky end of the world. Two boys with fishing poles propped on their bare shoulders trudged past, holding stringers of sunfish, their bare feet thudding on the dock.

"Let's go for a swim. What do you say?"

"I haven't a bathing costume." Ella's legs and arms were whiskey-heavy.

"Who needs one?" Lettie smirked and took another swig. She handed the flask to Ella as she stood, gave a resounding burp and unfastened her skirt.

"What if someone comes?"

"Stay underwater if you want to hide your cat's heads!" Lettie giggled and released the bow on her stays. She pulled her chemise over her head and threw it at Ella. Her skin glowed like the inside of a shell. Her hips were wide, but her waist nipped to a tiny diameter. She winked at Ella before she took a running jump off the end of the dock.

When Lettie broke the surface, she hollered, and her voice echoed. She pushed the hair from her eyes. "Come in! The water feels so good!"

"Shhhh." As if she could quiet Lettie.

It was like this to be with Lettie, large and thrilling, noisy and slightly dangerous in a way that made her heart beat faster. Ella licked her dry lips and cast a look around for watchful eyes. She dropped her shoes and stockings and quickly peeled off her clothes, covering her breasts with both hands.

"Jump!" Lettie commanded as she floated on her back.

Ella plunged forward, shocked by the cold, confused by the dark water and muddy bottom. She sputtered and flailed her arms to keep her head above the water.

"Come out farther. There's a sandbar." Lettie's hair clung to her breasts in tangled waves.

Ella pumped her arms and raised her chin to keep the lapping water out of her nose. Lettie drew a deep breath and, in a few fierce strokes, grabbed Ella's hand.

"I got you." Lettie flipped over on her back and began to kick until Ella's toes clawed the sandy bottom. Ella panted.

"Like this—on your back. Float with me. Oh god, look at the moon—round as an old man's belly."

Ella allowed the silky relief of the water to slide over her arms and between her legs.

"Isn't this somethin'? This lake bein' named after a murderer?" Lettie spit a mouthful of water like a fountain.

"Tell me more." Ella concentrated on how the stars seemed to pulse and move above her.

"Edward Phelan. He lived near here—bought some land, ran a business with a partner named John Hayes. One day, the partner's body washed up on the shores of the Mississippi River, near Carver's Cave. He was all cut up." Lettie kicked her feet and glided. "Edward was held as a suspect at Fort Snelling. They had a trial but let him go because they couldn't prove he done it. Now we're swimming in a lake named after him."

Gooseflesh puckered over Ella's torso. She longed for her bed, to drift into a murky sleep.

"I think he did it. Do you?" Lettie's voice sounded like a growl.

"How should I know?" Ella listened to the watery sounds of Lettie's movements.

"A witness said he found blood on Phelan's clothes and in his house. His dog tracked the path to the river."

Ella's teeth chattered with cold.

"Maybe someday," Lettie began, her voice wistful, "an important place will be named after me."

Chapter 25

The morning after their swim, Ella slipped her arms into the sleeves of her stiff blouse. Her fingers trembled at each button. Nerves and a whiskey headache were to blame.

"What time are we to meet them?"

"At half-past eleven—that's the last time I'm tellin' ya." Lettie positioned a chair near the screen door and fanned herself with a folded newspaper. She had hiked up her skirt and yawned.

"What's the name of the family?"

"Ummm, I dunno. Bergstrom or Dahlquist. Coupla Swedes."

"You don't know their names?" Ella fought to keep the coiled braid pinned securely to the top of her head. "This is important. This is the new surname for the boys!"

"You can ask them when you see 'em." Lettie sipped the last of the whiskey and dropped the bottle to the floor.

Lettie was mad that Ella wanted to meet the family. This proved to be the subject of their first fight.

"You take care of the little rats. I do the transactions. That's what we decided."

"They might have questions about the boys' temperament or health. You don't know one thing about them. You've never even held them. How will you manage the two of them?"

"Christ Almighty. Watch me push the thing." She grabbed the handle and shoved the carriage around the kitchen table. She clipped the chair, rammed the stove and startled both babies into vigorous cries.

"See? What will you do if they fuss?"

"The problem is that you are too attached to them. You don't want to give them up. You'd keep a hundred babies if you could."

"That's not true," Ella said, but her face flushed hot with the lie. She rubbed the boys' backs to quiet them.

"You need to start thinkin' about getting a man into your bed instead of those babies you cuddle."

"Connor's not been dead three months," Ella whispered. How could Lettie think a man could be the answer to easing her knife-sharp grief.

"And tomorrow, he'll still be dead."

Ella burst into tears, embarrassed that Lettie drove her so easily to sadness. After a few moments, she heard a sigh and felt Lettie's arm around her shoulders, the earthy smells of sweat and spicy perfume surrounding them.

"I'm sorry. My mouth can be real mean sometimes."

Ella renewed her tears.

"Now what's the trouble?"

"You think I cry all the time."

"I think you're sweet—something I'll never be. If it's that important to ya, come and meet the Swedes. But when this business gets rolling, I warn ya, there won't be time for that sort of thing. We'll be deep in money and babies." Lettie smiled, her grin wide and crooked.

Ella realized Lettie was right. She did love the boys, and it was harder than she ever imagined to give them up to someone else. The babies were both smiling. They pursed their lips and made noises of earnest conversation.

Unease crawled up her shoulders and pinched her neck. When she witnessed the mother reaching for the boys, then she would relax.

"Finish dressing! Let's go. I don't want to be late."

* * *

They walked under cool gray skies to the depot. Lettie complained about the distance to the station and her need for food and drink. Ella guessed that Lettie also suffered from a case of bottle-ache. She lagged farther and farther behind, stopping to talk to most everyone she passed. Men would lean in, whisper in her ear, and she usually offered a low chortle and a two-fingered caress of their lapels. Another man who was strolling toward them caught sight of Lettie and immediately dashed across the street. Lettie planted her hands on her hips and bawled after him, "May the hairs on your arse turn to hammers and beat your balls to death!" Ella quickened her steps, determined to put distance between them.

Ella turned the corner to see the broad face of the red-brick depot building. She admired the many arched windows and doors and the funny top of the building that looked like a pointed hat. The doors opened and closed with the swell of travelers who sprinted into the depot hauling satchels, packages and trunks. Women adjusted their hats. Two girls in matching striped pinafores held hands and sang songs. Ella struggled to push the carriage up the stair. Each time she bent over, her corset poked her sides. Suddenly, the front end of the carriage lifted, and Ella looked up to see Richard Gale.

"Let me be of some assistance, Miss Ella."

"Mr. Gale." The name rolled from her tongue as if she had been practicing in front of the mirror. She watched him lift the carriage and carry it as easily as if it were a small parcel. She pictured the long muscles of his back flexing under his shirt.

"Coming?" he called from the doorway.

Ella turned around to look for Lettie.

"Is something wrong?" Richard called.

Ella shook her head as she climbed to meet him. She flushed as he watched her move. Her breath came in fast little draws.

He pushed the pram inside the building and held the door open for her. Ella walked into the cool darkness and shivered in her damp blouse. Richard offered her his arm as they strolled under the high arched ceiling farther into the din of voices and noise.

"Since you carry no satchels, I assume you and your children are meeting a traveler?" He placed his hand over hers as they walked. His soft skin was free of scars and calluses—softer than her own hands. Ella smelled tobacco and shaving tonic.

"Mr. Gale, these babies aren't mine. I'm meeting a family that will raise them."

"No formalities needed. Please call me Richard." He tapped Ella's wedding ring. "Is your husband here?"

Ella pulled her hand from his arm. What would Connor think to see her strolling arm-in-arm with a man she barely knew? "My husband passed in March."

"Such a lovely to be left alone—this must be most difficult for you."

He didn't say he was sorry or offer prayers for Connor's soul like everyone else; he only spoke of her suffering. Tears blurred her vision.

"I have thought of you every day since we first met." He leaned in close enough that his breath brushed her cheek. Ella closed her eyes as something heavy bore down on her chest. The noise of the station was lost in the roar of her ears.

"There you are! I've been chasing after you."

Ella opened her eyes to see Lettie, breathless and disheveled, her hair a wild tumble around her face.

Ella looked around. Richard had vanished. "Hmm?"

"What's wrong with you? Did someone steal another one of your babies?" She winked, laughed wickedly and peered in the stroller. "No, I still count two."

"I saw someone I knew."

"Musta been a ghost by the looks of ya—"

"I'm fine. Nerves is all. So how do we find this family? Did you remember the surname?"

Lettie shrugged. "Maybe I just hold up a sign that says Swede? Or we wait until everyone's gone, and the ones that are left will be ours." Lettie smirked at her joke and then sobered when she read Ella's face. "Why are you upset?"

"This is a family for the boys. I want this day to be part of the story their parents will tell them at bedtime. It should be a happy tale—not one that begins with missed connections and—"

"What is all this to ya?"

"My family is gone. I want these children to belong to a family! I think about my mother every day."

"So do I," Lettie answered.

"Tell me about her."

"Mine are not the tales of games and warm bread." Lettie walked on and said nothing further, and Ella was afraid that was as much as would be revealed. They approached the chalkboard and looked for the train from southern Minnesota. "See there—number four is at the far end."

Ella's stomach clenched. She thought of Janna, who should be here with her brothers, and murmured a prayer and a promise that from now on all her future babies would make it to good homes.

The hands on the clock struck noon, and she heard the long groan of iron brakes. A stream of people spilled into the grand room, weary and limp; they carried the smells of sweat and the hot oily tang of the train engine. Ella searched each face. Could this be the new mother and father?

"Here is a story about my mother," Lettie began. "When I was a young girl, maybe twelve years old or so, she came upon me in my bed and had guessed that I had pleasured myself. I don't know if she had an ear for the noises a person makes or if she could just tell by the look on my face." Lettie shrugged, and Ella stared at the clock as blood pounded in her head. "Anyways, as she was screaming, 'whore, whore, whore,' she pinned me to the floor and poured carbolic acid on my notch. And that was that. I left that night, and I've been on my own since."

Ella stood shoulder to shoulder with Lettie, breathless and unsure what to do with this confession. Lettie didn't shed a tear or appear to show distress at the telling.

Lettie elbowed Ella, and said, "Looka those two."

The man's face and throat and forearms were tanned the color of chestnuts. His hair was cut close over his ears so that his pink scalp glowed. The furrows left by a comb made his head look like a newly planted field. He stood erect and barrel-chested, wearing a white shirt, frayed at the collar and bisected by suspenders. The tall woman next to him had a blunt, solid body, pale hair and a high forehead. She gripped a satchel in front of her with capable hands. They were both thin-lipped and grim.

Ella smiled. "Hello there. Are you the couple looking to adopt babies? She watched the woman lean over and look into the carriage.

"Hello folks. I'm Lettie. This is Ella. Well, here are the babies."

Ella wondered if Lettie was about to hold out her hand for payment without any more conversation.

"We are the Dahlstroms," the man said. He did not offer first names or a handshake.

They were older than Ella had pictured, maybe in their late thirties. Too old, in Ella's opinion for raising babies.

Gerick started to cry, loud and high-pitched. Lujan mimicked his brother. Soon they were both wailing, and Ella picked them up and jostled them over her shoulder. The blanket landed on the ground. Both of their diapers were soaked. Ella had one bottle remaining. She wished the new mother would offer to hold one of the boys.

Mrs. Dahlstrom whispered in her husband's ear. He made tsk, tsk, tsk noises, and when she finished, she closed her eyes and clenched her jaw.

Lettie looked at Ella and rolled her eyes.

"No tank you. We won't be takin' 'em home. Too dark looking. My wife say they look like gypsies." After his announcement, they spun around and walked away.

As if aware of their rejection, the boys screamed all the louder, their voices melded into one high plaintive note that floated toward the high arched ceiling.

"Wait," Ella called after them. "Come back!" The Dahlstroms didn't turn around, not even when Ella burst into tears in concert with the babies. "They need a good home," she screamed to everyone who turned to stare.

Chapter 26

Ten days had passed since the Dahlstroms had rejected the boys. Ten days since her horrid fight with Lettie.

"We will not be at the mercy of bad donations ever again!" Lettie screeched as they walked home from the depot that afternoon. It seemed to be their lot that day, to become public spectacles.

"It's not my fault the farmers didn't want them! Maybe if you had described their looks in the letter, it might have saved us from this trouble."

"Ella, these babies are homely! Looka that one—I think he has a lazy eye. We'll probably have to pay someone to take 'em!"

The argument continued when they got home. Ella swayed and jostled Lujan as he fussed in her arms. A hot rash climbed up his neck. Ella bit her lower lip, irritated with Lettie's feigned ignorance of the boys' names and the way she constantly pointed out their disfigurements.

"It's like trying to sell a lame horse," she complained. "They're odd looking and cranky." Lujan's limbs went rigid, and he pitched his head back with such force that Ella nearly dropped him. Lettie raised her eyebrows and spat, "What'd I tell ya?"

"It's the heat," Ella said, furiously patting Lujan's back.

The rest of the afternoon, Lettie grimly poured over the stack of response letters, drinking and cursing. Suddenly she announced she was off to send a telegram. She didn't return that night, as was sometimes her custom, and Ella was relieved to be alone. Most of the time, Lettie went to Bucket of Blood and would stumble home the next morning in sour spirits, a musky-man scent about her. She didn't return the next morning, and by the fourth day, as the heat pressed over the West Side Flats, Ella thought she might be gone for good.

Then Lettie strode in the front door the next day, as if she had only been absent for a few hours, and her announcement prompted another spat.

"All's I got was one letter to the ad. They want just one of 'em. Not the pair."

"I won't separate them. No."

"I'm nearly done with ya. Mule-stubborn will drive us out of business."

Ella's stash of money dwindled each week. Rent and food, flannels and rubber nipples and sugar and milk. Each night as she rocked and fed the boys, watching as the sky released its blue-black color, fear of running out of money caused her heart to flap around in her chest until it felt loose and pulpy. Ella muffled her sobs by pressing her lips to their silky heads, because if she allowed herself to cry outright, she might not be able to stop. Should she sell Connor's knives? His last earthly tie?

She dreamed Connor was holding baby Janna, but he was walking away from *her*. She tried to run after them, her fingers shaking with the need to caress the back of his neck, but when she looked down she saw her feet were crippled and riddled with weeping sores. When she tried to call out to him, she couldn't make a sound.

When Ella woke from her dream, she reached under the mattress and pulled out Connor's knife bundle and untied the string. The knives clinked and glinted in the thin moonlight that slid off the bed.

She shivered with the danger of what they could do.

Ella gripped the bone handle until her knuckles ached. The solution seemed so simple. The knife could cut away her grief. She pressed the blade against her inner arm. At first there wasn't any pain, and she wondered if she had returned to the dream, and then there was a sweet stinging sensation, like a high, quivering note. The grief and pain flowed from her until she felt heavy and sated. Relief.

She woke up that morning to the cries of both babies to discover the knives loose in the bed and blood staining the sheets and her night dress. That's how she ended up on her way to Martine's shop, embarrassed, and contrite. She had to do something to make money before the knives called to her again.

She pushed the carriage into the shop, and she prayed to St. Jude to keep them sleeping. Martine was with a customer, and Ella watched as she cooed and smiled, her thin fingers tucking the lavender hat into the box with tenderness. Martine fit the lid on the box and presented it to the outstretched palms of the customer. She waved and blew a kiss as the woman headed toward the door. Ella flashed to a memory of baby Janna's blue body curled in the hatbox. The bell jangled again, and Ella tried to control her breathing that sounded ragged in the quiet of the shop. Martine fussed behind the desk, stabbing the receipt on the spindle, opening the register to deposit the bills, and then slammed the drawer shut.

All this time she did not look up or greet Ella.

Finally, she came out from behind the counter and leaned against her cane. Ella's mouth went dry, recognizing the feelings of unease that were the same as the first day she had arrived there. Martine was dressed in a cornflower-blue shift, and Ella thought she resembled a delicate delphinium. She stared at Ella and shrugged her shoulders as if she had been asked a difficult question.

"How can I help you?" Martine's voice was the same tone she used with customers, overly sweet, like a spoonful of honey. Ella's foot tapped.

What did she want? A weekly allotment, sure and steady, to pay rent. Something to stop her frantic thoughts.

"I miss the learning. The hat business. I've…"

"Ah, it was your choice to be in the baby business. Isn't that the same merchandise you were peddling last time?" She lifted the blanket with the tip of her cane.

Ella had the urge to lie, *business is better than I dreamed.* She wanted to impress Martine, but her face burned, and the lie tangled her tongue.

"It's been harder to place twins than I thought. I've had offers for one, but not for the two together."

"Why not give the customer what she wants?" Martine's pursed lips looked like a heart.

"They are brothers, bound by blood."

"But they won't remember, years from now."

A picture flashed in her mind. The boys grown to stocky young men with voracious appetites and downy mustaches. They would still be living with her, and each morning she would send them off to work in the factories. Martine was right. God help them all, Lettie was right. She made up her mind to tell Lettie she could do as she wished.

"I have a business partner now," Ella began. "Soon we'll be making money, but in the meantime, I'm wondering if I can make any deliveries or help with—"

"How will you make time for both businesses? Your new partner has a tender heart for these discarded babies?"

Ella nearly laughed to think of Lettie showing a moment of tenderness. "If you give me work, I will manage."

"You think me cold, don't you, because I don't swoon over *les enfantes*. I've been told it's unnatural for a woman. Why doesn't everyone see they ruin your figure! They are often sick! Oh, and so noisy. They leak!" Martine's thin nose wrinkled.

Ella glanced at the stroller and hoped the babies wouldn't begin to demonstrate all of the characteristics Martine found so repulsive.

Martine leaned closer to Ella and looked her in the eye. "Ah, but you, my little one, you love these rats, don't you? I think you are maybe too delicate for this business." Martine touched the back of her hand to Ella's cheek. Maybe Martine still had feelings of affection for her? Then, Martine's eyes glittered with a look that frightened Ella. She pulled back. Martine gripped the head of her cane.

"Yes, I love them," Ella answered. How could she explain the wonderful feeling when a baby relaxed into sleep in your arms? How your heart swelled until it ached?

"I love my hat creations, too, but I send them out into the world."

Babies are not hats, she wanted to say. "As I took care of them, me feelings grew."

"Tsk, it is not a mystery. You have been sad, and they are something to love. Even though this one here has such a misshapen head!"

The shop bell jangled, and two women dressed in white linen skirts and blouses strode in and smiled. They held out gloved hands to Martine, and they all began to chatter in French.

Ella knew this conversation was done. She had been dismissed. The trip here had been a waste of time. The smell of soiled diapers filled the air, and she watched Martine's eyes widen.

Rather than maneuver the carriage around the threesome, Ella headed for the curtain that led to the work room. She pushed at tears that ran down her cheeks. As her hand parted the curtain, Martine touched her shoulder and pressed her lips to Ella's ear as she handed her an envelope.

"Please deliver the hatboxes on the worktable to this address down at the docks. I'm sending some of my creations back to Paris. The shops are begging for my darlings. Here is money to make the deliveries." A drop of spittle landed on Ella's earlobe, and she detected a whiff of anise. "Now go, before your putrid darlings drive my business away." Startled, Ella pulled back but saw Martine's half smile. She kissed Ella's cheek. "Your tears are sweet," she whispered and then turned back to her customers who were busy trying on hats as they cooed and strutted like pigeons.

She pushed through the curtain and gasped.

Martine had been drinking absinthe again, and that always meant Ella would be left with a terrible mess. The table was a jumble of sticky glasses smeared with greasy fingerprints and dirty plates studded with nubs of dried cheese and crushed cigarette butts. She claimed the Absinthe helped her to create beautiful hats. Snippets of ribbons, thread, and fabric were pinned to pages torn from French magazines. Melted candles lurched in a silver candelabra. Ella picked up crumpled pages of pencil illustrations and smoothed them with her palm. Ella turned to see the supply of Martine's hatboxes, dozens and dozens stacked on a pallet as if she anticipated making hats for all the women in Saint Paul.

Ella resented the hours she had spent sweeping, dusting, and sorting. She had warned Martine if she left food out, the mice would return to make nests in the fabric and leave their droppings everywhere. But the urge to scold Martine was dampened by her need to make money.

There wasn't time to clean. She pushed the stroller near the door, stacked the eight hatboxes in the stroller and hurried to her escape.

Chapter 27

Inez walked through a part of town called the West Side Flats. Murphy had sent her to the neighborhood after someone reported some abandoned children wandering the streets. Inez pushed up her spectacles and went off to handle the case, thankful she wasn't being sent to investigate more cases of women smoking in public. Inez rode her bicycle from the station across the Wabasha Bridge and began her search along State Street just past Mint's Shoe Store. She concentrated maneuvering over the uneven furrows of dried mud and tracked a child's cry.

She found three children crouched in the alley. Inez's limited exposure to small children usually left her at a loss to estimate their ages unless she had the opportunity to examine their dental records. The eldest of the trio, a boy, was barefooted, and his face, neck and hands were grimy. Crusty scabs framed the corners of his mouth, and he pressed himself against the brick wall as Inez approached. He gathered his younger siblings under his thin arms. They sniffed. The clammy air trapped between the buildings made Inez shiver.

"Hello," she ventured. "What are your names?"

The middle child placed two fingers in her mouth and squinted at Inez as she held out her other hand, begging for money. The girl's eyes were bright pink and oozed yellow pus. The youngest, of no discernable sex, hiccupped and lunged toward Inez with outstretched arms. Inez picked up the baby before it stumbled. The baby's feet were ice-cold, and the sour tang of the soiled diaper pinched Inez's nose.

"Come now, do you know your name?" The baby put a head against Inez's shoulder.

"Are you an angel," the older boy croaked, "from the church?"

Inez shook her head. "I want to take you to your home."

This was her duty, according to Murphy—*to look after the affairs of women and children—not to solve crimes*. Inez was instructed to leave that function to the proper officers. She admonished children who fended for themselves by stealing and twice carried young boys that had been maimed in factory accidents to the hospital. Women fell into three categories—those beaten by the men they were married to, those who worked at the brothels, and those who suffered from various diseases and malnutrition. In the last three months, Inez had recorded the complaints of women with black and blue faces, broken fingers and other injuries in private places. Last week, upon questioning, one woman had spit several teeth into Inez's palm.

Even if she had the power to arrest the men who indulged their whiskey-inflamed fists, no one at the station house had been interested in putting them in jail until a murder had been committed. She was sure her reports were fodder for jokes by the men at the station.

The weight of the child in her arms brought her back to the present and the oily air of the alley.

"Let's go then." She took the girl by the hand and motioned to the boy to follow. The girl shuffled along wearing scuffed shoes too large for her feet. The frayed laces dragged through the wet puddles.

As they made their way onto State Street, Inez blinked hard against the bright sunlight and sweat that stung her eyes.

"You there, where do these children reside?" Inez called out to an elderly woman, bent and shuffling along the street. She turned and looked Inez from head to toe and shook her head as if she were trying to clear her vision.

The girl stumbled, cried out, and stepped out of her shoe. Inez realized they were struggling to match her impatient stride. The boy picked up the shoe and slid it over the weepy blisters on her slender foot.

"Where's your house?" she asked him. He had spoken English, so he must have understood her question. He spun around and pointed to a vague area closer to the river. "Is it far?" He shrugged. The baby slept even as Inez adjusted its weight in her arms. The wet diaper soaked through Inez's white blouse. Surely, the mother must be worried about the location of her children! She would finally receive appreciation for her efforts.

Just when her arm started to burn with fatigue, the boy sprinted ahead down a dead-end street. She followed him to a battered porch and up the steps of a small white house. "Mama?" the boy called. The girl pulled her damp hand away from Inez's and followed the boy into the murky shadows of the house.

Quiet.

She strained to find the household noises over the footsteps of the children. A clatter of dishes, voices, the thwack of a cleaver on a cutting board. She quickened her steps to intercept the children, pushing her sweaty spectacles higher on her nose and waited for her eyes to adjust to the poor light. "Is anyone home?" Perhaps the mother had lingered after Mass?

Inez's mouth went dry as she walked down the hallway to the kitchen.

Flies crawled over the dirty dishes filling the sink. Inez bit her lip against the smells of soiled diapers and soured milk. The floor was sticky under Inez's boots.

The boy tugged at his mother's arm as she lay draped over the table, her pale face pressed to her arm. Inez circled the table to see the woman's eyes in a fixed stare.

"Ma'am? I've found your children." Inez watched the woman's back to see if she was breathing.

The boy whimpered and tugged harder on his mother's arm. His sister stood behind her brother and sobbed. The baby emitted an open-mouthed shriek. Inez pressed her fingers to the woman's neck beneath the jaw bone. The skin was warm, but when she moved her fingers about she didn't feel a pulse.

Suddenly, the mother sat up and blinked. She adjusted the shawl around her shoulders. Her hair was a worn shade of blonde, and she slowly pushed an oily strand of it that had escaped from a braided coil. Her movements were slow as if the air around her was viscous honey.

Inez stepped back, exhaled a long breath and said, "I'm Inez Laudenbach, from the police department. Your children were found wandering the streets."

"I sent them to the CSPS." The mother ran a distracted finger over her collarbone, and the vein along her neck beat a tender blue pulse. "In better times we would all go to the dances there and these two would fall asleep in the coats. My husband, he was in plays there. An actor." The woman's speech was thick with a Czech accent, and she smiled in a dreamy way to think about a different time in her life.

"Ma'am, I don't think they got a meal. I found them in the alley, alone." She motioned to the baby who continued to wail. A shiny filament of salvia dribbled over Inez's shoulder. "What's your name?"

"Chormansky. I am Paula." It sounded to Inez's ears as pool-la. "Maybe you could take them somewhere? I have no food here." She dabbed her nose on the back of her hand.

Inez wondered what was required from the job at this point. The needs here were clearly more than a bowl of porridge and some bread could remedy.

"And Mr. Chormansky is—?"

"Dead." She cut in before Inez could finish her question. "Ya, last January he was crushed at work." When she slapped her palms together, Inez pictured Cratos, the Greek god of power, compressing Mr. Chormansky between his massive hands.

"I'm sorry."

Paula stood, and the shawl slid from her shoulders as she reached to take the baby. Inez gasped. The great swell of the woman's belly in contrast to her thin arms reminded her of a black vine weevil. Inez watched a slow ripple of movement across her taut belly.

Paula set the baby on the floor. She spread her trembling fingers across the expanse of her belly, and Inez thought her nails resembled tiny pink shells. "I've been waiting for God to send a miracle, but I think He has forgotten about me." Her eyes filled with tears.

Inez wanted to tell her that the time she wasted in prayer might have been put to better use obtaining a well-fitted pessary to practice anti-conceptual methods but decided Mrs. Chormansky would not likely have had enough money to purchase such a womb-veil.

"Is there someone to help? Family in town?"

Mrs. Chormansky's face buckled. "My husband's brother, Milan, he fishes the river most days. Could you find him there, and tell him I need him?"

Chapter 28

Lujan lay on his belly across Beata's lap as she sat under the towering maple tree behind her brick house. He cooed as she bounced him up and down and vigorously thumped his back until he closed his eyes. A breeze lifted a tuft of dark hair at his crown. Ella sipped strong, sweet tea and pressed the glass to her forehead. She had pulled off her stockings and boots to cool her feet in the long grass. Gerick lay on his back on Beata's quilt, kicking his legs as he shoved a wet fist into his mouth.

"It's good for his belly-ache," Beata commented in defense of her thumping method, and Ella couldn't imagine how Lujan could sleep with all of that agitation. "I've missed you!" Beata grabbed Gerick's bare foot.

Ella was not sure who was being addressed. "How have you been feeling?" she asked as she shooed away the black flies that buzzed around Gerick's belly.

"Yeech, I get pains here." Her prodding hand disappeared somewhere under her breast. "It's like a poke with a hot stick, so I chew this." She tossed a tin into Ella's lap. "Try some. See, I put a little wad in my cheek." Beata pulled down her lower lip to reveal a clump of something dark and juicy.

Ella read the words on the tin. "Jolly Jack Plug Tobacco. Aids digestion and masculinity." Masculinity? Would this make Beata even more manly? "No thank you." She handed the tin back to Beata.

Beata shrugged. "Suit yourself."

"Can I ask you a question?"

"For the cards?"

"No. Do you think I should let the boys go to different homes?"

"I'd take them if my hair wasn't gray and I didn't have these pains."

"But if I find a family that just wants one boy—is that bad?"

"A family to love any baby is good." She clicked her tongue against her teeth.

"So you agree? I was going to tell Lettie she could separate them."

At the mention of Lettie's name, Beata leaned over and spat a brown stream into the grass. "I don't like that woman. I have heard things about her—bad things. I will tell you, maybe. I would suffer the sin of idle gossip, but it would be worth it."

"What things? Who said something?" The tea was suddenly too sweet as it sloshed around in her stomach.

"The cards. Certain people, they talk, and I believe them." Beata shifted Lujan to her shoulder and heaved herself out of the chair. She settled him next to Gerick on the blanket. He raised his eyebrows as if he were fighting to wake up but then eased back into slumber. Cottonwood tufts floated in the air and settled on the grass like delicate snowflakes.

"What have you heard?"

"Bad. She is with many men. She spends her time at a terrible place…"

Beata nodded her head toward the river while she pried the lid from the tobacco tin. She plunged two fingers into the dark mass and pushed a wad into her cheek.

"She writes letters for the men at Bucket of Blood," Ella offered in defense and then winced when she realized how ridiculous it sounded.

"Anyone who likes that Bucket of Blood place is up to no good. The cards—they tell me all I need to know. What comes up every time are the Queen of Swords in reverse and the King of Cups, also in reverse." Beata widened her eyes.

"What does that mean?"

Beata shook her head. "The Queen, it means evil intentions. The King speaks of someone who is a double-dealer. Someone who is vi-o-lent. It always means scandal," she whispered.

Ella pictured Beata laying out the cards each night, her hand fluttering over her heart as the cards repeated their warning.

"Lettie hates the babies. I've seen her with them. She would as soon spit on them." Beata looked up to the tree branches.

"Oh, she doesn't hate them. I don't think she's ever taken care of children. Besides, she doesn't need to like the babies to find them a home."

Ella recalled Martine sneering about 'leaking' babies. "Lettie has placed ads in the papers, sent telegrams and written letters. She has worked hard to—"

"She takes advantage of you. She eats your food and sleeps all day. She's no good, that one, I tell you."

"Once we find the boys homes, it'll be different. Lettie will pick the next little ones. When she's part of it, I promise, she will warm to them." Ella said that aloud to reassure her faltering thoughts.

At that moment, Gerick heaved an arm across his body and rolled onto his belly. His head bobbed with the effort as he tried to lift his chin from the blanket. He formed a wet, lopsided grin.

"Look!" Ella pointed and clapped. She knelt on the blanket and touched her forehead to his. "He rolled over! My little boy."

"Pay attention. Look at my face, *kotku*. I know you don't want to hear my words because your heart is too young. You don't have the years I do to see things."

"What Beata? What are you trying to tell me?"

"Remember this day with the blue sky. The birds are happy to be here. The grass is soft. The tea is sweet." She leaned over and caressed Gerick's arm but never took her eyes from Ella's.

"Someday, you will remember this—the day when I warned you that bad trouble is coming."

Chapter 29

Lettie greeted Ella from where she sat on the front steps. She stood, arms outstretched, and leaned in to embrace Ella. Lettie's face shone with sweat, and the kiss on Ella's cheek was damp. "I've been waiting forever!" The green skies surrounded them like a veil and birthed a wind that churned a strange mix of hot and cold air. The leaves on the poplar tree fluttered.

"Where you been?" Lettie cocked her head to one side and squinted.

"I stopped by to see Beata." She didn't mention the trip to Martine's to beg for a job. "I could ask you the same question. I thought you were gone for good."

Lettie gripped Ella's shoulders; her strong fingers reminded her of how Connor would pull her to him. His lean fingers would stroke her arms as he pulled her to bed. Her chest ached as her breath came in shallow waves.

"I've been licking my wounds. I was mad. Now I'm not."

Ella pulled back remembering the sneer that had transformed Lettie's beautiful mouth during their fight.

"Let me help you pull the wagon! Lettie hefted the front of the stroller up the steps. "I guess I have to get used to pushing this thing around town." Lettie's hair was gathered into a high knot on her head. Ella had only ever seen her hair in loose waves springing around her bare shoulders. The bun exposed small, neat earlobes.

"What do you mean?" Ella didn't offer help to lift the stroller.

Wet strands of hair clung to Lettie's neck, and she wiped her cheek against her shoulder. "I found a home for the babies. I'm dropping them off tonight." Lettie's medallion swung like a pendulum as she bent over the carriage.

Ella's heart flipped in her chest. "Who's taking them? Where're they going? Someone wants both of them?" Questions tumbled out of her mouth. The green sky darkened, clouds roiled overhead. Gusts of wind kicked up grit and cottonwood fluff.

"A man from Wisconsin." Lettie propped the screen door on her hip and yanked at the handle. "God Almighty, this wheel's as crooked as a dog's hind leg."

"Wisconsin," Ella repeated. "Does he know, did you tell him their skin is dark?" She shuddered to remember the words spat like spoiled milk from the mouth of Mrs. Dalhstrom.

"I told him."

"Then he'll take the both of them?"

Lettie nodded.

Noisy, choking tears burst from Ella. Her chest ached. Was she happy? Sad? Relieved? She couldn't tell. Thunder rumbled, and fat raindrops hit the brick walkway. Ella leaped up the steps and followed Lettie inside. The hair on her arms stood up, and she shivered.

"I'm taking them by myself, so you know." Lettie flopped herself into a chair that Ella had never seen before and hiked her skirts over her knees. "I don't want a scene like the last one."

"Where on earth did this chair come from?" It was large and looked like something that would have come from Mr. Cochran's dark study. "Lettie, I swear on me mother's grave, I won't cry." For some reason, this made her tears flow faster. The air in the house was as thick.

Lettie ran her hand back and forth over the dark upholstery. "I got the chair for you since you don't have much to sit on. It's so nice, like being held in the arms of huge man. Soft and hard at the same time!" She snickered, thrilled at her analogy, and then slapped her bare thigh.

Ella noticed that Lettie didn't say how she paid for the chair or how it got to Ella's house. She doubted the chair was meant for her. It looked like something Lettie had been born to lounge in.

Lettie's giggles stopped, and her face was suddenly drawn and serious. "We do this my way now." A whiskey bottle appeared from behind the chair, and Lettie tipped it, taking three long swallows before she wiped her mouth on her hand. "Feed them, change their disgusting drawers and then say goodbye."

Ella pulled a handkerchief from her pocket and wiped her nose. A dull pain throbbed behind her eyes, and her chest felt like it was being squeezed in the cinch of a horse saddle. This is what she hoped for, wasn't it? The brothers would be raised together.

"I should take them back to Beata's to say goodbye." Sheets of rain pelted the windows. The thunder rumbled.

"You just came from there! No more tearful sendoffs."

"She'll miss them."

"You're both hopeless. Soon there'll be lots of babies coming through here, and you won't have time to love them so much." Lettie burped and made a sour face.

Ella stood by the window, felt the cool of the storm skim over her face and neck, and breathed in the wet, green smell. Raindrops dotted the sill and the front of her skirt, and she had the urge to bare her arms, lie in the grass and receive the cool gift of the downpour. The heads of the peonies bent heavily to the ground, defeated by the winds, their deep pink petals laying like shards in the grass.

"Someday, you may find love like that, Lettie. For a baby or a man."

"Love is nasty and salty."

"Or wonderful."

She looked over her shoulder at Lettie who had cradled the whiskey bottle like a baby.

Lettie snorted. "So you say."

Chapter 30

Ella moved her bare foot across the cool of the sheet, hooked the arch of Connor's foot, and flexed her toes. This was her signal to pull closer to her, and even if he was in the deepest sleep, he would always move to fit himself against her back. Without fail, his lips would find the nape of her neck, his arm would drape across her hip. Oh, Connor, where have you been? In some way it felt like so much time had leaked away since he held her like this, and yet the touch was so familiar it felt like pulling a purse string of time and all the missing moments cinched together. Did she say this aloud to him or were her words trapped in her head? Ella squeezed her eyes shut with happiness. Her arm tingled where his touch grazed her skin, and she pressed back against him. She heard a deep sigh and then a sound, an animal-like growl, and she waited for him to nuzzle her earlobe. The need for him was sudden, a throbbing between her legs. In one movement, she rolled over and squatted over him, pinning his hips as her hands braced on either side of his head. Then, in this moment of heat and longing, a gray confusion rushed in, and she wondered why she couldn't feel him hard against her.

* * *

She opened her eyes, even though everything in this moment told her not to break the spell of happiness.

"Well, partner," Lettie grinned, "that's quite the greeting."

When Ella sprang backward, her foot tangled in the sheet, and she rolled off the side of the bed, landing on her hip and elbow. A sharp pain shot up her arm, and she scooted farther back from the foot of the bed and the sound of Lettie's chuckles.

Lettie propped herself up on her elbow and thrust a handful of crumpled bills at Ella as if she were offering a bouquet of flowers. Her cheeks were bright red, rubbed raw from too much kissing, Ella guessed. "Real money—not promises. And tomorrow there's another baby for us—well, for you. The letter said this one has yellow hair and blue eyes. That one will be easy to sell."

"What time is it?" The sweat on Ella's neck cooled, and she shivered. The feeling of Connor, so real, so wonderful, was seeping away. She could smell him. He was here, she wanted to tell Lettie. Every place he touched felt hot.

Lettie flung the bills in the air, and they drifted over the bed and the floor like dried leaves. Ella hated the word sell. She was finding homes for babies, parents to provide food and care and love. Lettie made everything sound sordid.

"You don't seem very excited." Lettie licked her lips. "I mean you seem excited, but not about the money."

"Why are you in me bed?" Ella tugged at the sheet to pull it around her shoulders, but Lettie's weight pinned it to the mattress.

"I wanted to share our good fortune!" Her dark curls fanned across the pillow. "It's not my fault you were looking for someone to throw your leg over." She pursed her lips and made a smacking sound.

"You could have come home last night and told me then. I waited up for hours." Ella had fought the urge to follow Lettie last night when she left to deliver the boys. She itched to catch a glimpse of the new family and to see if Lettie imparted the proper directions. Instead, Ella scrubbed the floors, washed and hung out all the diapers on the line, and washed the jumble of bottles, dishes, and nipples until her hands were raw and her muscles quivered with fatigue.

"I was out celebrating. I didn't feel like coming home to tears and questions."

"What was he like? The man from Wisconsin. Was his wife with him?"

"Naw, he was alone—didn't say nothing about a wife. He had money in hand—that's all I cared about."

"How'd he manage two babies? Did they fuss? Did you give him the letter I wrote? The bottles of milk?" Ella's breath came in short stabbing bursts.

"He put 'em in a sack and slung it over his shoulder." Lettie laughed and said, "God, I can see you want to haul off and slug me. It's a joke! He was like any man—not much to say. I handed him the goods, he gave me money, and off he went. Done." She ran her fingers through her hair and twisted it into a knot on the top of her head. Two black lacquered sticks appeared from a pocket in her skirt, and she stabbed the bun, reminding Ella of knitting needles in a ball of wool.

"Then it's real. They're gone." Tears spilled down Ella's face.

"See! I knew you'd be like this. Don't be sad. This is our business. You can't collapse into a sad sack of tears every time we do this."

Ella realized Lettie spoke the truth. The boys had a new home. Maybe it was a dairy farm where they would grow up playing hide-and-seek in a sweet-smelling hay loft with the sounds of cattle surrounding them. After they shared the morning's chores, they would fish in the nearby pond. The farmer would pass down the land to his new sons. They would never know they once had a sister.

Lettie rolled off the bed and squatted in front of Ella. She touched Ella's cheek and tugged at her earlobe. "You were a good mother to them. They were both happy. I forgot to tell you that one of them smiled at me."

Ella grinned. The tears were a mix of sad and a bit of happiness pinching at her heart. "You never did learn their names, did you?"

"Sure—the first one and the other one."

Ella shook her head. "You're hopeless." Her feelings for Lettie always felt like a tug of war.

"Come on. Let's go count our pirate's booty and get some food! Besides, you need to enjoy some time without a baby on your hip. It won't be long before we have a house full."

Chapter 31

The sun burned high in the cloudless blue sky. Inez found the break in the yellow blooms of a patch of ranunculus that marked the path entrance to the bank of the Mississippi River. Her shoulder ached from holding Mrs. Chormansky's baby. She breathed the thrilling mix of sweet and rotten odors she always associated with the churning of the glaucous river. The back of Inez's dress was damp with sweat, and she longed to capture a river breeze. Delicate cabbage whites flitted among the stalks of purple loosestrife and blooming hawkbits. The odds of finding Mrs. Chormansky's brother were remote, but Inez had longed to escape the sadness and clamor of the household while she organized her thoughts.

When she reached the strand, the sweet grasses waved and rippled, and Inez snapped off a handful and sniffed the clean vanilla scent. To the south, she saw the remains of an abandoned campfire and piles of spent clam shells.

The beach was deserted so she sat on a boulder, unlaced her boots and peeled off her stockings. She gathered her dress, raising the hem above her knees and waded into the cold water until her feet went numb. A small painted barge, low to the water with its weight of heaped coal, glided past. The worker shielded his eyes and waved at Inez.

The waves slapped at her shins, and Inez watched the tangle of dark weeds, rusted cans and bleached driftwood that was caught in the exposed roots of a pine tree. A white object bobbed in the center of the snarl. Belly of a dead fish?

The waves created by the barge crashed at the shore, wetted the hem of her dress and roiled the mass of debris. It was then that Inez saw a tiny hand bob along the surface. She pushed her glasses up on her nose and waded closer. She bent over and plunged her hands into the water to clear the sticks and weeds. Her toes sank into the mud.

A baby, floating face down. The flash of white was not the belly of a fish but a white dress and a diaper. Inez turned over the swollen body. She surmised it to be younger than the child she had held earlier today. There were gashes across the forehead and nose. Two fingers on the left hand were missing, and there was a white ribbon cinched around the baby's neck.

Chapter 32

Back at the station, the men slumped in chairs and reclined on the benches that lined the south wall. Sweat-stained shirts, unbuttoned at the throat, all offered a disturbing view of various shades of blooming chest hair.

Before she approached Murphy with the news of her discovery, she knocked on the door of the water closet to determine whether it was occupied. Inez rinsed her face and glasses as best she could in the greasy, stained sink. There wasn't a towel available, so she patted her face dry on the sleeve of her dress. She studied her sunburned face in the clouded mirror, smoothed her hair, and peeled a patch of burnt skin from her nose. Water dripped from the faucet. The set of her jaw, similar to her father's, made her look glum. Just then the door slammed open and Officer Bennati burst in, his belt undone and jangling.

"Oh, well then," he sputtered.

"I'm leaving." Inez gritted her teeth. She pushed past him into the hall.

Chief Murphy sat with both elbows planted on the oak desk, his face resting in his palms so that the loose flesh of his pink cheeks spilled over to cover his fingers. When he exhaled, a puff of air broke the seal of his lips that resembled mollusks. There was a ruler next to his elbow with a six-inch piece of screen affixed to the end. He made a contest out of how many flies he could kill during his shift.

"Chief," Inez began, trying to figure out how to wake him up. She squeezed the notebook where she had written down the street name, the time of her discovery, and the condition of the body, even though she had committed these details to memory. Inez gritted her teeth against the desire to reach over and slap him on the head with the fly swatter. *Wake up. Crimes are being committed under your red nose!*

Instead she said more loudly, "Sir!" Now all the men turned in her direction. Murphy opened one eye.

"Yeah," he licked his lips with a dry click.

"Sir, I discovered the body of an infant in the river near Emma Street off of West Seventh. By the condition of the body, it appears to have been in the water at least one day. There was a bit of cloth tied around its throat."

She expected he would pepper her for details. Instead, no one seemed interested in the discovery. A few men yawned and stretched, frowning as if perturbed at the interruption of their thoughts. Inez's heart beat loudly in her ears. Murphy slapped the fly-killer stick at the corner of the desk. Inez blinked but steeled herself not to flinch.

"Sir, I've just reported a crime, a murder." Inez pushed her spectacles up higher on her nose and held his gaze. Finally, he tossed the stick across the open log book and dispatched the officers with the wave of two fingers.

"I'd like to go back to the scene," she said, "to retrieve the body."

"Ah, stay behind and write your report."

"But it's my discovery." She saw two officers roll their eyes and turn away.

David Gabrielle swept in, straight faced and serious. He pulled her aside. "Say, Murph, maybe I'll bring her over later, all right?" He ran his hand through his hair and glanced over his shoulder. "Over here, Inez." He cupped her elbow and guided her away from the desk.

"I should be at the scene," she said, trying to ignore the tingling sensation snaking up her arm.

"You're upset. Maybe you should rest for a bit at home?"

"I am tasked with looking after the welfare of women and children. I think this case qualifies me to be part of the procedure." Her voice sounded coarse. "And I'm not upset, but don't the others care about a murder?"

"Inez, I'll explain," David whispered. He walked her over to the far corner of the room where his desk was located. He held a hand out to the chair, pulled open the bottom desk drawer and grabbed a whiskey bottle by the neck. "Need a taste?"

Alcohol was the last thing she wanted. It was imperative to keep her head clear when she returned to the scene to look for clues. He smiled, raised his eyebrows, thick and arched with good humor.

Inez paused and considered his offer might be in the spirit of the camaraderie she craved. She lifted her chin to the bottle in response. He produced two glasses, poured sloppy shots and offered one to her. When she reached for the glass, his fingers, wet with whiskey, touched hers for a moment, longer than any man had ever touched her hand. The sensation coiled in her belly.

He tilted his head back and downed the drink in a robust swallow. Inez sniffed and touched the tip of her tongue to the amber liquid and then took a small sip. It smoldered down her throat and bloomed through her chest. Her face flushed, and she exhaled carefully.

His dark eyes watched her. "It's a hard thing, to find a body of a young one like that."

"Have you? Discovered the body of an infant?"

Inez watched the hinge of David's jaw flex; the bone was rounded and protruded as if he had an egg tucked at the back of his cheek.

"Probably, if you ask all of them, they would say yes. A *bambino morto*."

Inez stared. She took another burning sip.

"Then why don't they respond with outrage? Or at least with mild curiosity? It's their job!"

David bit his lower lip and squinted one eye. He shifted in his chair and poured another shot. "It's not that unusual, to come across one."

"Really?" Inez wasn't sure what she was asking. The question was bigger than she could articulate. Why are so many babies murdered? Why did no one care?

"Sometimes, it's not always a case of murder. Sometimes they just die and the families can't afford to bury 'em proper. Others?

Another mouth to feed is sometimes too much." He shrugged his shoulders, and Inez thought of the very pregnant Mrs. Chormansky and her scarecrow children.

"They are not farm kittens in a burlap sack."

"No." The color of his eyes added to the warmth that swirled around her.

"You're not much for the Irish handcuffs, are ya?" His forefinger tapped the bottle.

"Should I be?"

"Well, on a day like today…"

Inez recalled the image of her father, late at night under the yellow glow of his desk lamp, his head bent over to illustrate his Book of Crime. He always had a tumbler of whisky as he labored over the illustrations. She wished she could watch him sketch and have the chance to ask questions.

Her glass was empty. She realized David was in the middle of a story about his first case, something about a father that had murdered his young family.

Inez interrupted him. "Will you take me to the scene?" She burped and covered her mouth. Did he hear that?

David pounded the cork into the bottle with the heel of his palm. She waited for his response—either to her request or the burp, but he said nothing. He tucked his shirt into his pants and pulled up his suspenders. She stared at his fingers as he pinched the white shirt buttons. Inez realized she was sad when the twin knobs of his collarbone disappeared from view.

"Let's go."

* * *

A crow landed near the top of one of the tallest trees that lined Emma Street. The bough bent and bobbed as the bird squawked, whaaa, whaaa, flapping its iridescent wings. Inez watched the two officers, DiPaola and Gorman, lug the stretcher up the gravel path to the waiting Black Maria. The sheet that covered the baby's body billowed in the wind and folded back on itself to reveal a white, swollen leg. The body looked inconsequential in comparison with the size of the stretcher and the broadness of the bodies that hoisted it and the blue sky that surrounded them.

Inez took off her spectacles and pinched the bridge of her nose to push away the black dots that pulsed and swam in front of her eyes. It was not the discovery of a murdered infant, but simply the lack of sustenance for the long day and the whiskey that sloshed around in her belly. She willed herself to take deep breaths to push away the layers of gauze wrapped around her brain. Inez burned to think of what would be said if she fainted at the scene.

As the officers made their way along the path, Inez realized that if this was the route used by the murderer, any possible evidence of footprints was now trampled. Inez stood near the Black Maria and watched their struggle; all the while, she was aware of David standing next to her. She registered a confusing mix of scents like spicy mustard and warm cedar. To add to the off-balance moment, David began to croon, low and sweet:

> "Shall we gather at the river,
> Where bright angel feet have trod,
> With its crystal tide forever,
> Flowing by the throne of God."

Jack Gorman smiled up at David as they reached the street and joined in to sing the chorus, a harmony borne of practice and brotherhood. Inez was taken aback by the musical tribute to the lost baby. They did believe this was a solemn moment and not just an inconvenience.

> "Yes, we'll gather at the river,
> The beautiful, the beautiful river,
> Gather with the saint of the river,
> That flows by the throne of God."

Two more verses of the song pulled the spectators closer. They craned their necks to see the stretcher as they covered their mouths to whisper from cupped hands to waiting ears. Inez searched each flushed face, some drawn and hard, others appearing to be watching a theater performance.

Could the killer be standing here?

Inez thought of the killer, carrying an indistinct bundle, skidding in the loose gravel down the path to the river.

"Ere we reach the shining river
Lay we every burden down
Grace our spirits will deliver
And provide a robe and crown."

When they approached the wagon, the crowd grew dense and hummed like insects. Gorman flexed an elbow to ward them off. "Should the people be questioned? They might recognize the infant," Inez asked David. The smells of the river and decomposition mingled with the shrub roses that clamored over the porch pillars.

"Not possible," David said. "The body, it's been in the river too long. It will be too troubling for them to look at."

"We should begin to interview all these people, then?"

"The women? What for? Surely a woman couldn't have done this."

"You don't think women are capable of murder as a general principle? Or just the murder of children? Themisto, the third wife of Athamas, wanted to kill the children of her husband's second wife, Ino. Instead, she killed her own children by mistake."

"You don't say."

"And the daughters of Pelias made mincemeat of their father and boiled him."

"Who's that? Relatives of yours?"

"No, they are stories from Greek mythology."

"Then they are just made-up tales then, not real crimes."

Inez clenched her hands in exasperation. "They are stories that explained in a literary way, the history of the Greeks. All stories are born of truth." The wind blew grit in her face.

"So you're a bookish type?"

Here was the moment that always arrived when men talked to her at length. They came to realize she was educated. She read dry texts. She became dull in their eyes. Unladylike. They assimilated this information and then draped it over a summation of her looks: large hands and shoulders, mannish height, pale skin and white hair. She was dismissed then as odd and ugly. She had seen the stares and could almost hear the grinding gears of their thoughts.

"Oftentimes I've found that books are better companions than people."

"Surely, you have lady companions."

Inez cut him off. "No, I am by myself most times. I do have a housekeeper." Inez gazed up to the apex of a stand of pine trees, now flexing in the renewed winds. The crows complained in a cacophony of dissonant chords. She watched the narrowing of his brow, the crooked line that bisected his forehead.

"Damn noisy magpies—they scrape my ears raw!" He motioned to Gorman who was positioning the stretcher in the wagon. "I've heard Jack say the magpies always come when they smell death. You ever see how they pluck out the eyeballs of something dead?"

"Any scavenger will go for the eyes because they are a soft natural opening for the body." There was no need to disguise her tongue or her thoughts to him. He must already think her a misfit.

He frowned. "That doesn't bother you? Most women would be made faint by such things." David looked at Inez and then stared at the ground.

"It's science in nature. Why would I be offended? I admire crows."

"Admire? How's that?"

"Crows are from the genus corvis, the family corvidae." Inez went on. "They have remarkable intelligence. They have been known to use tools to get food. Crows eat almost anything—other birds, fruits, nuts, seeds or mice. This has made them efficient survivors."

"I didn't know that, but why do they peck out the eyes?"

"According to Greek legend, Princess Arne was bribed with gold by King Minos of Crete, who punished her for her avarice by transforming her into a jackdaw that forever sought shiny things." Inez stepped around to face David, to stare into his eyes. It felt like a sickness, the need to validate his repulsion. She would revisit this look on future nights whenever she thought of his collarbones framed by a white shirt. To her surprise, the look of scorn or disgust was absent. His look was not something she could identify. She turned and climbed into the wagon.

"But that's just a story—it doesn't mean anything," he called after her.

"If that's what you choose to believe," she answered. Her voice was so quiet she doubted if anyone heard.

Chapter 33

Martine's cramped handwriting led Ella down to the shipping docks just east of the Robert Street Bridge. In a matter of a few hours, the heat of the last few weeks had disappeared as if summer had suddenly packed its bags and left town. It was a shocking relief from the high temperature that had pressed her into a heavy-limbed fatigue. As Ella shivered under her green cape, the silk lining rustled. It felt odd to push the stroller without the boys, for tonight it served as a cart to deliver hatboxes to the docks.

A fine mist dampened her hair. The gas lamps glowed, creating halos. She wondered why she was being directed to make a hat delivery at dusk. Hopefully, this would be the last time she would walk the city to make a delivery. After tonight, she would concentrate on the baby business.

As the wheels of the carriage groaned in complaint, Ella pictured the blonde baby promised by Lettie. How would it be to have her heart captured each time by these motherless children? Would she ache each time she took them into her arms only to send them back into the world? As the wheels thudded along the wooden decking, she pictured the boys asleep in their new crib, handmade by their farmer-father. Now there would be money to pay rent, buy coffee and meat. She and Lettie were true partners.

Suddenly, a wheel of the stroller caught on a pile of rags, and two of the hatboxes tumbled to the wet planks of the dock. One of the covers rolled to the edge of the dock. Ella gasped to think of the airy hat sucked into the dark waves. How would she explain the loss? She picked up the lid, searching the darkening shadows on the dock for the shape of a hat. There were only wads of straw—no hat at all. One by one, Ella tore open the other boxes. They were all empty.

Martine had said she was sending hats to Paris. Had she lost her mind? Ella replaced the lids and stacked the boxes with trembling hands.

The barges were tied to the dock pilings with ropes as big as her arm. Ella wrinkled her nose at the smells the river pushed at her; sewer and fish and wet wood planking became something she could taste. As the shadows grew dense, she began to hear the chatter of prostitutes who scavenged for men like seagulls after bits of gutted fish. Ella flinched as bats swooped overhead. She heard the pounding of heavy boots, the sound of glass breaking, and she spun around to hear a moan, low and long in the manner of sex. A shriek—or was it laughter? What was she doing down here? Unease pricked across her shoulders. She feared a man would attack her from behind, pressing the jagged edge of a boning knife to her neck.

A sob escaped her, muffled by the wind and waves. She pushed at the tears that blurred her vison with the palm of her hand as she jerked the handle of the carriage, determined to make her way back to the road. She didn't care about the delivery and would gladly hand the envelope back to Martine. Suddenly she wished for Lettie at her side. Lettie would scoff and scream, hurling rocks or obscenities at the men and the shadows.

"Hey you, girlie."

Where did the voice come from? Ella stumbled and twisted her ankle. A hot pain, like an awl driven into the bone, caused her to gasp. She blinked hard to make sense of the shifting shapes.

"Come closer." The voice swirled around her.

"Leave me be." Every step was a fresh jolt of pain.

"Keep me warm, will ya? Just for a minute anyway." The voice was closer now. It scratched at her skin like wool. A flare of a lantern light sliced across her shoes.

"Can I see your babe?"

"There's no baby," she yelled. She limped faster, following the path of moonlight painted on the dock. She looked up to see the clouds had parted, thin and wispy over a heavy, glowing moon.

She felt a finger trace along her shoulders, her braid tugged as the length of it passed through someone's hand. Ella shrieked and squeezed her eyes shut. She fell and curled up, pressing her knuckles into her eyes. Panic roared in her ears.

"You there, get away from her!"

"Get your own. I was just looking for a bit of fun."

"Move. Now." The voice was familiar, a smooth comforting caress. Ella turned her head to see two men looming over her. They took a step closer to each other. The attacker gestured, two fingers curling, *come here.* He swung a fist in a wide arc, bouncing on his heels. The other man stood still.

"What do you want, a bunch of fives?" He raised both fists now, rolling them like engine pistons. She could see his shape now, dense and bulky, bullish. His cap was pulled low over his eyes.

Ella saw the other man reach into his coat pocket. He tossed an object from hand to hand. She heard a click and saw the blade of a button knife. "Leave her or you'll be wearing a wooden coat."

The voice. Calm, steady. Mary, Mother of God, it was Richard Gale!

"She's just a fancy girl. Get your own." The bullish man's voice was slippery.

Richard lunged and kicked the man between his legs. His movements were swift and graceful. The man grunted, vomiting a thin stream before he sank to his knees. As he pitched forward, Richard pressed a boot to his back and bent to flick the knife across his cheek.

"Can't say I didn't warn you. You're dumb enough to prefer shitting through your teeth." Richard smiled as he stepped away.

The man groaned and pushed himself up with wobbly arms. Ella saw his cheek was dark with blood.

"You're up to another go, then?"

"Aurggg." He spat and felt along the dock until he located his cap. "No more." He staggered to a standing position and reeled off into the darkness.

Ella burst into tears. She huddled and pressed her face to her knees.

"Miss Ella, are you all right?" Ella felt him kneel next to her, his words like a gentle touch.

"Did he hurt you?"

She shook her head. Her nose ran.

"Can you stand?" He took both of her hands and guided her to an upright position. Her arms and legs felt hot and loose.

"What on earth are you doing down here?" He closed the knife and slipped it into his pocket.

"Me employer, she told me to deliver some hats here, for shipping. Trouble was, I didn't know who I was supposed to meet or where they were going. I just have an address—here." The fear bubbled up again, and she started to cry. "And then I found out all the boxes are empty."

"Where are the babes?"

"Adopted." Ella sniffed. "We found a home for them on a farm!"

Richard pressed a folded handkerchief into her hand. It seemed this is how she knew him—as someone who rescued her and dried her tears.

"What are *you* doing down here?" she asked but wanted to say that he didn't belong in this place of brawling and thieving. He shrugged and adjusted his cuffs as if he had just finished a game of chess.

"The stevedore is an acquaintance of mine. Listen, why don't you unload those boxes. I will see that he gets them. He'll know what to do with them."

"Would you do that?"

"Of course. You should get back to the street and hurry home. Tell your employer not to send you out at night."

"But the boxes are in my charge!" Ella clenched her hands as Richard began to stack the boxes in a pile next to a shack.

"They're empty, you said so yourself. Thieves won't be interested."

Ella remembered Janna's body in the hatbox.

He leaned over and retied the bow on her cape.

Ella wanted to go home. Her ankle throbbed, and her palms stung.

146

"Thank you so much."

"Take this and use it if you need it." Richard took both of her hands and slid the button knife into her palm. The soft pad of his thumb stroked the back of her hand. He bent and kissed her hand.

Ella's legs trembled as she walked away. The handle of the knife was warm in her hand. She cast one last look over her shoulder and watched the dusk consume him.

Chapter 34

"Are those his teeth?" Ella whispered in Lettie's ear. She pointed to a pile on the bar that resembled several brown stones. They glistened in a puddle of sticky, dark blood. A few feet away, a man cradled his head in his arms and snored; a string of pink drool hung from his lip.

"That's how this place got its name. Most nights there are enough bloody brawls to fill a bucket. Isn't it fun?" Lettie smiled as she walked through Bucket of Blood, acknowledging greetings from some, ignoring others. Ella followed the sway of Lettie's hips and twice stepped on her heels because she was following too closely.

The bar smelled of sweat and greasy meat. Lettie had persuaded Ella to celebrate out on the town, claiming Ella spent too much time alone in her house with the babies. This felt different from the times she had gone to the pubs with Connor. The feeling of trouble hung around her neck, so Ella refused to meet the eyes of the men in the crowded bar. There were men of all ages and manner of drunkenness. A few men sported bruises or fresh cuts as they slapped cards on the table, threw dice or sang songs. A few hands grazed her backside. The heat of the entire summer was stored in this room.

"What if the police come?" In the space of a few minutes, she witnessed gambling, as many guns on the table as empty glasses and the flash of a knife buried in the web of someone's hand.

Lettie slung her arm around Ella's shoulders and pointed to one of the dice players. "See that fellow there? The one with the ginger hair? That's a policeman. They have an arrangement with Charlie, the owner, to overlook certain things, so no need to worry."

Lettie leaned in to whisper something in a man's ear. He was the same height as Lettie, but powerfully built. His eyes were half-lidded, and he pursed his lips as if he were deep in thought. Ella watched Lettie run her hand across his chest. He responded by tugging on her earlobe and pulling her close for a kiss that she returned with gusto.

"Ah Lettie, sing us a tune," someone shouted. A mug of ale appeared in Lettie's hand, and she passed it over to Ella. It was bitter and warm, but it quenched her dry throat. The song request was followed by hoots and whistles and one loud burp.

"Come on, will ya? We're achin' for your angel voice!"

Two sets of hands lifted Lettie to perch her on a wooden table. She crossed her legs and slowly inched up her skirt to her knees, stirring a chorus of howls and yips. Ella felt the crowd surge forward, merging together as if they had formed one large, sweaty man that pressed against her damp back. She squirmed when someone sniffed her hair.

"This one, you'll leave alone. She's with me," Lettie shouted and pointed to Ella. She waggled her finger as a warning. "You'll answer to me, if you do."

"Come on," they called.

Ella smiled at Lettie as she heard her start to hum a tune, low and rich. Eyes closed, Lettie dangled her pendant back and forth like a metronome, and the notes gradually swelled and grew bolder. Ella saw the men smile and sway. In this beery moment, she felt absolute love for Lettie. She admired her for making her own rules, for coming and going as she pleased, and for telling men what to do. She was someone who could command her safety—even in a place like this.

> "We'll drink, a drink, a drink
> To Lydia Pink, a pink, a pink—
> Savior of the human race,
> For she invented a medicinal compound,
> Most efficacious in every case.
> Now Mr. Brown has a very small penis,
> He could hardly raise a stand,

So they gave him the medicinal compound and
Now he comes in either hand."

Ella blushed to hear Lettie singing of such personal matters, but the beer blurred the edges of her discomfort. She began to laugh and cheer along with the men who professed their love. A few offered promises of marriage. As Lettie belted out more verses, building in gusto, Ella looked around the bar and spied Aldo, her old boss, sitting in a back booth, the man who fired her without a backward glance, sending her out into the streets to starve.

Aldo was the only man ignoring Lettie's performance. He sat, legs splayed, his shirt unbuttoned and stained. Beads of sweat slid down his temples. He had one of the working girls by the wrist; his thick fingers pinched her white skin as she struggled to get away. Ella stared, unable to move.

Tears stung her eyes. She hated Aldo and blamed him for Connor's death. If only Aldo had promoted Connor to floor supervisor. Her hands clenched into fists, shaking with the urge to punch Aldo, like a man would. Oh, to pummel his fat nose right off his face! Lettie slid into another song.

"Oh, this is number one and the fun has just begun!
Roll me over in the clover,
Roll me over and lay me down,
And do it again ..."

Ella walked over to Aldo and kicked him hard in the ankle. He squawked and immediately released the woman's arm. She rubbed the red marks and mouthed *thank you, honey* to Ella before she ducked out the back door.

"Whadja do that for? You wanna take her place, Missy-girl?" The drink caused his tongue to grow too large for his mouth, and it protruded from his lips like a panting dog.

She realized he had no idea who she was, a former Seeger's worker, the widow of his fastest cutter. The sweat that had soaked her back in the creation of a thousand seams meant nothing to him. A storm of anger simmered in her chest.

She watched his tobacco-stained fingers waggle, reaching out to touch her. She registered the applause and whistling, but all sounds were muffled. It was how he saw the rows and rows of seamstresses. Faceless. Replaceable.

She slipped her hand into the pocket of her skirt and squeezed Richard's knife. Her thumb found the release button.

Suddenly, she felt Lettie's arms around her. Lettie pressed her cheek to Ella's. "Aldo, you old dog. If you want this girl, you have to put your money on the table. She's not as foolish as she looks!"

"Ah, Lettie." Aldo sniffed and licked his lips. He pushed himself up from the booth bench and leaned heavily against the table. "You always make my balls hurt."

"All the girls here talk about you. Wanna know what they say?"

Aldo smiled slyly.

"I'll tell you." Lettie leaned in, pressing herself against the length of him. Her leg curled around the back of his calf. She tugged his earlobe, and her lips grazed his ear as she whispered. Aldo's eyes closed.

When Lettie pushed back from Aldo's chest he swayed as if he'd been shoved. She picked up his glass on the table and drank the rest of his whiskey.

"Come on, Ella. Let's go home."

She slung her arm around Ella's shoulder, that now familiar gesture that warmed Ella as they turned their backs to Aldo and made their way to the door. One man reached to kiss Lettie's hand and bowed.

When they burst out the front door, Ella breathed in the night air, so clear and cool in contrast to the smoky sweat of the pub. She felt the anger and tension float away from her arms and shoulders.

"Remember when I told you about the floor boss who fired me from Seeger's? That was him. Aldo." She pulled the damp hair from her neck.

"I know who he is. I know his reputation. Here, this is for you." Lettie slipped something into her hand as they walked. "Aldo sends his apologies."

As they passed under the gas lamp, Ella saw it was a money clip.

"I don't know how much is there. He was always a cheap sonofabitch, but it's the thought that counts." In the golden light, Lettie winked.

Chapter 35

Inez winced as Louise pressed the folded flannel soaked with apple-cider vinegar to her forehead. Her housekeeper's touch was gentle but sure. The sharp smell pinched the back of Inez's nose and made her eyes water. The last sun of the day had retreated behind the green-tinged clouds, tinting the kitchen with long shadows.

"Your skin's as red as a brisket!" Louise frowned, her gray eyebrows pressed to narrow her eyes.

Inez held the flannel with one hand as she tipped the glass, slippery and cold, to drain her third glass of lemonade. The tip of her tongue prodded the blister on her lower lip.

"Are you going to talk to me or do you need more time to yourself?" Louise asked.

Inez closed her eyes and sighed. The kitchen smelled of vinegar, sardines and rain. Louise's voice was soothing and low, but the image of the baby's body bobbing amid the floating twigs and pine needles pulled her back to the lapping waves of the river.

"You're like him, you know… your father." Louise took the cloth from Inez and dipped it into the bowl, rung it out, and dabbed the back of Inez's neck. "He would come home and sit right there where you are now, quiet, thinking, his lips moving but not saying anything I could understand."

"I'll tell you everything." Inez's mind snapped back to the kitchen, to Louise's voice and her concern. She knew she had hurt Louise's feelings. She was a constant. Always ministering and offering opinions thinly veiled as advice. Rain pelted the windows, and Inez felt chilled from the sunburn and the lemonade. She pulled off her spectacles and pushed at the throbbing spot in her temple. For now, she preferred the world to be blurry and soft.

"Here, take these." Louise turned over her cupped hand and dropped what looked like two buttons in her palm.

"What are they?"

"Bayer aspirin. You're working up to a fever."

"It's not a powder?"

Louise pulled the tin from her apron pocket and set it on the table. "They're new. The pharmacist called them tablets. Put them in your mouth and take a sip of lemonade, tip your head back, and swallow."

Instead, Inez bit down on the tablet; the bitter taste flooded her mouth and cleared her mind.

"I found the body of an infant today… in the river."

Louise unfolded a section of newspaper and set out a tin of shoe polish and a brush. "And you reported it, I expect."

Inez relaxed into the telling of the afternoon's events. Louise was a careful listener, not shocked by horrific details. She didn't interject questions. For years, she had listened to Joseph Laudenbach recall details of robberies and murders.

"Yes, I went to the station, and then we were sent to the scene with the Black Maria." She watched as Louise cleaned the boots she had peeled from her swollen feet, the leather still damp and stained. They looked as tired and worn as Inez felt. Sand and grit crusted the laces and eyelets.

"It's part of the work, you understand. It won't be the last time."

Inez nodded and poured another glass of lemonade from the pewter pitcher. She couldn't bear to eat anything. Thunder rumbled bass notes.

"The infant had a ligature cinched around its neck."

"Such an awful thing, to murder an innocent. Anyone come forward? A witness?" Louise's hand and arm disappeared inside the boot while she whipped the brush back and forth over the toe. Her jaw was set in a manner that matched the exertion of her task.

"No, and the other officers didn't even ask questions of the neighbors at the scene! It was confusing. The officers, they seemed to have a reverence for the body—they sang as they moved it to the hearse. But they seemed so matter-of-fact about the death. David—I mean, Officer Gabrielli..." Inez felt odd saying his name aloud. "He told me they frequently find infants. Probably will be buried at the Ramsey County Poor Farm is what he said. And that will be the end of it."

"So you want to know what happened?"

"Of course."

"Go figure it out. You're a clever woman. In most ways, you're smarter than your father. Solve this crime."

"But I'm not allowed. I can't act like a detective."

"They don't need to know what you're up to now, do they?" Louise set the brush on the table and scrutinized her progress.

"But my work on the Tombstone Thief case was dismissed. Ignored." Inez put her spectacles back on and brought her glass to the sink. She lifted the curtain to peer outside into the darkness. A breeze wafted through the window to cool her hot cheeks.

Inez listened to the furious pace of the brush on leather. "So, is it the notoriety you're craving, or do you want justice for the baby?" Louise asked.

Inez spun around to see a small smile tug at Louise's mouth. When she set the boot on the paper, the leather glowed buttery and dark.

"Is it wrong to covet both?"

"Not in the least." Louise attacked the second boot. "But if you could pick only one."

Inez stopped, remembering the heart-pounding moment when she had solved the crime and then the slice of pain that flared again when she recalled how her work was stolen.

Inez walked back to where Louise worked, the floor cool to her bare feet. Louise had a smear of boot black through her brow, and she frowned at the boot as if it were a misbehaving child. "I'm guilty of the sin of pride, is that what you're saying?"

"Oh, sit and eat something. I'm saying you can be quietly prideful and find justice for the baby that will never be able to speak."

Inez picked up the slices of toasted bread with sardines arranged in a precise row and bit a salty mouthful. There was a flash of lightning through the window followed by a deafening clap of thunder. The storm thrilled her in exactly the same way it had when she was a child. Zeus was flinging white-hot bolts of lightning at earthly targets. The heat and booming reverberations rippled through her chest.

When she closed her eyes, she pictured the baby wrapped in a white sheet on the table of the coroner, the smell of death and the river filling the room. And then an eternity in an unmarked grave in the poor cemetery.

"I want to know what happened."

"Is there a fellow at the station, maybe someone who knew and respected your father, who's interested in justice for this baby?"

Inez nodded, thinking of the way David's shirt parted to show olive skin.

"Let this man be the front for your crime solving." Louise capped the tin of boot polish.

At that moment, thinking of David, his brown eyes, the peculiar way he stood with his hands bracing his lower back, Inez wasn't sure what she wanted.

"I have something for you," Louise said as she rolled up the stained newspaper. "Wait here."

Louise left the kitchen, and Inez heard her rummaging in the hall closet. Inez finished the last of the sandwiches and set the plate in the sink. She sat down at the table and licked the oil from her fingers.

Louise reached over her shoulder and placed a package in her arms. She squeezed Inez's shoulder with a strength that pinched her bone.

Inez pulled the string to release the bow and unfold the brown paper. It was a leather-bound book with gilded edges. When she opened the cover, she found the heavy cream pages blank, save for the first one. Inez recognized Louise's prim penmanship.

> What we have in us of the image of God is the love of
> truth and justice.
> —Demosthenes

"I figured it was time for you to start your own Book of Crime," Louise whispered.

Chapter 36

Inez couldn't sleep. Every time she closed her eyes she pictured David's mouth, the way he bit his lower lip when he concentrated. The cracks of thunder, her sunburned face and full bladder only added to her agitation. More images of David crowded in, the contrast of his white shirt against the olive skin, the way he gestured with both hands while he talked. She put a pillow over her mouth and screamed.

Inez flung off the damp sheet and swung her feet to the side of the bed. Her feet felt the cool of the wood floor. Even though the storm had pushed the heat away, the second floor stubbornly held the warmth of the past days. Inez's clammy nightdress clung to her shoulders and back, and she tried to peel it away as she maneuvered the creaking stairs. She didn't want to rouse Louise who would immediately fuss over her.

The kitchen smelled of citrus, fish, and the dying sweetness of flowers. Inez preferred to keep the room dim and walked by feel in the creamy moonlight. She opened the icebox and grabbed the bottle of milk, poured a glass and drank thankfully. She couldn't swallow fast enough, and the milk ran from the corners of her mouth. A pulse thudded in her ears.

As she wiped her mouth on her sleeve, she heard a creak. Inez turned toward the sound coming from the porch. Her nose caught the spicy aroma of tobacco. Her heartbeat quickened. She was a police officer without a weapon! Inez pulled open a kitchen drawer, and her fingers glided over the edges of serving spoons, the pointed tip of a spatula, and the rolling pin. Then her fingers found the head of the meat tenderizer.

When she was young, she thought the blade on the back end of the head looked like a miniature ax. The metal felt cool to her hot palm as she pulled it from the drawer.

There were footsteps on the porch floor, just twenty feet from where she stood. A bead of sweat raced between her breasts. Inez moved toward the sound, her weapon raised in front of her. She felt unprotected wearing just a nightdress. A burglar? She thought of the pickpocket she had questioned at the hotel. Or maybe it was an imitator of the Tombstone Thief.

A shadow moved at the end of the hall. A civet smell, the oily odor of the Central Station.

It was the scent of a man.

Her stomach churned with greasy fear. For a moment, she thought she might be dreaming. The shape wavered, but the only sounds were the last raindrops falling on the tin roof. Maybe she wasn't here after all, standing in her nightdress clutching a meat tenderizer. Maybe she had fallen back to sleep in her narrow bed. This was just part of a fragile dream that would fade away when her eyes opened.

This thought made her bold. She strode toward the shadow-shape, her weapon high over her shoulder.

"Inez? Is that you?"

The voice stilled her gait. Her arm cramped. The voice was leathery, familiar. Her breath came in husky bursts.

"Oh, it's me, David. I shouldn't be here." He hiccupped. "I started walkin' and ended up here."

A breeze swept through the porch, hardening her nipples and releasing her coiled fear. Her weapon banged against her thigh.

"Say something, Inez."

"David." His name was all she could manage.

"Say, I'm sorry for the fright." His words were thick and twisted in drink. "God-awful-damn, I don't know why—I just had to see you. Alone, is all. Without everyone watchin'." He sagged against the wall. "I wanted to ask you to maybe help me with the absinthe case. I've gone over and over it. Your mind works different from other women. I thought—oh, I dunno."

Inez's eyes adjusted to the dim light. She walked to him. Under the promise of a dream, she reached out and touched the curls that sprang over his ears. Barefoot, she was exactly his height. The skin at the back of his neck felt hot.

He gasped. "Inez?"

There was something coarse about him in this state, but he was also loose and inviting. She stepped in closer. It was a dream after all. Why not?

An urgency welled up in her—the need to know what his mouth felt like. In her youth, she had been spared the pawing attentions of young men. Now it all seemed so different. Her thumb grazed his full lower lip. Then she cupped the back of his neck and pulled him closer. She felt the buttons of his shirt through her thin gown. Her thumb followed the curve of his collarbone to the hollow of his throat. Of course, this was a dream.

His mouth pressed her lips, and she tasted ale and salt. Inez was surprised by the softness of his mouth. She felt his hand on her waist as his fingers began to knead her lower back. It must be a dream.

Eyes closed, she responded in kind, drinking from him like the cold milk. His mustache scratched her raw skin, but the pain only made her draw him closer. It was hard to breathe because his fingers pleated the nightdress, drawing it up past her knees. She thought of Poe and for the first time understood the words, "*Let my heart be still a moment and this mystery explore—'tis the wind and nothing more.*"

Her grip relaxed, and the meat tenderizer slipped from her fingers. "Ooompf," he howled, and he pitched forward, hopping on one foot. His forehead slammed into Inez's nose with a blunt stab of pain.

"Inez, God, I should go." David backed away from her and staggered against the wall.

The porch door rasped and slammed shut, and Inez stood, slick blood running over her lip.

Chapter 37

"Such a pretty baby!" Mrs. Lynch leaned on her cane, calling from the street. Ella sat on a blanket in her yard holding the new baby. The old woman began to click her tongue as if she were calling chickens. "What's her name?"

When Ella waved away a fly, the baby gave a toothless grin and vigorously kicked her chubby legs in the air. Ella grabbed the baby's soft little foot and kissed the tiny toes.

What was her name? Ella had no idea. Lettie had wheeled the buggy home last night, just as the purple dusk spread over the heavens. She told Ella she didn't remember if the mother ever relayed the baby's name, but happily displayed the ten dollars that had been handed over in exchange for their services.

"This one'll fetch a good fee! It's a better looking creature than both of the dark ones put together!"

"What did she tell you?" Ella needed to understand the long list of desperations separating mothers from children.

Lettie shrugged. "Said something about her husband's feet getting chopped off."

So what do I call this baby? Ella watched the baby blink her crystal blue eyes when the hot breeze fluttered across her face. She threw an arm across her body, rolled over to the edge of the blanket and grabbed a fistful of grass. She stared intently at her hand as she crushed the green blades.

"We call her Little Blue," Ella called out to Mrs. Lynch.

"What's that?" The old lady cupped her hand to her ear. Her thin hair that barely covered her scalp was gathered in an egg-size knot at the top of her head.

"LITTLE BLUE!"

"Oh cheese and mice, what kind of name is that for a baby? Say, I heard of your husband's passing last winter. Beata told me." Mrs. Lynch made the sign of the cross. "At least you have this baby to remind you."

At the mention of Connor's death, a stab of pain sliced through her chest, fresh and hot. There he was sitting on the same blanket next to her, his hand pressed over hers... the same quilt he had dubbed the kissing blanket because they would haul it down to the riverbank last summer to escape the heat of the house.

"She's not mine." Her voice was choked with tears. "I'm just minding her for a bit of time." She focused on the white butterfly alighting on the cabbage rose pattern of the quilt. It pressed its wings together like hands in prayer.

"Say again?"

"She's not mine!" The porch door slammed, and Ella heard the thud of footsteps. She yipped in pain when Lettie's fingers pinched her arm.

"Get back in the house," Lettie snarled. Her hair was pressed in sweaty waves along her neck.

"What's wrong? Ouch! You're hurting me." Lettie tugged at the blanket, jostling the baby.

Mrs. Lynch's toothless mouth hung open.

"Mind your own business, hag! Shoo, get outta here." Lettie darted at the old woman, kicking up clouds of dirt.

Ella picked up Little Blue and set her on her hip. The baby squinted in the sun and laughed when Ella shook the grass from the underside of the blanket. Ella was embarrassed. Why did Lettie make her feel like a scolded child? She stomped up the steps into the house.

Ella flung the blanket over Lettie's chair, pushed aside the curtains, and opened all the windows. She walked to the kitchen and surveyed the dirty plates and sticky whiskey glasses Lettie had left on the table. Lettie's footsteps trailed after her, but she ignored her. Ella set the baby in the buggy, handed her a spoon and started a kettle of water on the stove. She had the urge to slam things and make noise, or break plates, but she was afraid of startling the baby.

"You can't tell people what we're doing here with the babies." Lettie took a bite from a half-eaten plum and put it back on the table. She wiped her hands on her skirt.

"Why not?" Ella tied the apron around her waist. The baby babbled as if she were participating in the argument.

"Do you want the police at your door?"

"Why would they care? We're finding homes for babies!" The minute these words were out of her mouth she immediately questioned herself.

"That's the work of the churches. You're getting paid for it. They might look at that with a different eye."

"That's crazy."

"It's your reputation I'm worried about."

"Mine?" Ella set the dishes and empty bottles in the sink.

"The police know me as a pickpocket."

Ella carved a few curls of lye soap to drop into the sink and put a stopper over the drain.

"What if anyone started counting?"

"Counting what?"

"Babies. Remember the one that died? Suppose someone asks questions? What if they say you did something to her?"

Ella spun around, and droplets flew from her wet hands. Janna, that poor scrawny sick baby. The image of the cold blue body on the bed appeared.

"I did the best I could!" Ella pulled the buggy closer and picked up Little Blue, kissed her wispy curls and reveled in the solid feel of her soft skin.

"I know your heart is made of gold, but maybe the police think differently."

Ella placed her hand across her chest, feeling her golden heart kick a fast beat.

"Do you know they've even got a policewoman now? You should see her! A giantess! Big and pale. Serious and mean, I bet."

Was that a lie? Ella didn't know what was in Lettie's heart. Not exactly a heart of gold, but was it black and rotten? The baby popped her thumb into her mouth and regarded Ella with wide eyes.

There was a loud thud against the back door. Ella gasped, and Little Blue startled and began to cry. Ella ran to the door but didn't see anyone standing there. She sighed, relieved there wasn't a giant policewoman with a grave expression. As she opened the screen door, the frame nudged a blackbird lying on its back, its dead eyes staring up at nothing.

Chapter 38

As the last spoon of rice cereal disappeared into Little Blue's mouth, she rubbed her sticky fists into her eyes and yawned. Her head lolled back and forth as the heat of the day and a full belly drew her to sleep. The baby relaxed into Ella's arms as she wiped the baby's hands with a cloth. Ah, what a lovely child. Such an even temperament! She rarely fussed, slept for long periods of time, and ate heartily. Her skin was clear, and her back was strong. Ella found herself chattering to this baby, and Little Blue took to bobbing her head in agreement as if she understood all that was said to her.

Ella carried the sleeping baby to her bed and laid her toward the middle, placing a pillow on either side. She brushed the sweaty curls from Little Blue's forehead and watched her mouth move as if she were telling a story. The room was still, and Ella was pulled to the same call of slumber. Just a minute's rest, she promised herself, and then she would get after the chores. She curled her body around Little Blue, and the last thing she remembered was the cool greeting of the pillow.

When she awoke, the room was dark and thick with warmth. She heard the sounds of children outside on the street, boys calling to one another. Ella licked her dry lips. There was only a fog of a dream remaining, Connor yelling, his eyebrows furrowed. Ella tried to apologize, but no matter how wide she opened her mouth, no words came forth. And then the wisps of the dream drained away, and tears ran across her temples.

When she reached out to check the sleeping baby, her hands patted the quilt. No baby! She sat up, her hands still moving across the empty bed as if she had somehow missed her in the folds of the sheets.

Had she tumbled off the bed? Certainly, she would have heard her cries. She looked on the floor and peered under the bed. Gone. Where was she?

Kidnapped? Maybe Lettie was right—the news of this babe in her care had spread to the wrong person. Maybe someone else figured out the price this pretty baby could fetch! She pictured one of the men from Bucket of Blood following them home, watching and waiting. Or what if the mother had changed her mind and came back for her? Ella paced the bedroom floor and then ran to the front room when she heard a knock at the door.

"*Kotku,* it's Beata. I bring you a slice of chocolate cake."

"Beata, do you have Little Blue?"

"What's this talk?" The screen door slammed shut. She set the plate on the table by Lettie's chair.

"The baby was sleeping. We were sleeping. When I woke up she was gone!" Ella balled a fistful of apron.

"No, it can't be." Beata took Ella's hands.

"It's my fault. I shouldn't have slept." Ella burst into tears. The skin at her temples tightened.

"How long did you sleep?"

"I don't know." The warmth of the room, the graying light, told Ella the long afternoon had passed.

"And where is that one?" Beata peered around the room as if Lettie were poised to jump out.

"Lettie didn't come home last night. Oh, Beata, she will be furious with me!"

"Ah, she's off drunk somewheres or with some man while you are the one here taking care of the baby!" Beata wagged a face of disapproval. She dropped Ella's hand and shifted her weight back and forth.

"But Little Blue was in my care!" Ella bit down on her knuckle.

"Let's go look in the bedroom. Maybe she crawled off on her own. She's a very strong baby!"

"She's gone. I think someone stole her!"

Beata walked down the hallway and pushed aside the curtain to the bedroom.

"The window is shut."

Suddenly, Ella remembered when she was still living in Ireland, and Da would smoke his pipe after dinner and tell her of the female faeries that often gave birth to deformed children. "The faeries prefer the beautiful Irish babies," he would say, "and they come into the mortal world looking for them."

"Should I call for the police?" Ella faltered, thinking of how to explain Little Blue's presence in her house. She feared Lettie's rage.

"What would they do? We have no proof someone took her. It's only ideas spinning in your head. I know those men. They will laugh and walk out the door."

"Where should I look?" Ella sat down hard and sobbed. The wood planks felt cool and gritty. One baby. She couldn't take care of one child. Beads of sweat mixed with tears and rolled down under her chin. Something tight twisted in her chest, a tension and pain that was like a musical note soaring higher and higher. She wanted to unwrap Connor's knives that were hidden under the mattress. She needed that first sting of pain. Beata's scuffed shoes moved closer, and her eyes blurred with tears.

"Maybe the neighbors have seen something? Come, we go look. I will bring some cake—they will talk if they have seen anything. You pray now to Saint Anthony, the finder of lost things."

"Then everyone will think I can't properly mind a baby."

"Your pride is for another day. Come now. Let's go."

Ella mopped her face on her apron and stood on shaking legs. Beata's arms went around her shoulders. "There, there, *kotku*. You have had too much sorrow." Beata's hand thumped repeatedly across her back. Ella's nose was so clogged she had to breathe through her mouth.

"If you will listen to an old woman for minute." She took Ella's face in her hands and looked her in the eye. Her plump hands were damp and warm on Ella's cheeks. "It's impossible to be ready for life. You think you've lived through the worst thing, the loss of your Connor, but there are always bad things unimagined coming for you."

Ella shivered in the hot room. She wondered if Beata had read something dark in the tarot cards.

"Come, let's wash your face and get a drink of water. Then we go. The wringing of the hands will do no good."

Ella nodded and followed Beata down the hallway into the thrumming heat of the kitchen. The folded flannels were nestled in the basket on the table. An empty milk bottle sat in the sink. A fat fly trapped between the windowpane and the screen buzzed as it repeatedly threw its body against the glass.

"*Kotku*, where is the carriage?" Beata paced around the kitchen.

"I left it here." Ella pointed to the place next to the stove.

They turned when the front door slammed and listened to the wood floor creak with each footstep. Ella rushed down the hallway to find Lettie sitting in her chair, wriggling her bare toes. Lettie's face was flushed as she balanced a plate on her knees and picked up a piece of cake.

Lettie. How to tell her about Little Blue? Ella's words were trapped.

"Ella-bell, you see a ghost? Maybe one of your leprechauns?" Lettie took a bite and chewed. "Mmm, this is so good."

Beata followed Ella into the front room and stood, arms folded across her chest. Her hands balled into fists.

"Oh, it's you," Beata muttered. "I see you enjoy the cake not meant for you."

"I see you are wearing out your welcome again." Lettie smiled. She took another bite, and Ella saw the crumbs tumble into the crease between her breasts. Beata made clicking noises with her tongue.

"Lettie, Little Blue is gone. Someone has taken her! I know you don't like the police but—"

"Stop fretting so much!"

"Fretting? She's gone!"

"No one's taken her. I delivered her tonight. Look at this!" She reached into her cleavage and pulled out a number of folded bills. "People will pay a lot of money for a pretty, fair one."

"You came into my room and took her? Did she have a change of flannels? A bottle? Why didn't you wake me?"

Lettie shrugged. "Didn't see the need." She sucked the frosting from her forefinger, her eyes closed in pleasure in a way that made Ella turn away. "Listen, we agreed. You take care of 'em, and I move them around town. What's bothering you?"

"I thought someone stole her."

Beata stomped over and wrestled the cake plate from Lettie's hands.

"Wait!" Lettie cried. "You're a jealous old bat. Ella and I are like sisters, and you can't stand it."

"This one," Beata pointed to Lettie, "she will bring ruin to you. She's bad."

"What's the saying? Love without jealousy is like a Pole without lice?" Lettie grinned.

"And I say, after shaking hands with a Greek, you should count your fingers." She stabbed her finger in the air and muttered a string of Polish curses.

Lettie stood her ground. "Apologize to me or get out, you old *flotch*. At least I bring in money to pay the rent." Lettie knew some Polish words too.

"Don't talk to her like that, Lettie. She has been nothing but good to me." Ella trembled as tears spilled down her cheeks.

Beata stooped to pick up the towel Lettie had dropped to the floor. She covered the massacre of cake and frosting. "I'm not going to tell you my tongue got in the way of my eye-tooth, and I couldn't see what I was saying. No apology for the truth."

Beata yanked open the screen door.

"Wait, Beata. Don't leave," Ella called. It felt like she was being asked to choose between them. Beata kept walking, shaking her head. "That one will always be the thorn on the rose," she muttered.

"That was rude, Lettie!"

"Well, she was rude to me. Who grabs a plate cake out of someone's hand?"

"I'm leaving." Ella retrieved her coin purse from her room and pinned her hair to the top of her head. She slipped out the back door so she wouldn't have to talk to Lettie.

"Suit yourself," she heard Lettie call. "Is there any more cake?"

Chapter 39

The air moved briskly under steely gray skies. The coolness was a welcome gift to Inez who hated the sun as much as the sun hated her. Clusters of broad maple leaves littered the muddy streets. Robins hopped in the puddles and ruffled their feathers as they bathed. Inez walked and walked.

She didn't sleep again after David fled the porch. She passed the hours in her favorite chair, staring at the wall where they had stood and kissed. The sky lightened by degrees as the birds chattered. She relived the encounter over and over again, and the humiliating conclusion crested. It was time to start her shift, so she got dressed, ate a few slices of buttered bread and headed to the neighborhood where she had discovered the body.

The puzzle helped to occupy her thoughts. The walking urged her mind to arrange the details of what she knew. Inez began her search near the footings of the Robert Street Bridge. She wanted to learn more about the currents, how they flowed this time of year after a heavy rainfall. Her father's book contained several drawn maps as they related to other crimes, but he hadn't recorded any helpful information about the strength or directions of currents and eddies and the effects of tugboat traffic. Inez decided to work her way upstream to see if she could discover any gossip. The world was growing. Many young girls traveled to the downtown area to work in the factories. If the mother of this infant was such a worker, someone might have heard talk about a mysterious swell of pregnancy that failed to yield a baby.

This is how she would begin her Book of Crime.

The collection of these details eased the hot bands that bound her chest. At this very minute, was David telling the story of the hulking woman in a nightdress who leapt at him in the middle of the night? She could hear their laughter and lewd comments. Maybe the others had put him up to sneaking into her house to frighten her so she would quit the job. A plan concocted in the fellowship of whiskey to scare off the big woman who dared to walk a police beat and steal the work that so rightfully belonged to the men.

Inez distracted herself from these thoughts by talking to everyone she encountered. She asked simple questions. Did you hear about the baby found in the river? Do you know the mother? She queried a woman pinning wash to the line, another sweeping her front porch. She waylaid a priest who was walking to the rectory. She asked young girls walking to the market and an old woman on a bench. Most of the time the responses were similar—eyes narrowed, lips pressed together to keep observations from escaping, brows furrowing in suspicion.

They didn't trust her.

The incredulous reactions could be categorized in three ways. The mothers minding children seemed the most resistant to her presence. "Such a shame, that baby," they said as they made the sign of the cross, "but you should send a policeman to talk to my husband."

The factory girls seemed protective of the clan of fellow workers. "I don't want any trouble," they would say as they studied their shoes. These girls held their secrets.

And then there were the prostitutes who doubled over with laughter. "Then it's not a rumor? There is a white ghost police girl? Now getting into bed with the law will be interesting for sure!"

Of course, of the dozens of people she spoke to, not one offered any information of use. If they weren't off-put by her sex or her size, certainly their poverty created a line of demarcation. Shoes tied with twine, tattered dresses, stringy hair and sallow faces. Inez recalled a quote by Aristotle: "Poverty is the parent of revolution and crime." If these assertions were true, then was poverty responsible for the murder of the baby? If it was her duty to look out for women and children, how could she prevent crime when they didn't have enough food in their bellies, or clean and decent clothes, let alone books to enrich their minds?

She swung her arms to make her stride long. She felt strong. The hollowness in her stomach made her feel lean and powerful. She came to the south end of the Wabasha Bridge and watched an empty barge, shaped like a gar fish, glide under the bridge. She liked the predictability of bridge design, the golden hues of the limestone blocks that faced the stout pilings and the repetition of the wooden skeleton that framed the passageway. A peddler at the far end made his way into the city as the roar of the river muffled the clatter of horse hooves. The sun parted the clouds, and irregular patches of blue sky appeared. She stepped up her pace to catch up to him.

Peddlers.

They covered large territories. They knew the city and watched people. Inez felt a hot coil of excitement. If not this man and his wagon of wares, then others like him certainly must have seen something of note. She began to run across the bridge, her boots thudding on the planking. Inez felt like the hawk swooping over the shoreline in the world of wind and waves. She watched the peddler make his way west where the mansion of Nina Clifford, the woman who ran the large brothel, perched on the bluffs of the Mississippi near Bucket of Blood Bar.

Chapter 40

Sweat soaked Ella's back as she stomped past houses and gardens, hedges and wooden fences lazy with age. She had no destination in mind but walked as fast as she could. Mothers called children to dinner; birds scolded a tomcat that sprawled in the dirt under a pine tree. Ella saw a man called Bones pulling a cart heaped with burlap bags down the alley off Concord Street. He was known for scrapping horseshoe nails and old rags. He also sold bones used to make knife handles that made his coat shiny with grease. He stared at her with milky eyes as he poked at a pile of ash with a hook affixed to a long stick. Ella's stomach clenched at the sight of him. Would she be reduced to selling old rags and bottles? Tears stung her cheeks as the late evening sun blasted her face.

She felt such loss for the dead and the living. Her family, Connor, Janna, Amolia, the boys, and now Little Blue. Gone. Each loss like a bright slice of stinging pain. Even Richard Gale, who seemed to appear at the oddest times, always vanished. And how long would Beata live given her growing list of ailments?

Then there was Lettie. Often, she seemed like a sister, and then she could be cold, mean, and embarrassing. Ella watched her feet as the dust of the street settled on her shoes and the wide hem of her skirt.

Lettie had said she would find homes for the babies, and she did. Think of the future profits if babies came like Little Blue! Lettie had never committed to help with the day-to-day care of the babies. That was Ella's duty, so why was she so annoyed? Lettie spoke her mind, caroused and drank like a man. Ella pressed her shirt cuff to her temples. A darker thought snaked in—was she jealous of Lettie's spirit?

Ella bent over, breathing hard as she pressed her hand against the stitch in her side. Oh, she was so thirsty! Dark spots darted beneath the pink of her closed lids. Oh, to share a pint with Connor like the old days! She realized she was close to the path that led to the river. Her muscles trembled with exhaustion and memory.

One night last summer when it was too hot to sleep, he had led her to this place. They had followed the glow of moonlight as the path became soft sand under her feet, and the tall grasses grazed her bare calves. They sat near the water that night because the breeze pushed away the mosquitos. Ella had dug her heels and flexed her toes into the cold, wet sand and leaned against his shoulder, listening to the lapping waves. They watched lanterns glinting on the deck of a tugboat. For once, Connor was quiet, no stories of Aldo or wild plans for the future. They slept there until the sun came up.

Now, as the sand began to give away under her feet, it felt familiar because each day without Connor felt like the world sliding out from under her. This was a place of Connor's choosing. The light blushed bright to the west, and the churning waters moved downstream. Ella smiled to find a stillness in this place of movement and heat.

"Is your name Ella?" The voice came from behind her.

Ella turned around, shielding her eyes. A mother, holding a baby swaddled in a blanket, called from the path. There were three children straggling behind her, identical thin faces, scratched and bruised legs.

Ella nodded.

"Then you are an answer to a prayer. The first one in a long time." The woman's voice was weak, and Ella strained to hear her words as she walked towards her. "They said you had red hair."

The woman's heavy accent sounded similar to that of Beata. She breathed deeply. The youngest boy held up both arms but was ignored.

"I came here to find my husband's brother," the woman began. "Milan fishes down here sometimes." She stopped her story to cock her head and consider Ella. "Oh, you are so young! I don't know why, I thought you were much older."

"I don't know your husband's brother," Ella started even though she knew the brother was not part of this story.

"People say you help, with babies, like this one." She nodded at the baby in her arms, its face so still and serene Ella's heart fluttered to wonder if it had taken a first breath. The older children sat down in a clump of skinny arms and legs.

"I find homes for babies," Ella answered.

She approached and displayed the baby for her. She then whispered in Ella's ear, "I came to the river to give him back to God. And here you are, so God must be working through you." Her green eyes teared. The setting sun glowed.

Ella pictured this mother, standing thigh-deep in the river, the muck pulling at her feet as she released the baby to the sparkling waves. The blanket would billow and then disappear. Would she have a moment of regret? Would she reach out and try to snatch him back or would her heart be cold?

"Please take him." She pushed the small bundle into Ella's arms. "I don't have money for you, but here, take this." She pulled a thin gold band from her thumb and cupped it in her palm.

"Go to the CSPS for a meal for you and the children," Ella urged.

"We've already come from there." The woman turned and walked away. Her children stood and stumbled after her. None of them looked back at the one they were leaving. Ella felt the baby moving in her arms as if he were trying to levitate toward his departing mother. He produced a small whimper.

"Shhh, maneen," she said softly. "You're safe with Ella."

Chapter 41

Inez lingered across the street from the police station, behind the horse-drawn cart heaped with fruit. Occasionally she would rise up on her toes to peer over the twitching ears of the horse at her counterparts as they departed from the station.

They sauntered off, adjusting their jackets, setting the angle of their hats as they scattered east and west. Some whistled tunes she didn't recognize or shouted insults to each other. William Gorman dragged his feet and pressed his fingers against his brows as he squinted into the morning sun. Inez smelled manure and over-ripe fruit.

She hated that she hid from David this way every morning. She couldn't face him. She was embarrassed that her heart lurched at a glimpse of him. He was always the last officer to leave. He was headed toward the docks again. She liked the way he bounced on his heels and swung his left arm to propel his walk.

"That's the last of 'em. They've all gone now."

Inez startled at the voice behind her. She turned to see the driver of the cart stroking the gray coarse mustache that overwhelmed his mouth. He gestured to the station as he offered her a paper cone filled with strawberries. The fruit was deep red and plump.

Inez could only nod. She was behaving as if she were a frightened child, or worse, a skulking criminal. Her cowardice was even obvious to the street vendor. She rubbed the horse's velvet nose, and the dense ripple of his muscles reassured her.

She strode across the street, and the sun touched her face without its usual menace. She pushed her chin upward, determined to be stronger, honorable. She would complete her duties without distracting thoughts of David Gabrielli. She would push aside this folly to collect the salient facts for her Book of Crime.

As she pulled open the door to the station, the hallways echoed with wailing sobs.

"God, where have ya been?" Murphy bleated. "Take care of this girl, will ya? We haven't the time to sort through womanly hysterics!"

Murphy's stare felt like a shove. A woman sat on the bench. She sobbed into a dirty blanket. Inez knew she should offer an embrace or comfort of some kind, but her arms remained stiff and immobile at her sides.

"What's your name?" Inez sat next to her and set the cone full of strawberries on the bench. She licked the pencil tip and turned the notebook to a fresh page.

"I made a mistake," the girl sobbed. She lifted her face to peer up at Inez. Her bright-blue eyes were red-rimmed, and she repeatedly pressed her chapped lips together. Inez frowned as she tried to determine her age. At first her diminutive stature led her to believe this was a child, but then she saw evidence of a womanly figure.

"Your name," Inez prompted when fresh tears rolled down the girl's blotchy cheeks.

"I'm Annah. My baby, my darlin' Madeline. You understand, I did a terrible thing."

Inez nodded, holding her breath, picturing the new realities she had learned about desperate mothers.

"We've had hard times! My husband—he worked at the railroad yard. He slipped on the icy rails when he was pulling pins on the cars." The last part came as a whisper. "The wheels ran over his legs."

"He perished then," Inez said.

"No, he's living. His feet, they're gone." She stared at the floor, and Inez knew they both pictured the moment when the steel rolled over his ankles, severing tendon and muscles; the crisp snap of bone.

"So your child…"

"Our Madeline was born on Christmas Day." Annah positioned her arms as if she were holding a baby and swayed. She made a face that was part smile, part grimace. "After the accident, we had no money comin' in. Not much food to eat but what people gave us. My milk dried up."

Everything about the girl was thin. Her lank blonde hair, her frame. Her hollow cheeks confirmed her account.

"It's a terrible thing to be so hungry. I can't work because Michael can't properly look after the baby—not in his condition."

"So what did you do?" Inez looked over at Murphy, but he had ceased to pay further attention now that the quiet had been restored. She wondered if Annah was about to confess to smothering the baby. She heard David's voice in her ear telling stories about the poor, unwanted babies.

"I answered this here ad, from the paper." Annah offered a page of newsprint from her pocket. Inez unfolded the ragged, smeared paper.

> If you are unable to provide proper care for a newborn, consider putting the child in the care of a competent woman who will find a loving family for your child. Also offering temporary care for infants and children. Discreet transactions assured for nominal fees. P.O. Box 114, Saint Paul.

"I sold my wedding ring and gave the money and my baby to this person. I thought if someone else could look after her for a few months…" Annah paused and pointed to the paper. "…then maybe things would improve for us." A fresh round of tears welled up. Inez handed her the fresh handkerchief Louise always tucked in her pocket. "I cried all the way home. When I told Michael what I'd done, he wouldn't speak to me—wouldn't even look at me. It was a mistake—I knew that straight away."

"I'm sure you wanted better for your child," Inez said, thinking of Mrs. Chormansky and all of her starving offspring. "You were behaving sensibly considering your circumstances." Inez slumped against the back of the bench, realizing she had been holding all of her muscles rigid as she awaited a worse confession.

Annah shook her head at Inez's praise. "No, no. It was wrong. I waited a week, and then I decided to go back for my Madeline. The woman could keep the money. I didn't care. I just wanted my baby."

"What happened next?"

"The address she gave me… it's a boarded-up place. I asked some folks around there, and they told me it's been closed for years."

"Could you have remembered the address incorrectly?"

"She wrote it herself—see? On the back side of the paper."

Inez flipped over the newsprint. "An error?"

"I don't know what to do. The policemen, they won't help me." Annah's sobs gained intensity. Pete McCoy walked past escorting a man in cuffs. He shook his head in disgust at the sight of the women.

"I am a police officer," Inez said quietly, hoping their conversation wasn't being overheard.

Annah wrinkled her nose and sniffed. "Oh, I see."

"Please realize, it might all be innocent. You paid a fee to someone to care for your baby. You were clear about the temporary nature of the arrangement, yes?"

Annah clutched at Inez's arm, pinching her skin. "You have to believe me—something went wrong. When she wrote to me, the cost was ten dollars. When I brought Madeline to her, she said it was going to be two dollars more. She said the baby looked sickly, and the money would go to pay a doctor. She said I would have to pay each month after that. Why would she write down the wrong address if I was supposed to pay each month?"

Inez sighed. Annah was getting more distraught. "Here, eat these strawberries." She picked up the cone and offered it to Annah. Inez closed her eyes and tried to ignore the salty-sour smell of Annah and the laughter of the men behind the front desk. "Tell me what the woman looked like."

Annah held the cone like a bouquet of flowers and bit half a berry. She chewed and licked her lips. "Mmmm, that's good. Well, I met her at the Wabasha Bridge at dark. About as tall as me, she was. Not stout, not thin. She wore a cape even though it was warm."

Inez flashed to the day in the cemetery—the crying girl in the cape next to the grave; her bright red hair fanned in the green grass.

"What color was her hair?"

Annah picked up another berry and shrugged, her face full of misery. "A hood, she wore a hood. Then she asked for more money so I gave her all I had. She wrote the address and a minute later she was gone." Annah was breathless with the telling.

Light slanted through the windows, creating oblong rectangles on the scuffed floor. Annah scratched at the flakey skin alongside her nose. Everything about the young woman's distress caused Inez to think about the Daimones, the spirits of pain and suffering who brought tears to the sorrowful. Inez tapped the pencil again as she considered her next words.

"The men here…" Annah dabbed her eyes on her sleeve. "…they don't care about me and my baby. You don't know how it feels to be ignored over something so important." Her fingers were stained with the red juice.

Inez handed Annah the pad of paper and pencil. "As it turns out, I do. I will investigate for you. I make no promises, understand. Write down your full name and address." She watched Annah's tears and wondered if it was possible for someone to cry until she was a dry husk. Annah handed the paper cone back to Inez full of green hulls.

Murphy's nostrils flared. "Laudenbach!" The sharp tone meant she should conclude the interview.

"My name is Inez. I will be the officer assigned to your inquiry." She pulled a bill from her sleeve and pressed it into Annah's palm. Annah blushed a furious shade of defeat as she stood to leave.

Chapter 42

Inez swirled her paint brush into the ink wash. The number of illustrations in her Book of Crime grew daily, the pages drying in permanent river waves. She often found herself at the kitchen table, on nights when sleep abandoned her, putting form to the images that bloomed in her mind. Sometimes it was the depiction of a place, like where she had discovered the body of the child in the river. More recently, the brush had turned to portraits—the tear-streaked face of Annah and the stony, lost look of Mrs. Chormansky.

As Inez waited for the ink to dry, she found herself ordering her thoughts, creating theories, making decisions. She often jotted notes in the margins. Questions that led to other questions. Inez's brush followed the lines of the abandoned building near the docks that Annah claimed as the address of the baby broker. She had ridden her bike there early the previous morning as the first light softened the sky.

This was the best time of day, in Inez's estimation, before the noise and heat and bother of people buzzed like bees. Most of the windowpanes were gray with grime or broken out of their frames entirely. The steps had rotted through, and tufts of stubborn weeds sprouted along the foundation. The roof sagged like the back of an old nag. Inez satisfied her curiosity about the building. The door was nailed shut, and the interior was crammed with stacks of wooden crates and broken chairs. Had the baby broker intentionally misled Annah?

Inez sipped from a glass of warm milk and picked up the pen to expand the scene. As the street curved, the perspective of the distance shrunk the details. Behind the building, the road led to a ruddy four-story brick building set back from the street. As the pen scratched the paper, she remembered crossing the tall grasses to the empty lot as a pair of voices drew her attention to the open delivery door. It was the furtive look on the face of one of the men that compelled her to move closer. His dark head darted out the door, looking both directions. She had scooted to the side of the building and stacked crates under the window. She grabbed the drainage pipe and hoisted herself up, pressing herself to the ivy leaves.

One man nestled bottles into rounded containers filled with straw and then loaded them into the wagon. The other man in a gray long coat watched, his hands clasped behind his back. She caught the green glint of the bottles. Absinthe. What the man at the station had called *la fée verte.* This is what David had been chasing. The absinthe must have come here by boat and then was transferred into the containers. In a matter of minutes, they finished the packing, and the cart drove off.

Now, as the gray light seeped into the kitchen, she captured the details of the man in the gray coat. He had a thin, straight nose and a particular wave to his hair. The page rippled with the wet of the ink wash. Her jaw clenched in anger. She was witnessing part of a crime, but she had no means to stop them, neither with threat of authority nor weapon.

Maybe this drawing would help David solve his case.

Chapter 43

"Why on earth would you just take a baby off the street? I thought we agreed I would bring 'em in and send 'em out." Lettie leaned against the post on the back stoop and pressed her palms to her temples.

"The mother, she said she'd put the baby in the river! She had three other little ones, and they all looked hungry." Ella looked at the newborn sleeping in her arms. Somewhere close to the steps, a cricket chirped.

Lettie sneered. She picked up a stick and poked at the dirt near her feet.

"So you'll find a home for this one?" Ella asked. "I don't see what the fuss is about." With one hand, Ella shook open the quilt on the grass. Two squirrels chased around the tree trunk, their nails making a high clattering sound on the rough bark. "Little Blue is gone, and we are on to the next one."

"Did you get a payment?"

A prickly blush skittered up Ella's neck. "Yes," she answered as she squatted on the blanket and positioned the baby on his back.

Lettie stepped off the porch with an exaggerated sigh and stood next to the quilt. "All right, let's have a look." She poked at the blanket with the stick. "Go on. Unwrap him."

"He's not a rasher of bacon."

"Why's he so red and wrinkled? He looks like he's been boiled."

"Babies look like this when they're first born." Ella matched Lettie's sigh. How could she be so ignorant of infants? Ella touched the swatch of sandy hair that curled in a cowlick at his temple. Would his eyes be green like his mother's?

The air was starting to cool in a way that felt delicious on Ella's neck, and the dimming of the day painted long shadows that softened the look of the backyard and made the sparse grass look purple. The laundry hung in regular bright squares on the sagging line. Ella unwrapped the blanket, not because Lettie demanded it, but because it must be time for a diaper change.

Freed from the swaddling, the baby's skinny arms waved, and his tight fists punched the air like a boxer. When Ella pulled the blanket away from the baby's legs, Lettie gasped and pointed.

"Look at his feet! They're broken! That mother did that, I'm wagering."

Lettie was right, they did look broken. Both feet twisted at the ankle, curved so they resembled the letter U. Ella stroked the top of each foot as if the touch could straighten the bowed legs and set the feet to the proper position.

The boy had been born with club feet.

She couldn't meet Lettie's eyes. She remembered a family back in Ireland with a boy that, as he grew, could only stagger on his ankles. He begged by the side of the road. Michael was his name. He would be twenty years old by now.

"Whatever you got paid, it wasn't enough."

Ella's cheeks burned as she quickly pinned the dry diaper in place and wrapped the blanket around those sad legs. When she was done, she fished in the pocket of her apron and pulled out the gold wedding band. "Here." Ella held it out to Lettie. "See what you can get for it. I know you're good at that."

"Well, if you're going to be stuck with him for the next fifty years, you should keep it." Ella heard the thick rage in Lettie's voice, heard the stick striking the steps. Ella flinched with each blow as if Lettie's anger had brought the stick across her back.

"I'll find a home for this one—by myself. I swear. You won't have to lift a finger, Lettie." Lettie stormed into the house. Mosquitos buzzed about her, and when she slapped her wrist a tear-shaped smear of blood appeared. She scooped up the baby and headed into the kitchen.

"Lettie, I'm sorry. I just couldn't let that woman drown him!" The air in the kitchen hung heavy with the pall of vegetable rot.

"Maybe it was a bluff. Ever think of that?" Lettie poured herself a drink. "She knew you wouldn't say no."

"Is your heart like a stone?" She looked down at the baby, who opened his eyes. He pursed his lips. He would be wanting to eat soon.

"Leave my heart out of this! How many times do I have to explain? We are running a business!"

She clenched her teeth, and a muscle flexed across her jaw. "Remember how you cried, 'Oh Lettie, I'm so worried I'll be tossed out on the street.' If you want to take in frog-legged babies, the two of you will be shaking a tin can on the corner!"

Ella cringed to hear Lettie's perfect imitation.

"If that's your choice, Ella, I'm washing my hands of all of ya."

Ella hated her husky words. "Don't leave me. We can be partners."

The baby started to fuss. The quilt was heavy in her arms, and she stood, unable to move.

Lettie cocked her hip. "Fine. Get rid of this one or I will."

The baby moved his head back and forth. Ella swallowed a dry click. "What do you mean? I told you I would find him a home."

"Get rid of him." Lettie refilled her glass, sat on a kitchen chair and propped her feet on the table. Her eyes locked on Ella.

"It may take time…" Ella started, knowing this was the wrong answer.

"Maybe this will make it clear for you. You get rid of this one or I go to the police and show them the grave of your little hatbox baby. They have a big, white policewoman now. I've met her." There was a smirk, the look of a poker player displaying a winning hand.

The edges of Ella's vision grew blurry. The quilt fell in a tangled heap at her feet. Baby Janna. The stolen hatbox outside of Bucket of Blood. It was Lettie all along.

"You stole…" Ella's lips were numb. She remembered her panic after the theft. The blur of faces on the street.

"Your dead baby? I did! Imagine my surprise. At first I thought I was getting myself a fancy hat, and then I realized it weighed too much. I figured you were stealing silver, same as me." Lettie wiggled her feet as if she were doing a jig.

"The police know you as a thief. You said they don't like you."

"And I'll tell 'em you smothered it because you were tired of taking care of a sick baby."

The baby screeched, red-faced and insistent. Lettie stuck her finger in her ears. "So first I hid the box and followed you to see what you were up to. I mean, a baby in a hatbox! You caught my attention."

Ella placed her knuckle in the baby's mouth, and he sucked hard. Her tears splashed on his blotchy cheeks. She kicked at the quilt that tangled around her feet. Oh, dear Lord, Beata and her cards had been right all along. "I thought we were friends!"

Lettie smirked. "Of course you did."

She sipped her whiskey and stroked the medallion at the end of the chain. "So then I buried that dead baby of yours." She rubbed her mouth with the back of her hand. "You know, in case of a rainy day."

Chapter 44

"Laudenbach, you got another one here," Murphy bellowed.

Inez stood, drew a deep breath and watched a woman lumber toward her. A nest of gray hair sprouted from underneath her battered hat, and she huffed with the effort it took to cross the station.

"That man..." she poked her thumb over her shoulder, "...he say to talk to you."

Inez motioned to the bench. "Please, have a seat. I'm Inez Laudenbach. What have you come to report, Missus...?" She turned over a new page. The woman pursed her lips and hummed three short notes.

"I am a police officer, if that is the expression of your concern."

The woman grinned, and the sharp slap of her palms echoed. She nodded her head. "This I like. A woman to stop the robbing and the killing. Good. I am Beata Pavlak."

She dug into a cloth sack and pulled out knitting needles and a shapeless mass of gray stitches. Inez was impressed with how the woman's thick fingers moved nimbly over the points of the needles by feel, not observation.

"OK, what I want to tell you is that I know a bad woman."

"A bad woman," Inez repeated. "What is her crime against you?"

"It is not for me I come here. It is for my neighbor."

Inez tapped her boot heels on the floor. She had learned she must wait out the way people told their stories, how their minds meandered to the important facts, but her impatience always pounded a thick beat in her temples.

"This bad one is Lettie. She stays with my Ella, who is an innocent. She sleeps there, eats her foods, sometimes gets her drunk."

"But what is her crime?"

"I think she steals."

"From you?"

"No."

"From the neighbor, then?"

"This Lettie woman, she has things she can't afford. There is no husband. She does not work—at least not at an honest profession."

"Are you telling me she is a prostitute?"

Beata sniffed and wrinkled her nose as if an odorous prostitute had chosen that moment to strut past the bench. "It would be no surprise to me. Her apple dumpling shop is always open."

"Pardon?"

"Her bosoms." Beata abandoned her needles to thump her large breasts, flattened by age and the cut of her wool vest. "She shows them around."

"Has your neighbor reported anything to you?"

Beata's thick eyebrows cinched as she resumed her furious knitting. "My neighbor, Ella Byrne, she is a living saint. She finds home for unwanted babies." Beata crossed herself. "She is a poor widow, and this Lettie takes advantage of her."

Inez gritted her teeth. "What does Ella say?"

"She says nothing. She never complains, but I see all of it in the cards," she whispered. Beata rummaged in her bag and handed a worn card to Inez depicting a crude drawing of a scowling creature perched on a throne. He had curved horns like a ram and scalloped wings sprouted from his shoulders. A five-sided star was stamped on his forehead.

"Every time I read the cards, I see this. The cards tell me of selfishness, swindles and death."

"You understand, I can't have someone arrested because you think they might commit a crime or because they have bad manners."

"Why not?" Beata snatched the card from Inez's fingers.

Inez leaned in to whisper in Beata's ear. "The other officers, the men, they won't allow it."

"Yeah, the men. Always, they are in the way."

Inez looked up to see David walk in the door dragging a man by his jacket collar. He nodded in her direction and pressed his lips into a tight line. She made a motion to wave but then her hand appeared before her eyes as something large and not at all hand-like, floating in the air like a pale mallet. At the last second, she aborted the wave and instead pushed her glasses up on her nose. The notebook curled in her clenched hand, moist with sweat.

"Whatcha got, Gabes?" Murphy asked.

"Found him at the docks. He had a cartful of absinthe stashed in ladies' hatboxes. Now we know where it's comin' in. I gotta find out who's involved."

"That's the spirit that animated our forefathers." Murphy beamed at David.

David shook the man as if the information was something he could dislodge as easily as loose coins from his pockets.

"I told you I saw the Green Fairy with my own eyes. She was the real thing, not a sprite! She was down at the docks, I tell ya." He squinted at Inez. "Now I sees a white ghost!" He began to sob.

The man was small in stature, slight as a boy. His dark hair thinned back from a widow's peak. His brown shirt was tattered and stained.

"What's wrong with him?" Beata whispered.

"Sounds like he's been imbibing Absinthe. They make it by soaking wormwood leaves in wine. Some say it makes a person go insane or have epileptic fits. Others say it creates a peculiar state of alertness. Absinthe was banned for sale a few years ago."

"He has the same look as my cousin who went crazy with a cleaver," Beata said.

"Ahh, la fée verte has done terrible things to my mind." He held his head between his hands, whimpered and then vomited a watery, green-tinged stream.

Inez stared at her splattered boots. Beata had scooted back on the bench so that her feet were off the ground, exposing swollen ankles. David swore, shook the man, and lifted him so that his bare feet dangled off the ground. He looked over his shoulder at Inez, a brief, stern look. Shame and embarrassment crawled up her neck. Inez watched the muscles flex across David's back as he dragged the bawling suspect away.

"Tell you what..." Inez was breathless. "Why don't you watch this Lettie, and as soon as she commits a crime, you come to me."

Beata pinched her bulbous nose. "And on that day, I will read your cards to see what your future holds."

Chapter 45

Ella sat bare-legged on the edge of her bed. The curve of Connor's bone-handled knife lay smooth in her palm. This brought back a memory of Connor, naked, standing before her last summer as they grew comfortable and bold with each other. In the dusky purple light, his pale skin glowed. She pulled him closer, and when her fingers grazed his belly, following the stripe of downy curls, she thrilled to hear that sound, the raspy hitch of breath, the satin noise he made in the dark when she brushed against him.

Grief crushed her heart. A raw moan escaped her throat. She was alone, cradling his knife. He was gone, and she was alone. Now there was another baby with problems, and Lettie's angry threats hissed in her head.

She scratched the tip of the knife across her inner thigh. Painless. A series of tiny dots of blood welled. She held her breath, pressed harder this time, connecting the red teardrops, seeking that tart sting. Blood flowed down her leg, tiny streams merging into a dark river. The fear that she had gone too deep mingled with the thrill of relief. She pressed a folded linen square to the cut and reveled in the dull throb of pain.

* * *

There was a sharp rap at the door. Ella wiped the knife on the linen and pushed the blade under the mattress. She watched the trail of blood as a mix of thrill and shame cramped her stomach. Three more

190

taps at the door, a pause, two more. She unrolled a length of fabric and wrapped it around her thigh and tied a knot. Her skin puckered around the linen.

"Coming." She checked on the baby sleeping in the crate on the end of the bed.

Ella's mouth was dry, and her head pounded. A shadowy shape loomed on the porch. Moths fluttered against the screen.

A woman stood at the door. Tall, bigger than most men. Broad shouldered.

"Excuse me, I'm looking for Mrs. Ella Byrne. My name is Inez Laudenbach. I'm a police officer." Her tone was firm. In the distance, a dog yipped and howled.

"Yes, I'm Ella." She recalled Lettie's words, *They have a big white policewoman.* Had Lettie already made good on her threat to report baby Janna's death? Something loose lurched in her belly.

"May I come in? I have some questions."

"Questions?"

As the door opened, the springs groaned, and before Ella had a chance to answer, the officer's bulk filled the entryway. She gestured to the chairs in the front room. "May I?"

Connor had fashioned a small table from crates that sat between the two chairs. The neck of one of Lettie's whiskey bottles stuck out from a basket of laundry. The light in the front room held the last yellow glow of the day. Officer Laudenbach perched on the chair, her knees drawn high.

"There has been a complaint issued with our office."

Ella's shirt clung to her lower back. "About me?" The officer's face was pale, sweaty. A web of violet veins at her temples disappeared into the white-blonde hair. Ella's breath sounded too loud. The officer opened a small, leather-bound notebook and pulled a pencil from the depths of the bun at the top of her head. When Ella pressed her legs together, the cut on her thigh pulsed.

"A woman came to the station and reported she had entrusted her infant to a woman. Her husband had been maimed in an accident and could not work. For the benefit of their infant daughter, she thought it would be best to have someone take care of the child until their circumstances improved."

Ella held her breath. This was not about baby Janna.

"So this mother met with a woman who agreed to take care of the baby for a sum of money."

Ella nodded, unable to keep herself from staring at the officer's queer green eyes and white lashes behind her spectacles. Ella recalled a story from her childhood of a woman who had been lost in a sudden snowstorm. After the winds ceased, she was found sitting against a tree, her hands folded in her lap. Her skin was frosted white as if she had somehow swallowed the blizzard. Her hair, brows, and lashes were adorned with crystals that sparkled as the sun rose.

"I hear you're doing 'God's work,'" the officer started.

"Who told you that?"

"Actually, your neighbor, Mrs. Pavlak, came to the station. She said you were finding homes for unwanted babies."

Her thoughts banged around in her head like the moths at the door. Why was Beata talking to the police about the babies? What if the new baby awoke and began to cry? She pressed the cut on her thigh to make it throb. *Concentrate!* Her palms were slick with sweat at the thought of Lettie bursting through the door to announce the location of Janna's body.

"I was a seamstress at Seeger's. A friend there had a baby. It was out-of-wedlock, you see, so she begged me to find him a good home."

"How kind of you. What is the name of this family?" The officer adjusted her spectacles, and Ella saw her nose was blistered.

Ella pursed her lips. "I can't tell. It's a family of wealth. I was sworn to secrecy. The man's wife—well, he didn't want her to know their child died."

"So you were paid for your secrecy." The officer held her gaze, and Ella was unsure how much to say. "Were there other babies?"

"Twins. They were left at me door." She missed the boys fiercely at that moment and felt her body sway as if she were comforting their cries. She also felt a bloom of pride. "They were in poor health, and I nursed them. I was stubborn about keeping them together, and now they're living on a farm in Wisconsin." Ella smiled and lifted her chin.

"No wonder your neighbor proclaims you as a saint! You are like Demeter, the Greek goddess. She is a protective and caring mother."

Demeter? Who was she talking about? "I'm not a saint."

The officer flipped back a few pages and ran a finger over the notations. "Do you know anyone else providing a service like yours? Others that might be doing the Lord's work as well?"

"No, ma'am, I don't."

"You can call me Inez. The woman that made the complaint—she changed her mind about the arrangement, and when she went back to retrieve the baby, the address was false. The baby, it seems, had vanished along with the woman."

Ella nodded in agreement. This visit had nothing to do with Janna's death. This was about another infant, and the officer was just asking questions. She wiped her hands on her skirt, waiting for the cool night air to bring relief. Near the window, a tomcat yowled in a way that made the hair on her neck stand up.

"If I give you a description of the infant, will you watch for her?" Ella nodded.

The officer referred to her notes. "These are the mother's words— 'The infant is seven months of age. She is very fair with blonde curls. She has blue eyes and an agreeable temperament.'"

Suddenly, the officer's face went out of focus. *Little Blue! It had to be the same baby! What did Lettie do?*

"Are you unwell?" Inez's large eyes blinked behind the spectacles.

"I feel for the mother—her loss." She stood and opened another window and peered into the shadows. A dead June bug lay on its back on the sill. Ella's thighs were sticky with blood.

"Can I ask how you manage this by yourself?"

Ella shrugged. "Oh Beata, Mrs. Pavlak, she helped me so many times. She rocked them when they were fussy. She even sewed gowns for the boys and embroidered the hems. I'll show you." Ella knelt and pawed through the clothes, stiff with the day's sun, until she found one of the gowns. She handed it to the officer. "I told her, the babies don't need adornment. Maybe she wished for little girls? I don't know." Ella was breathless. She babbled to avoid talking about Lettie.

One pale eyebrow on the officer's face arched, but her expression remained smooth. Ella had the sense she had said something wrong. Some bit of the telling had landed solid and sharp between them.

"Do you have the address for the family that took the twins? A name?"

Ella looked out the window again. She heard voices down the street raised in an argument. Had Lettie even told her the man's name? She remembered her plan to keep a ledger of all the babies she had placed, the family names and addresses. It was to be part of her history. "There's a telegram. I'll have to look for it." She watched the officer running a finger over Beata's needlework, following the twists of vines and flowers.

"Your neighbor, she came to the station because she was worried someone was taking advantage of you."

"What does that mean?"

"She wasn't very specific, but she was concerned about a woman that stays here with you." The officer spoke in a low voice and didn't blink. Ella felt as if she were being examined without her clothes.

"Oh, Beata worries over nothing. A friend was here for a while, but she's gone now." As she crafted the lie, she detected a whiff of Lettie's musky scent and wondered if she was lurking in the hall, listening to the officer, waiting for her to reveal their secrets.

Ella's heart pounded. This could be the moment, a chance to confide to this woman about Janna's death and Lettie's friendship and rages. Would the officer believe her?

The officer stood suddenly, her chair scraping the floor. She handed the gown back to Ella and closed her book. The pencil disappeared into her bun. Ella was again surprised by the woman's height, confused about her role. She had not witnessed so much as a smile or a nod of understanding.

"I have seen you before, Miss Ella," the officer began. Ella startled, her hands cramped around the gown. "At the Calvary Cemetery."

Ella blinked. Connor's grave. The grave of another man. She hadn't been there for many weeks. Did the Gavin family tend the grave and bring flowers? Again, Ella felt the officer's scalding look. "Me husband died in March. He had an accident at Seeger's." Ella wiped her sudden tears with her palm.

"My condolences. Thank you for speaking with me. Please let me know if you find anyone else caring for a baby that matches the description." The officer pulled open the screen door but paused for a moment, staring at the hooks by the door. Connor's coat hung next to Ella's cape.

"Goodbye, then." The door banged shut, and Ella watched the officer hike up her skirt and perch on the seat of a bicycle. She leaned into the pedals, and after a minute the purple dusk had swallowed her.

Chapter 46

Ella paced as she fed the baby. Not that he needed the jostling movement. He was calm, peeping like a chick when he was hungry.

Officer Laudenbach's quiet questions chased Ella up and down the hall. When she had fixed her magnified eyes on Ella, the scrutiny felt like stones piled on her chest. The baby's limbs grew heavy, and his mouth fell open, so she nestled him in the stroller.

By now she knew most of the places Lettie hid her whiskey, and it didn't take long to find a flask hidden behind the stove. Ella emptied the last dregs into a greasy glass, swallowed, and closed her eyes as the harsh burn swelled low in her stomach. She slumped at the table and pressed her forehead against her arm as hot tears dripped from the bridge of her nose.

Ella yearned for that moment when the whiskey would bloom through her chest and her breathing would ease. She wanted that peace of the perfect moment when everything seemed possible and right. She took another mouthful, worked the bitterness over her tongue, and swallowed again. She chased the hazy memory of the pubs after the shifts at Seeger's when her hands and arms buzzed with fatigue, but there was a sweet, slow warmth from the beer and Connor's smile as his arm draped across her shoulders. Try as she might, she couldn't get back to that feeling again.

Lettie. Something had gone terribly wrong. She was bundled with sly secrets. What had happened to Little Blue? Why had Lettie lied about that?

Of course, the answer was plain. Money. Time. Lettie would never agree to take care of a baby for months and months, only to hand her back. There was no profit in that. She could get money up front from the mother, place the baby for another fee, and then go on to the next infant. No guilt over the mother who would ache and cry for her child. A fly skittered up the side of the bottle and perched on the rim as it twitched and rubbed its legs.

And why did the policewoman have questions about the boys? What did they have to do with Little Blue? Ella sensed the woman had a head full of questions hidden behind that broad, quiet face. She wiped her mouth on the back of her hand and tasted salt. Tears blurred her vision. Trouble was a creature crouched behind her chair, threatening to grab her by the throat. Once the first sob escaped, a storm burst from her chest. Ella glanced at the baby. His arms were thrown over his head, and he slept. He was probably used to the sounds of his mother's cries.

The screen door slapped in the frame. Each hitch of breath felt like a dull saw blade cutting through her chest. She wanted to confront Lettie and shake her by the shoulders. She feared this moment too. She could not hold her own when she was weeping and sad. Lettie would laugh and push her aside.

To her great relief, it was Beata running into the kitchen, her heavy hips swaying and her arms spread wide for balance. When she embraced Ella, she knocked over a chair.

"What's the trouble? Did that witch hurt you?" Beata's plump hands squeezed Ella's shoulders and hands, checking for injury as if she were a lump of dough.

Ella slumped into Beata's embrace, heavy-limbed like a baby.

"I can hear your wailing all the way to my house."

"I'm sorry. Please don't be upset with me."

"Upset? No. Maybe my heart is heavy. That one, ack ya, the one with the devil under her skin, she makes me mad."

The baby bleated. The tumult finally sliced through his slumber.

"Who is this baby?" Beata released Ella and crouched over the buggy.

"A mother…" Ella hiccupped. "…I met at the river. She gave him to me."

"He's a handsome one."

"Lettie is furious! His legs, his feet, there's something wrong with them."

Beata peeled back the blanket, her tongue clicking as the baby's crooked legs waved in the air. She crossed herself, murmuring, "*Deformacha stopy*. Poor baby."

"His mother was going to drown him!" Ella shivered, thinking of the mother's dead eyes.

Beata gathered him to her chest and covered his face with kisses. "I can bind his legs. I can fix them. I'm sure of it." Beata's cheeks looked like cooked beets.

"Beata, can you take him to your house?"

"*Kotku*—what's wrong? You have a look like there is a knife in your belly."

"I need to find Lettie. I have to ask her some things about all the babies. The boys, Little Blue. A woman was here from the police."

"The big one? Like a white archangel? I talked to her, *kotku*. I was worried about you—I told her about that no-good snake."

Ella nodded. "She was here. Tonight. She asked all kinds of questions." Tears stung her face. "I was so afraid Lettie had told her about Janna."

"What does that devil know about our dearly departed baby?" Beata draped the baby over her shoulder and thumped him soundly on the back.

"Remember when someone stole the hatbox with her body?" Ella whispered.

Beata crossed herself, including the baby's back in her motions.

"It was Lettie. She buried Janna somewhere. She said she would tell the police that I smothered her."

The knuckles on Beata's clenched fists were shiny white knobs. "You would never hurt one of the babies! You love them!"

"She said she would tell them I killed Janna because she was sickly."

Beata set her jaw. "The cards, they told me this story."

Ella recalled Lettie's threat—Get rid of that baby, or I will. "I need to find out where the boys are—if they're safe."

"Gerick and Lujan? What is the worry?"

"The officer, she asked me where they were. She had questions about the Wisconsin family. She knew something. I could feel it. She wouldn't tell me. That's why I have to find Lettie."

"Tonight? Don't go. I smell rain. Besides, the boys are fine. If something was wrong, I would have seen it in the cards. I think the whiskey is making your tongue brave."

Ella grabbed Beata's hands and squeezed. "Please take him home. I don't want to think of what will happen if Lettie comes home and finds you and the baby here."

Beata snorted. "You know what I do to snakes?" She righted the chair, sat down, and hiked up her skirt. Her thick calves were covered with dark hair. A bone-handled knife sprouted from the top of her tight boot. "I cut their heads off. See, no worries about me."

Ella's tears flowed again. She pictured Lettie knocking Beata from her chair and wrestling the knife from her hands as the pitch of the baby's cries grew louder. "Please, no. Take him somewhere safe." Ella's hands shook as she folded them in prayer.

"So how do we settle this? I say, don't put your hand in the hornet's nest!"

"I can't sit here every day waiting for Lettie to come back. What will she do next? I was stupid to think she wanted to run a business with me. She's a thief. I invited a thief or maybe worse into me home. It's me own fault. I have to settle things with her."

"Maybe you, stubborn one, should take my knife, then?" Beata leaned down to pull out the knife.

"No, keep it. I have Connor's knives." As she said that, the cut on her thigh throbbed in agreement, calling to her.

"Fine. You will win. As soon as this little one wakes, I'll take him home."

Chapter 47

David's desk was bare, save for a wooden box containing two pencils, the graphite worn to shiny blunt nubs. Inez sat in the chair positioned next to the desk, her scapulae pressed hard against the curve of wood. She crossed her arms over her illustration book, positioning it like an armored chest plate. As the men filed past her, she lifted her chin and bit down on her tongue hard enough to draw the salty tang of blood. It was folly, she realized, to work so hard to compose a neutral expression, because no one paid her the slightest attention. Every once in a while, she cast a glance at the contents of a partially opened drawer and at the crumpled paper in the wastebasket. David's penmanship demonstrated as thick, precise slanted strokes.

The sun found the top of the desk, warming the history of scars, insults, and a light coating of dust. He didn't spend much time here at the station or at his desk. He preferred to walk the beat, talk to people and observe. Inez moved her thumb over a gash that resembled an eyebrow.

"Inez." David's voice boomed from behind. She had been watching the door for him and practicing her discourse. *I discovered some evidence that I believe is related to your Absinthe case. I have identified a suspect in your absinthe case.* She wondered if she should speak of their encounter on the porch to clear the air as if it were of no importance. Her thoughts slipped around in the coppery taste in her mouth.

"Is something wrong?" He came around the side of the desk, and Inez yanked her hand away as if she had been caught stealing. She burped bitter coffee as his face moved in close enough for her to see one curved eyelash balancing on the swell of his cheek. He smelled of sun and tobacco.

"David," her voice cracked, and she coughed to clear her throat. "Are you ill?"

"No, I… your case. I've seen something…" Of course, at his inquiry, she did feel immediately ill. A sour stomach and a flush of prickly heat swarmed across her chest. She hated the corporal betrayal. She had not been this close to him since the morning on the porch.

"Yes?" David looked ill as well. Sweat formed along his temples like so many glistening blisters, his face drained of its usual olive glow. He must be disgusted to see her. Repulsed. She looked at her hands, like big ghostly doves in her lap. There was an intersection of purple veins at her wrist that resembled the letter "H."

"I should tell you…" she began and faltered. Where to start? It was a mistake to talk to him. She hoped Murphy would call him away.

"What's this?" He motioned to the book. His fingers were blunt and strong. She flashed to the feeling of those fingers at her lower back. Her throat constricted.

"A Book of Crime," she whispered, her words and voice stolen. She could not meet his eyes.

"Zats so? Can I have a look?"

Inez set the book on the desk. She had marked the pages with a bookmark. The illustrations of the buildings at the dock, the profile of the man in the gray coat—all these images burst from the pages.

He gave a low whistle. "Inez, did you draw these?" His hand hovered over the drawing, and she stared. He turned the pages and revealed the swirling river, the clouds that curled to resemble a scalloped saw blade. Inez closed her eyes and let her mind go back to the riverbanks, the lapping waves, the birds, and the rustle of leaves.

"They're so real!"

Inez reveled in the sensations of the river. The noise of the men and the smell of cooked cabbage disappeared. A river breeze cooled her skin, and she began to tell David about Annah and her missing baby and why she was at the abandoned storefront. She described the warehouse, the two men, and the wagon loaded with absinthe bottles. She became stronger in the telling, behaving more like herself.

"When was this?" He turned the page to the illustration of the buildings.

"Yesterday morning, just as the sun rose." She could hear the excitement in his voice. She pointed to the building in the background and the window of her vantage point. "The man in the gray coat, when he left this warehouse he headed south."

"I know this place. I thought the absinthe was coming in at the docks. Shipped from New Orleans, I've been told. I snooped around cargo shipments and as many storage sheds as I could find—but nothing. Believe me, nobody down there is doing any talkin'."

She looked at him and a small thrill flickered. He was sharing his case, his ideas with her. If he wanted to ignore her or escape this encounter, he could have done so at any moment. He *wanted* to talk to her.

"This man here," she pointed to the portrait. "I think he's in charge. He carried a gun."

"Tell me about the containers—the ones they hid the bottles in."

Inez tried to recall the look and size of them. "Round? They had some kind of script on the lids."

"Like a lady's hatbox?" He leaned on the edge of the desk and picked up the book. One leg rested on the exact place where Inez had placed her hand minutes ago. This made her heart pound. Of course, the round containers must be hatboxes! Why didn't she think of that? Inez owned only one hat. It perched on her head at an odd angle like a tiny bowl, and the black color was a harsh contrast to her white hair. Louise had purchased it for Inez to wear to her father's funeral, and after the services she returned the hat-coffin to the back shelf of her closet. She remembered the box was adorned with the letter "M" scripted in gold.

"Yes, a hatbox," she answered. "I believe the purveyor has a shop downtown." Her linen blouse stuck to her back, and she had the urge to peel the limp material from her skin.

"Why do you do this? These drawings?" The suddenness of the question surprised her. They were talking about the facts in the cases, and this question seemed to be about something else entirely. His voice was low, thoughtful, and his eyebrows knitted in his familiar way. He was looking at the page that depicted the body of the baby, the wet gown clinging to his leg.

"It helps me to think about things, maybe to recall an important detail. My father, he recorded the cases he worked through illustrations and notes." The moment was a mixture of pride and embarrassment.

He wiped his forehead with his sleeve. "I had something I wanted to tell you, as well."

Don't talk about the kiss on the porch, she pleaded silently. It was best forgotten, but yet, in thinking about it, she flushed remembering the feel of his lips, the scratch of his beard on her sunburned skin. Her vision blurred at the edges.

"The other night... I hafta say something. I was a drunk ass. I remember yelling outside your house. I hope I didn't wake the neighborhood."

Inez nodded as if she understood. Yelling? What was he recalling?

"This Absinthe case, I don't know how I ended up in front of your house. Can't remember how I got home. It's all part of fat headache now." He slapped the side of his head.

Was he telling the truth? Inez's intuition faltered.

"Am I forgiven?"

He didn't remember anything about the porch or the kiss? Inez was surprised to be a bit disappointed. Maybe it wasn't real after all.

Chapter 48

Ella pulled the hood of her cape back from her hair as she entered Bucket of Blood. Rain drops, big as coins, stained the front of the cape. This was the only place she could think of to find Lettie. Lettie never mentioned friends by name, and Ella had no idea where she stayed when she wasn't nested in her stolen chair.

The bar crowd jostled her into the mix of bodies, and the dank air smelled of spilled lager, dirty clothes, and piss. A short man with a wiry white beard perched on an upended crate. He played a low, sad melody on his squeeze-box that led the other patrons to loll their heads back and forth to the despondent beat. Another man held a glass of stout to the musician's lips. He drank greedily, fingering the keys and buttons without pause. He wiped his chin on his shoulder and sang:

"Oh, the rain, it rains all day long, Bold Riley-o,
Bold Riley.

And the northern wind, it blows so strong. Bold
Riley-o, has gone away.

Goodbye my sweetheart, goodbye my dear-o,
Bold Riley-o, Bold Riley-o.

Goodbye my darlin', goodbye my dear-o. Bold
Riley has gone away."

Ella pushed up on her toes to better scan the crowd. In a dark corner, a man pressed against a woman, his hands woven through her dark hair. His body hunched over her like he was poised to devour her. Ella's heart ticked faster as she recalled Aldo's advances. Was it Lettie? Then Ella saw the curve of the woman's mouth, the heavy eyelids, and the way she laced her fingers across the man's neck to pull his face to the bare curve of her breasts. Ella blushed and turned her head away although her mouth parted to remember the taste of desire, loose and warm. It wasn't Lettie, and this was not a girl in any trouble she didn't invite.

The crowd sang and swayed with the squeeze-box player. A man with a long beard pushed a wet mug of beer into her hand as he snaked an arm around her waist. When Ella turned to protest, he produced a gap-toothed grin that was all sweetness and charm. Ella smiled back and took a sip, warm and sour on her tongue.

"I remember you, Reddy-girl. You were here before. I couldn't forget your angel-face!" His forehead was slick with sweat.

"Do you know Lettie?" she yelled. He cupped his ear toward her. "I'm looking for a woman—she has dark hair and is about this tall…" Ella indicated Lettie's height with her hand. "I was with her the night you saw me. She sang a tune." He shrugged and pointed to the man serving beer.

Ella held up her mug in thanks and pushed her way to the bar. A man raised a mallet to punch a spigot into a wooden barrel. His arms were thick and muscled and bore a long, curved scar from the wrist to the elbow. The wall behind him was covered with yellowed IOU notes and wanted posters, most of which bore splatters of dried blood. In the middle of the papers, affixed to the wall with a ferrier nail, was something that resembled a bit of cured bacon, rounded and curled at the edges. Ella leaned on the wooden plank of the bar and stared at the contents of a jar filled with murky liquid. She squinted in the yellow glow to see that the jar held dozens and dozens of teeth—of all sizes and colors.

"I'm Milo. What's your pleasure?"

"What's this?" Ella pointed to the jar.

"Teeth from all the fights—we decided to save 'em." The bartender tapped the lid of the jar with the mallet.

Ella pointed to the wall. "And that?"

"That's Baldy-Bill's ear. It got bit clean off one night when he was in a brawlin' mood, and we thought we should save it in case he wanted it back."

Ella reached for her ear and pulled on the lobe. "I'm looking for Lettie. She's here lots of times. She told me she writes letters for some of the fellas."

Milo used a grimy rag to mop his face and squinted at the crowd. "I know Lettie, darlin'. I don't think I've seen her tonight."

It was foolish to think she could track Lettie down. And what if she did manage to find her? Lettie, here in the company of fellow thieves and brawlers, would laugh at her. Her arms and legs were heavy, and the sounds of the bar pounded in her temples.

Suddenly, a table upended. Glasses shattered, playing cards flew in the air and the music stopped. The first punch connected with a man's face. His head bobbed, and then he wiped a bloody mustache. Next, the attacker rushed in and pressed a pistol to his throat. After he growled a string of insults, the man spit in his face, and they tumbled to the floor, all arms and flailing legs, groans and grunts. The crowd cheered.

A policeman appeared and knocked the pistol out of the man's hand, then grabbed the man by the back of his collar and yanked him clear of the tangle. As he did this, the pistol got kicked, glanced off the leg of a stool, and came to rest at Ella's feet.

"Go to Minneapolis if ya want to kill each other. Not in my town," the squat policeman proclaimed to the room. The man with the broken nose scooted backward on his elbows until he reached the back door.

The other man dangled in the grasp of the policeman. He squirmed and weakly kicked his feet. The policeman looked down and raised his dark eyebrows in surprise as if he had forgotten what he held in his hand.

"Get on yer prayer bones," the policeman barked, and dropped the man to his knees. When his head sagged, the policeman holstered his gun, took the man by the hair and stroked the muzzle of the gun under the man's chin. Ella watched the man's eyes dart back and forth like a frightened horse.

"I'm not gonna waste a bullet on ya." He released his grip, and the man slumped over as if all his bones had been removed. "Now go back to your whorin' and gamblin'!" The policeman slipped his gun back into his holster.

The woman from the back of the bar wove herself into the circle of onlookers. "Why don't you leave 'em alone. They can work out their beefs without the likes of you." She stood before the policeman, hands on her hips, her bottom lip quivering.

"Maybe I should cast you out into the storm with the other vermin?" the policeman asked, laughing, and placed his palm against her forehead when she swung her fist in a wide arc without connection.

"Why don't you find out who is drowning babies in the river? That's the real crime if you ask me. Not a bar fight!"

"Milo, what's she talking about?"

Ella blinked, her heart flapping against her ribs. "Babies in the river?"

"A bit of time ago, they found a youngin' a floatin'. Didn't ya hear?"

Ella shook her head.

"I heard accounts that the police lady found him." Milo threw the rag over his shoulder and squinted at Ella. "Ya all right there, darlin'?"

"Officer Inez found a baby?"

"Don't know the name. Just heard talk of the big police girl around town."

"What else do you know?" The sour taste of panic and ale mixed in Ella's mouth. Her stomach ached as if she had been punched. The front door slammed behind the officer. "Good riddance," someone yelled, as the first few notes of the accordion introduced a new ballad. Sounds of laughter burst from the group, and the two men righted the table and collected the wet cards from the floor. Milo opened the spigot and filled more glasses.

"I've heard stories about someone seein' a hooded form, like death, you would imagine, on the bridge throwing a bundle over, like so." Milo balled up the rag and launched it over the bar where it landed in a heap. "'Course, people throw things they don't want in the river all the time."

She touched the hood of the cape as tears blurred her vision. Her toe clipped the gun, and, not quite knowing why, she bent to pick it up and hid it under her arm.

Milo held up the tooth jar. "Free drink to anyone who finds a tooth!"

Chapter 49

As Inez worked at the desk in the library, she heard the sturdy clip of Louise's shoes advancing down the hall. The sound was instantly muffled by the thick rug in the study. Louise set a glass of tea next to Inez's Book of Crime and placed her palm, cool from the glass, on the back of Inez's neck. She smelled of lemons.

"What a lovely girl! She looks troubled though."

"I talked to her tonight. I think she's involved with the baby's death."

"Involved? How?" Louise clasped both hands over her bony chest.

"She admitted to having twins in her care for a period of time. She possessed a gown that matched the one the infant was found wearing." Inez paged back to the drawing of the river and the gown and pointed to the depiction of the needlework. "It looked exactly like this."

"She doesn't look as if she would harbor such a cold heart to murder a baby. However, your father always told me that everyone has secrets. What did she say when you asked her about the murdered baby?"

"I didn't ask directly. She told me she found the babies a home. When I inquired about the family, she seemed startled. Confused." Inez stared at the portrait of Ella; the crimp of a worried brow and the shadows under her eyes. She swept the brush, heavy with ink wash to render the curls that sprang loose from their pins.

"Perplexing, certainly." Louise pulled a chair to sit next to Inez. "Mind if I watch you work? It does so remind me of your father sitting at this very desk."

"Sit. I like the company. I've been alone with my thoughts too long." Inez held the brush aloft as if it were a cigar and gulped the crisp tea. "I wonder if he minds me sitting here, attempting to carry on his work."

Louise snorted. "It's your study now. What's gotten into you? It's not like you to be maudlin or impractical. Besides, you have more artistic talents than your father. You evoke more details and feelings. These portraits speak to the state of your suspects."

"I'm not sure she is a suspect or not, but I do wonder about the soundness of her mind. Her neighbor told me her husband died a few months ago. Would that loss cause her to—?"

"Murder an infant? You make her sound like she should be in a mad house! Did she seem that bad off to you?"

Inez sighed. "In some parts of the interview, she seemed perfectly earnest. Even proud of her work. And then she appeared lost and sad. It was like she wasn't listening to me."

"Have you been reading from the Freud person again? All that talk about people's urges and dreams—if so, don't let the others at the station know about that." Louise pulled a rag from her apron and began to dust the wide expanse of the desk.

Her own dreams might be the subject of one of Freud's studies. Dreams that left her drenched in sweat and longing. Kissing David, crouching over him as he lay in the sand. When she lays the full length of him—they fit together. At that thought, her throat ached, and she closed her eyes and brushed her bottom lip, but she couldn't match the feeling of the dream-kiss.

"Did you hear me?" Louise tapped a finger on the desk. "Do you think she's the sort that could put on an act?"

"Lying? Perhaps, I'm not sure." Inez was tired of the brushwork. The Book of Crime felt heavy tonight. She rinsed the brush in the clean water and then pulled the tip through a rag. She stared at the portrait as the colors lightened and the page rippled.

"Your father told me of things to watch for if a person was a liar. Tics and such."

"Do you remember the details?"

"Of course I do! There were lots of things that common liars did. He said it would start with their mouths—sometimes they would cover them like this…" Louise curled her fingers around her mouth and hung her head low. "Or their mouths would go dry, and they would complain of thirst or lick their lips too much. He always said that at the precise moment of the lie a person's eyes would dart away. And then there were some that would begin to fidget the way a young child might. You know, crossing their legs, folding their arms or working over an object, like a button or a coin."

Inez's heart suddenly ached with missing her father! What kind of advice would he offer? Maybe he would hop up and drag out one of his volumes of his past work and find the precise case to quote. "I wish I could ask him these things."

Louise snapped her fingers. "Here's an idea. Why don't you show this young girl that drawing? Ask her about the infant you found. Arrest her if you believe she put that poor baby in the water."

Inez shrugged. "You forget I can't arrest anyone. I've as much clout as a clergyman. No wait, I can't even send a guilty person to hell!"

"The girl doesn't know your restrictions. Why don't you scare her a bit?"

"How?"

Louise set the rag on the desk and walked over to the wall of books. She paused, looked up, and moved the sliding ladder to the far side near the window. She gathered her skirt in one hand and scampered up the ladder with the grace and speed of a much younger person. Inez laughed. She watched Louise rearrange a few volumes of books and then pull out a metal box. Inez rushed over to the base of the ladder and reached to take it from her hands. The contents shifted with a dull clank.

"What's this? Who put it there?"

Louise stepped down and brushed the top with her rag as if cleaning it were part of her daily chores. "I hid it there after he died."

Louise flipped the hasp and opened the lid to reveal a pair of handcuffs nestled next to a wrapped bundle. Louise unfurled the cloth and handed Inez her father's pistol.

The oily sheen glinted, and the weight of the wooden grip, its girth, fit neatly in her palm.

Louise smiled broadly, a rarity as she usually pursed her lips over her crowded teeth. "Don't worry. It's in good working order. I clean and oil it every month."

Chapter 50

Sheets of rain careened from the awning of Bucket of Blood to the slick deck of the boardwalk. Steam billowed from the gas lamps. Ella watched the currents of water rush over the streets seeking the river. Everything led to the river. She yanked the hood over her hair. Tears and rain mingled as the humid air filled her chest. Her fingers grazed the rough contours of stone along the side of the bar.

Body of Baby Found in the Mississippi River

Ella sees Milo's news as a headline printed in the *Saint Paul Pioneer Press*. In her mind's eye, she is a witness to a person tossing a bundle from the bridge into the churning waters. Lettie. It all flowed back to Lettie. The truth was revealed like Beata's tarot cards. Lettie had murdered one of the boys. Probably poor Gerick whom she always described as ugly and deformed. Or maybe she got rid of both of them. There was no family farm in Wisconsin. No warm woolen blankets or cups of rich milk. No loving arms to hold them. The boys were too much trouble. Something to be thrown away.

Thunder ripped through her chest, rupturing a membrane of pain. Oh, she had been such a fool to believe one word that came out of Lettie's mouth. *You become who you befriend*, Beata had warned. Ella had known Lettie was a thief who would do anything to save her own hide, and yet she had welcomed her help. How she must have laughed at her idiot partner! Guilt pressed like someone kneeling on her chest.

Ella's heel skidded, and she pitched forward, the toe of her boot tangled in the hem of her skirt. She tumbled, hitting her head. A sharp pain throbbed at her temple. Her palms stung with splinters and grit.

An arm wrapped around her shoulders and strong hands pulled her up. She pressed her face against the smooth cotton shirt and the warmth of Richard Gale's chest. His voice, his warm utterances, filled her ear. She couldn't make sense of what he was saying. Her mind diced the sounds, rearranged the words, but she recognized his cadence and tone. She felt as if her bones had softened as she melded to him. Richard's tonic smelled of oranges. He drew his cape around her shoulders and urged her to walk. Ella didn't ask where they were headed.

They wove through the streets and alleys as the thunder rumbled. Ella felt like they were following a labyrinth of rabbit furrows in the soft rain. They didn't speak. Ella's head throbbed, and her wet skirt clung to her legs.

Richard turned abruptly and guided her up a set of stone steps that led to a house with a broad porch and stained-glass windows that glowed greens and purple. The turret made Ella think of a castle in Ireland.

"This is your home?"

"I rent a room there." He pointed to the tower. "From Mrs. Murray and her son William."

Something like a bright flame of fear or excitement flared deep in her belly.

They entered through a small door on the side of the house. The hinge of the screen door screeched. They stood on the narrow landing that led to a set of winding stairs. When Richard pushed the button, an electric bulb cast an amber haze over his shoulders. Parted from his warmth, Ella shivered.

"Follow me."

Ella paused, hand on the railing, and watched the shadows swallow him. Four stairs, landing, turn, four stairs. She watched the hem of Richard's cape as each step creaked.

He turned the key and pushed open the door that led to a compact room. Rain dampened the stacks of books that sat near the open windows. She pictured Richard reading poetry. There was a small table and one chair next to a shelf that held dishes and glasses. In the corner, a bureau was partially hidden by a dressing screen. Ella flushed when she gazed at the bed, neatly made with a white blanket. She stood like a rain-soaked tree. Richard untied her cape and slipped it from her shoulders. When his hands ran over her arms and down the length of her waist, Ella trembled.

"You're damp and chilled to the bone. Wait." He slipped behind the screen and returned with one of his shirts. "Put this on." He smiled. Kindness crimped the corners of his eyes.

Ella unlaced her shoes and pulled them off. She walked behind the screen and worked the buttons of her cuffs and shirt front. The top of the bureau held a tray with a comb and brush set and a bottle of hair tonic. The chilled air seeded gooseflesh across her arms and nipples as she slipped out of her shirt. She hesitated and then unbuttoned the waistband of her skirt. When it collapsed in a damp pile, the gun in her pocket hit with a dull thud, making her jump. As she peeled off her stockings, Richard's footsteps thumped about the room. The kerosene lamp glowed, and she heard the clink of glasses and silverware. She slid her arms into the softest shirt she had ever touched, and this made her throat ache. When she came out from behind the screen, Richard was waiting to drape a blanket across her shoulders.

"Come, have a drink. Something to warm you." He gestured to the table and held out the chair. Ella clutched the blanket at her throat and sat down. In the middle of the table there was a bottle of green liquid, a glass next to a slotted spoon, a bowl of sugar cubes, and a pitcher. Ella stared at the bottle with the curled script letters that looked like ivy. She recalled Martine's favored brand.

Richard gathered her clothes and draped them over the screen. He said, "Big gun for a small girl."

"Just a little protection. Does it bother you?"

He laughed and came back to the table, poured water from the pitcher into the glass, and balanced the spoon across the mouth. He lincd up two sugar cubes on the face of the spoon.

"Now the Green Fairy arrives. This is absinthe, my dear."

Richard's fingers were lean, and each nail was buffed and rounded. These were hands that should wield paint brushes to depict flowers or beautiful women. She knew his touch would be different, smooth and soft on her skin.

"I've drank this once." Her words sounded like they had been dragged over gravel. The afternoon she had celebrated her new employment with Martine seemed so long ago. A dull pulse throbbed where her head had hit the ground, and her fingers probed the tender swelling.

Richard slowly poured a measure of the green liquid over the sugar cubes. Each droplet broke the surface with a series of delicate plinks. The liquid in the glass glowed like the milky green of the sky before the storm. Ella shifted in her chair.

"Why is it green?"

"The grande wormwood is an herb. A plant."

"But there's light! It glows!"

"*La fée verte* will free you. You desire escape, yes?" Richard dangled the bottle by its delicate neck. The sugar cubes lost their hard edges and slumped tiredly against one another. Drip, drip, drip. Oh, the ache of waiting filled her bones.

Finally, he removed the spoon, took one of the cubes, and placed it on his tongue. He plucked the next one and held it out to her. Ella opened her mouth, and Richard carefully slotted the sugar cube between her lips. An unholy Communion. Sweet, cool licorice. She shivered with the sweetness.

"Now for the Green Fairy." He held the glass out to her.

Noticing her ragged nails and the scabs across her knuckles, Ella flinched as she reached for the glass. She snatched her hand back and balled both hands into fists, but Richard stilled her movement. He gently took her hand and cupped it between both his, as if it were a tiny bird. When he pressed his lips to her fingertips, nuzzling open her clenched palm, Ella shivered again and stood up. Richard slipped behind her and sat in the chair. His hands found her waist, and he pulled her into his lap.

She picked up the glass, sipped twice, remembering how the sugary sweet mixed with the edge of bitterness. Pleasant. She passed the glass to Richard. Her empty stomach cramped, and she heard him lick his lips and swallow. A groan, a note of pleasure, escaped his throat. He draped his right arm over hers, his thumb stroking her fingers. They sat in silence. He didn't ask why she was crying outside of Bucket of Blood. Even if he asked, she couldn't bring herself to admit her part in the baby's death. That part of her had splintered and sat in sharp pieces in her chest. When his chin rested on her shoulder, she leaned into his chest. They were melting into each other like the sugar cubes. With each swallow, the warmth swelled and filled her.

"First you will see things as they are," he murmured in her ear. "Then you will see things that aren't."

His chest was warm against her back, and there was a tingling sensation in her shoulder blades. Was she growing fairy wings, light and green, that would lift her from the chair and out the window over the rustling wet trees? A giggle escaped her throat at the silliness of wings and flying, but the want of flying pinched her chest.

"Since the first time I saw you, it was this hair that captivated my thoughts." His fingers released the pins, and her damp hair fell over her shoulders and grazed the table. She watched as he coiled a strand around his finger.

"In front of Bucket of Blood?" The day Janna's body was stolen. The memory bloomed hot panic through her chest.

"No. I watched you many days walking to work. Across the bridge." He sighed. "I know of your hardships. Your husband's death. Your babies." His words were warm against her neck. Richard poured more water into the empty glass and repositioned the spoon and fresh sugar cubes.

"How do you know these things?"

"People tell me what I need to know."

He splashed more absinthe over the cubes. Ella closed her eyes. Her arms and legs vibrated like they were filled with bees. Her thoughts became thick and drowsy. The gossamer wings of the Green Fairy fluttered against her cheek.

"She's here," Ella giggled, "your fairy."

She stood and took Richard's hand. He turned down the lamp, and they walked over to the bed. The back of her legs brushed the cool sheet. The bedsprings gasped under her weight. When her heavy head tilted back, his mouth found hers. His fingers stroked her eyebrows, forehead and cheeks. Fairy wings. Her body plummeted backward, falling, falling, and she waited for the splash into the river. His arms enfolded her just in time to save her from the churning waters. His kisses rushed along her temples and neck.

She kissed the side of his mouth, tugged his lower lip with her teeth. Richard's palm brushed her nipples through the shirt.

Ella could see Connor through the wrong end of a spyglass, his movements small as he walked toward the horizon. She felt the release of each button, and then he eased the shirt from her shoulders. The bed creaked again when he knelt over her. The swollen moonlight rippled across the bed, and Richard's face became shadows and planes of glowing skin. She wrapped her arms around his bare shoulders, fingered the rounded bones, like robin's eggs, down the length of his back. Could he feel the buzzing in her arms? The fairy had warmed her, turned her blood green and roiling. The night breeze brushed her hot skin.

He untied the linen strips around her leg and then traced the cuts on her thighs with his finger, then bent to tongue her green blood. The cuts tingled as if she had just dragged the knife, sharp and sure over her skin, and that made her groan. Richard's knee parted her legs as his fingers tangled in her hair. And then he was inside her, and the Green Fairy gasped. She dug her nails into his thighs to pull him deeper, away from the grief, away from the loneliness. The slow rocking movement was the familiar current. She rode the waves and swells with him. The Green Fairy whispered in her ear, "Enjoy. You crave this, so let go." Ella obeyed and was amazed how easily the feelings wound to the pulsing release. She cried out when her body betrayed her loyalty to her only love. Like a thief, she stole this perfect moment thing of theirs for her own pleasure.

She became the fairy, leaving Richard to soar above trees to the black sky of winking stars. She lingered, wondering if this was the path

Connor traveled when he left the earth. Quiet. There was no trace of him here in the darkness. The heavy loneliness tugged her downward, rushing her back to earth, and Richard's room. She hovered over the bed, and the sound of her whispered beating wings filled her ears. Ella watched the ropey muscles of Richard's back and the way his shoulder blades pinched the curve of his spine. She saw a girl under Richard, her hair spread across the pillow and her scarred hands that held his hips. She watched tears slip over the girl's temples.

There was a sudden stab of green pain as Richard's collar-bone bumped against the tender bruised egg on her temple. Her wings collapsed, and then she was pinned under him. His breath hitched, and he gasped when his muscles seized taut. Then his hands fell away from her shoulders, and the slick weight of him crushed the hollowed bones of her wings.

Her tears were the watery melancholy of being left alone on earth.

Chapter 51

The tall grasses wet the bottom of Inez's shift as she followed the path to the river's edge. Bottles clinked against one another in the rough crate. She breathed the sweet morning air and surveyed the small cove. Wisps of smoke curled from an abandoned fire, and she thought the charred curve of driftwood resembled an animal's spine.

Inez perched the crate in the wet sand and balanced four empty bottles across the end. The sun winked off the blue glass as she walked backward, counting off ten paces. She unwrapped the Smith and Wesson from the square of flannel and loaded each of the five chambers with bullets. A robin landed on a low branch of the pine tree. Inez squinted into the eastern sun as her thumb rubbed the knurled grip.

Inez had never fired a pistol.

Her father had always encouraged learning. When she watched him clean the gun, she inquired as to the names of the various parts, the extractor rod, the safety, the hammer, cylinder, barrel, and the front sight. While he understood her need to learn the language of how things worked, he had never taught her to shoot.

She held her breath and raised her right arm, pointing the muzzle at the line of bottles. Her thumb pulled back the hammer. The gun felt heavy and bobbed in her outstretched hands. When she squeezed the trigger, the explosion kicked the gun with enough force to bounce her hand upward in the air. She stumbled. A robin burst from a branch in flight. Pain flared through Inez's wrist.

The bottles remained undisturbed.

This time she cupped the grip with both hands, stood with her legs slightly apart and bent her elbows. She aimed and fired. The muzzle jumped up again, but with more control. Hitting the target was much harder than she had expected! Inez pictured Artemis, dressed in her knee-length tunic and sandals, a quiver full of arrows strapped across her shoulders, her bow in hand.

Inez gritted her teeth hard enough to make her jaw ache and continued to fire until the gun made a clicking sound. She felt for the handful of bullets in her skirt pocket as she emptied the cylinder of spent shells into the sand. Then she tilted the pistol so that each bullet slid into place.

Now the sun moved higher in the sky, blazing through the smudges of orange and pink. Inez fired again and again until her hands cramped and the pad on her finger was tender and pink. The secret to accuracy was steadiness, but the sound and the kick of the pistol caused her to flinch.

Suddenly, she pictured David walking up behind her. He would put his arms around her to brace her shoulders. She would smell tobacco and sweet sweat. His fingertips would prop the underside of each arm. *Exhale as you pull the trigger*, he might whisper, his bottom lip brushing against the curve of her earlobe. *Control the breath. That controls the shot.* She shrugged her shoulders as if to push him from her thoughts, as if any of this was real. Did it help or hurt her concentration to have him slide into her mind?

Be Artemis, she commanded. Aim careful and sure. Inez crinkled her nose to adjust her glasses and swelled her lungs with a big breath until her chest ached. Slowly, she forced the air over her pursed lips as she squeezed the trigger. The blue bottle on the right side exploded. She repeated the process, missed her next shot, but hit the crate, causing it to tip over in the sand. She wiped her forehead.

Progress.

Chapter 52

"Girl," Murphy barked. "You, girl—where the Sam Hill have you been?"

Inez raised her head from her notebook. She had the urge to shove her hands into her pockets as if he could tell she had been firing a gun. The thrill and forbidden nature of the gun practice made her feel guilty and secretive.

"A lady was here complaining about stolen pies. Go talk to her, will ya? She was pestering me all morning."

Pies? Inez pushed her glasses higher on the bridge of her nose. Was she supposed to look for a thief possessing a fruit-stained upper lip? Should she ask what variety of pie had been stolen? A pulse throbbed behind her left eye.

"Name's Inez, sir." She stood.

"Didn't I just say that?" A barbed-wire brow crimped over his bloodshot eye. "Here's the address."

"Say, Chief, we took care of that already—just a couple of scallywags out stealin' food. We kicked their asses all the way to the river."

Inez froze. David leaned against Murphy's desk as he smiled and winked at her. Her tongue was a dry piece of burlap.

"Don't do her job, Gabes."

"No, sir, no bother at all."

"OK. How are ya, anyway?"

David grinned, his white teeth gleaming in precise rows. "I get better every day! I can't wait for tomorrow!"

"That's the spirit that animated our forefathers!"

"Inez?" David said.

"Yes?" Should she call him David, or Gabes as the others did? The moment passed, and she didn't call him anything. He was bouncing on his heels with coiled energy. His apology for the nocturnal visit seemed far from his mind, but Inez was all awkward, heart-pounding, stomach-churning tension. Should she ask him about the absinthe case? She wanted to tell him about the shooting practice, but she was afraid his easy smile would turn to disdain. It's one thing for a woman to draw pictures of a crime scene, quite another to pick up a pistol and behave as if she were truly in the brotherhood of officers.

She blushed then to remember her thoughts of him... his arms wrapped around her as she squeezed the hammer.

"Are you ill?" Concern pinched twin lines between his eyebrows.

That was the second time he had inquired after her health. She wondered if her pale, solemn ways made others think she looked infirm or if it was just a particular look she took on in his presence. Yes, she was ill. Her body had run off like a thief with her solid, orderly thoughts.

"Hey, you again," Murphy snapped. "Laudenbach—there's a letter here, and I'm guessin' it's for you. It's addressed to the White Ghost. If I was a bettin' man ..." He waved a piece of paper over his head as he gave a phlegmy chuckle.

Inez's face burned as she approached the desk. Of course, all the men who ignored her most days now paused to watch. Their eyes snagged her back like meat hooks. As she reached for the note, he jerked it out of her reach.

"Now, Gabes, don't you go wasting time on this. You're close to cracking that absinthe case, am I right?"

"You got it, sir."

Murphy nodded.

Inez raised her hand again, and Murphy crumpled the note into a ball and tossed it to her.

"Laudenbach, do you think you could bake a cake or something for us? My sweet tooth is achin' something fierce today."

She bit the inside of her lip and pictured the look on Murphy's face if she brought in a baked good made by her own hand. Even under Louise's tender instruction, Inez produced cakes that were burnt or raw, salty or flavorless. Eventually, Louise had praised Inez's other fine talents and discontinued the baking tutelage.

"What's it say?" David's voice whispered in her ear, his breath on her cheek.

"Probably an invitation to a tea party or a complaint about laundry stolen from someone's line." Both of these things had happened last week. Her voice was sharper than she intended.

"Ah, don't give him any mind. Someday I'll tell ya all the things he said to me when I was fresh on patrol. Really. Come on, what's the paper say? Let's get away from Murph." He cocked his head toward the desk area.

That smile again. She glanced around. The others had already lost interest and gone back to their conversations and papers. Inez followed David, and he gestured to the chair.

She smoothed the note with trembling fingers as David sat on the desk and peered over her shoulder.

> Ghosty Police,
> I heard tell you found a baby in the river. There's a girl you should know about. She's killed another one. She's the one wearing the green. Go behind Bucket of Blood. A path leads to the river. Find a crooked tree struck by lightning. Dig there.
> A citizen.

"Bucket of Blood, that's a rough place. Most of the men I've arrested are probably having a pint there right now." David scratched his cheek, and the sound of fingernails on beard filled Inez's ears. All his male sounds were amplified… licking lips, a sharp intake of breath. Inez clenched her fists at the quickening in her gut. The same feeling as when she trapped the Tombstone Thief. The excitement of his warmth next to her, and the thrill of a new clue.

"'The one wearing the green.' I s'pose that's tellin' you she's an Irish gal?"

224

"I think it means something else, or maybe both." Inez remembered Ella, crumpled in grief at the grave, the green cape spread on the grass. The same cape that hung on a peg by her door.

"Ya know Bucket of Blood is just down the street." He pointed over his shoulder.

"I remember my father talking about Chief O'Conner. He said the chief and several of the officers had a financial arrangement with the Bucket of Blood owner. They were paid to look in the other direction regarding most illegal activities."

"I guess that was true for some time under O'Conner."

Inez bit her tongue. Why did she feel the need to bring that up? If she had learned anything, it was that the brotherhood was strong. "I didn't mean to infer…"

"It's a five-minute walk from here. I'll grab a shovel from the Black Maria."

Inez looked at David and then Murphy. She was unsure what he was announcing. Was he planning to check out the clue and report back to her? Was he irritated about her comment? "I should wait here in case there's another rash of pie-thefts."

He laughed. "If he asks questions, I'll make up something. Come on. What are you waiting for?"

He was walking, curling an impatient finger at her. Inez followed as he adjusted his pistol in the holster. A prickly rash moved up her neck as her heart jittered. His voice dropped when they reached the door. "After all, this is your case." Something like pride and gratitude swelled in her chest as the door to the precinct closed behind them.

Inez walked with David. He shouted greetings to people they passed on the street. A few cast frowns in her direction, but David appeared not to notice. She was glad all of her walking and bicycle riding had prepared her to match his stride with ease. She was equally glad to be free of the corset. He chatted about the sport of baseball, waving his hand in excitement, talking about an assortment of players with odd names like Zip Zabel, Ty Cobb, and a new pitcher he called the Babe. He swung the shovel in the motion of a baseball bat. He complained bitterly about the dead baseballs, explaining that because they were so expensive, there was only one ball allotted per game. By the end of the game, it was a rare event to hit a home run because the ball was so misshapen. All of these details were new information to Inez, but she was impressed by his command of the language associated with the game.

The sun arched higher in the midday sky. The thick air filled her chest, and she wiped her forehead with the cuff of her blouse. Bucket of Blood was made of crumbling limestone, and the windows were smeared dark with smoke and dirt. They passed a puddle of vomit studded with flies. A hive of voices came from the propped open door. David walked along the side of building, kicking through trash and rotted leaves, pushing aside overgrown weeds with the head of the shovel.

"This way," David called. Inez worked to untangle a branch that snagged her ankles as David skidded down the steep dirt path. The hill declined sharply, and she could smell the river below. Wild asters, bellwort and wild honeysuckle studded the hill along with rusted cans.

"Watch your step!" She heard David's voice from below. Inez cursed the narrow cut of her skirt and wondered if Louise could fashion her a pair of trousers. This terrain proved she had to be able to move with practical ease. She smiled to picture the horrified look on Murphy's face if she walked into the precinct wearing men's trousers.

"I think this is it—the tree hit by lightning." David wiped his face with a handkerchief.

At that moment, Inez's boot heel slid on loose gravel and, to her horror, she pitched forward toward the base of the tree. David dropped the shovel and grabbed her by her upper arms to prevent her from tumbling down the hill. The shovel spun around.

Inez found herself face to face with David, and the kiss in the porch, his warm smell, flooded back. There was a jolt, a heavy-lidded look to his eye that made her think he remembered standing this close.

"Sorry," Inez mumbled. "I didn't mean to send us both to our death."

"I'm glad you didn't have a fall. Did you twist an ankle or anything?"

"No, I'm quite sound, as you can see." She paused. "You can let go of me now." She immediately regretted saying that. How could this nearness be both so awkward and wonderful? His arms dropped, but they were still standing chest-to-chest.

Inez shifted her attention to the tree, and she ran her hand on the rough bark. "American Elm," she stated. "Certainly the description of the lightning strike was accurate." The burnt tree stood asymmetrical, like a person waving one arm.

"It's a wonder it still lives. That must have been a helluva strike."

"Most likely the damage happened just as the storm began. If the bark had been soaked, the charge would have gone into the earth. There are moist tissues just under the bark, and when the electrical charge heats them to high temperatures, the limb explodes."

"You sure know a lot of things."

She listened hard for the disdain she expected in his comment but couldn't detect any. "I like knowing how the world around me works. The rules of nature are more predictable than people."

"You know things about trees, but I can spot a shallow grave. Look there." He pointed to an area near the damaged tree where the earth had been recently disturbed. There was a rounded mound with stones heaped over the top. David pulled off his police coat and flung it over a branch. He retrieved the shovel, and when he pried the rocks from the mound, they tumbled downhill into the brush. As he dug, Inez viewed the scene as something to render that night in the Book of Crime.

"There's something here, a box of some kind, I think." He dropped the shovel and brushed the dirt away with his hands. Inez crouched to get a closer look. The round container, softened and stained by the damp earth, was still intact. A distinctive scrolled letter "M" was on the lid. It was the same design of hatbox as the ones she had seen at the docks. She wondered then if they had been led on a wild chase, and this was really a clue to David's absinthe. Then, as David cleared the dirt from the sides, a sickly-sweet smell wafted over them.

"Whoa, you might want to step back. You will never get that smell offa ya." David pressed his handkerchief to his nose and mouth. "I don't think I can move it because it will fall apart."

Inez had knowledge of the decay process gleaned from her father's Book of Crime. He had noted that the moment a person died, the process of autolysis began. The body digested itself as organisms entered the alimentary canal and enzymes broke down the cell walls. This caused a buildup of gases. The body bloated, and the skin split, allowing the gases to leak from the body. David was correct. The cardboard would be wet and soft.

"If you want to go back to the station, I understand. It's always hard to find one like this." His voice was muffled behind the handkerchief. His eyes shifted back and forth from the hatbox to Inez.

"You forget, I found the first baby. If you are worried I might be squeamish or am prone to a faint, don't trouble yourself. I understand the biology of death. In fact, I admire it. It's very efficient."

"If efficient means stinky, I agree with you. Suit yourself. I'm going to take a look here."

"This is the same as the hatboxes the absinthe bottles were stored in. Could this all be part of the same crime?" A gray squirrel made a chittering call on the branch above them and twitched his tail.

David shrugged and then pried the soggy lid from the box and flipped it over. Curled inside of the box was the decomposing body of a baby. Maggots and beetles were eating what was left of the flesh.

David made the sign of the cross. "How long do you think?"

"Well, each fly that lands on the body lays over two hundred eggs. They hatch as maggots, pupate and become adults."

"No. How long do you think the babe has been buried?"

"It's hard to tell. We don't know how long it was from the time of death until the box was buried. Hours? Days? The soil here seems fairly moist. Rainfall runs off from the streets above us and soaks this part of the hill, but there are a few pine trees, so the soil might have a higher acidity and that would slow decomposition. It is my understanding that the bodies of children putrefy more rapidly. It's also hard to tell if there was a wound of some kind before death. That would hasten the process because bacteria can enter the body faster."

"Doesn't this bother you?"

"The odor?"

"I mean, to be here, see this. Find another dead baby."

"I want to be here. I want to solve the mystery."

"You seem different is all. You are a thinker. Not a—"

"Feminine? Woman-like?"

"I guess another gal would be puking in the bushes and crying up a storm. I dunno," he mumbled, and his forehead creased with misery.

"Would you prefer that?"

"No. Forget it. Never mind."

Inez wanted to admit to her awkward ways. She wanted to tell him she had never fit in anywhere in her life. Not as a child, not as an adult. Not with other women. Certainly, not with men. She knew she was different, and the way her mind worked made her suspect. As they knelt over this grave though, she was unable to tell him any of these thoughts. Instead, she talked about the evidence before them.

"This death is related to the baby I found in the river."

"How's that?"

"See this dressing gown? The needlework along the hem?" Inez pointed to the rotting fabric. "The river baby was wearing an identical gown, and I've questioned the young girl who had these babies in her care."

"I should arrest her then?"

"I'm not sure just yet. First I think I need more information from the woman that runs this hat business."

Chapter 53

Ella's head throbbed. Her fingers found a tender lump near her temple, and she remembered the fall outside of Bucket of Blood. There was a bitter taste in her mouth. She turned her head to find Richard sleeping next to her. He was stretched on his side facing her, naked and uncovered. In the early light, she considered him, his hands resting between them, his muscled arms, his smooth chest. She realized he didn't have any scars. Not one. Life had not injured him as it had Connor, Da, or her brothers. He snored lightly. Her heart had not been moved by his lovemaking. At first, she was surprised that she felt nothing at all for him. And then she wasn't. Half her heart was with Connor in his grave.

She slipped out from under the sheet, pulled the chamber pot from under the bed, and went behind the dressing screen. As she squatted to release her urine, a thick pain chugged behind her eyes making the room spin. She had to get dressed and get home to Beata and the baby. She needed the quick release of Connor's knife. There was an excitement to deciding where to place the next cut. The calling hummed through her body.

If she left before Richard awoke, maybe he would question whether she had been there at all or if the Green Fairy had bewitched his memory. Gooseflesh bloomed over her skin as she slipped into her chemise and blouse. The weight of the gun in her pocket brought back the scene at Bucket of Blood. Her face in the mirror was pale save for a purple bruise forming at the corner of her eye. She ran her fingers through the wild tangle of snarls.

Richard stirred. Ella sat on the chair where they had shared the drink. When she bent over to tie her shoes, her stomach churned, and she forced a sour swallow. The sticky remnants of his absinthe ritual were strewn across the table. A fly ambled over the lip of the glass.

She hurried to the door, eager to be away from this room, and just before she turned the knob she took one last glance at Richard, his face buried in the pillow. A plume of hair stood up at the crown of his head. Then there was the sound of a key turning in the lock, and Ella stared at the turning knob. The door swung open, and Ella found herself face to face with Martine.

Martine's mouth formed a perfect tight circle. She slipped the key back into her pocket. A new hat creation adorned with cornflower-blue ribbons made her brown eyes shine. Martine and Richard. All those mornings when Martine stumbled into the shop in a woozy state. She had been lovers with Richard all along! Martine would be attracted to his lean refinement. They would have sat at the table together, just as Ella had last night, and shared absinthe, awaiting the arrival of the Green Fairy. Did it matter to Richard what body he kissed?

Martine chuckled, leaned on her cane, and called out, "Why, Richard, I didn't know you had developed a taste for the red!" Richard sat up in bed and looked at both of them. Ella's face burned, and she pushed past Martine as Richard called, "Wait, Ella." Martine's laughter chased her down the stairs, out the door, into the wet street.

* * *

The walk home was a blur. Her stomach roiled, and she stopped several times preparing to vomit, but the feeling passed even as heavy pain stirred through her head. Of course Richard had other lovers. He had that look about him, but she cringed to think it was Martine! She felt just as she had that first day in Martine's shop... poor, disheveled, and something to be pitied. That throaty laughter caused a wave of dizziness.

Standing water filled the ruts in the muddy streets. The storm washed the air clean, but the sun felt too bright, and her eyes teared. The sight of her house, the way the front door hung like a crooked tooth, made her legs weak. Hopefully, the baby would sleep, or she could impose upon Beata for a few more hours, drink some weak tea and close her eyes against the pain.

The front door was open. This was not unusual, but there was dread attached to this that seized Ella's chest. Please let Beata be in the kitchen stirring a pot of *bigos*. Or sitting in a chair, knees spread, a pile of knitting on her lap. "Beata?" she called.

The house was silent.

Ella walked the hallway to the kitchen, fear pinching her belly. An overturned chair with a snapped leg started to tell the story. Glass shards, some with blood on them, glittered across the floor. A shattered plate lay next to the baseboard, bits of food stuck to the wall above it. Beata's orange tomcat, the one Ella was named after, crouched on the floor, ears flattened. He growled. Blood shaped like a giant tear smeared the top of the table. Where was the stroller? Where were Beata and the baby now? Who had been hurt?

Lettie. She had returned to unleash her rage on Beata and this deformed baby. In her irritation and hatred, she had murdered one of the twins. Or both of them. Then she'd tossed the bundle off the bridge.

Ella ran to the bedroom. Maybe Beata had put the baby to sleep on her bed? She clutched her throat to see that someone had been in this room too. The sheet and blanket were heaped on the floor. The bundle of Connor's knives had been pulled out from under the mattress. A note rested on the pillow, impaled by the shaft of the largest knife. Ella yanked the handle to release the piece of paper.

> I know you talked to the White Ghost. You mean to betray me. It's a mistake to think you are smarter than I am. I wore your cape. People will remember the girl in a green cape. Right now, the White Ghost is reading a letter that will lead her to the grave of your hatbox baby. Meet me at the bridge tonight at dark to save your broken baby. If you tell anyone about me, I will do what I have to do.

Ella sat on the floor. Where was Beata? Had she been hurt? *Oh, Connor.* Her throat ached with loneliness. She missed the way he would rub her shoulders when she was troubled. *Connor, what should I do*? It was too late to confide in the policewoman. Lettie will lie and say Ella had killed Janna and hid the body. Everything had gone wrong. The baby business. Martine. She was alone. Grief crimped tight bands around her chest until she couldn't breathe.

She crumpled the note and threw it on the bed. She pulled her skirt high on her thigh and drew the blade crossways over the scabs so that the wounds resembled the letter "H." The knife dropped to the floor, and she slumped against the bed. There were no beating wings or feelings of flight, but she reveled in the warm blood that ran between her thighs.

Chapter 54

When Inez pushed open the door to the hat shop, the bell jangled against the glass. The owner of the shop paused her conversation with a customer, looked Inez up and down, and held up a delicate hand. "I will be with you in one moment, please." She leaned over the glass counter as she tied a bow on the hatbox and spoke French in low tones.

Inez turned her attention to the store. They were all silly and impractical hats of all sizes, featuring bows and ribbons that looked like they would itch under her chin. Tiny hats that couldn't keep off the sun or rain and large-brimmed hats in garish purples and greens and golds, featuring plumes that rose from the crowns so that they looked like nests for exotic birds. Inez lifted a black felt toque hat from the form, placed it on her head, and viewed her reflection in the gilded mirror behind the case. The angle was wrong, as was the scale. Her head looked enormous, and the harsh color made her skin appear all the paler.

"Au revoir," the woman called to her customer. She kissed her on the cheek and held the door open. The woman cradled her hatbox and smiled brightly.

"This one is not right for you." The woman slunk behind her, stood on tip-toes, and snatched the hat from Inez's head. "I am Martine. This is my shop. If we cannot find the perfect hat here amongst these offerings, I will create one suited to your, umm, unusual coloring." Inez suddenly understood the liberal use of feathers. The woman was bird-like, thin and all hard angles. Even her narrow nose resembled a bird's beak. She smelled of oranges and sharp spices.

"I'm not here to purchase a hat. I'd like to talk to you."

"Talk?"

"I'm an officer with the Saint Paul Police Department."

"A woman police? I don't think so." Martine sniffed and slowly retreated behind the counter. She picked up a cane that was leaning against the glass case. "Where is your uniform? Badge? Maybe you investigate the crimes of women wearing ugly hats?" She laughed but picked at her cuticles, and her eyes darted about the shop.

"I have been tasked to look after the welfare of women and children."

Martine pulled her shoulders back and tilted her chin upward. "I take care of the welfare of women who come into this shop. I make them feel beautiful and special. And there are certainly no children about as you can see." She leaned on the cane, and Inez wondered what infirmity plagued her. Inez had trouble estimating Martine's age.

"I think you, your business perhaps, may be connected to a case we're working on."

"And you want to talk to me, why? I am just a shop owner who makes hats." Martine averted her eyes from Inez and moved a rag over the spotless glass counter.

"An infant was found yesterday," Inez said, pointing to the stack of boxes behind the counter, "in a shallow grave, inside one of your hatboxes."

Martine rolled her eyes. "And if the bébé was found in a peach crate you would be at the grocer bothering him now? My hat creations are all over this city. Some are even in Minneapolis! Lots of women have these boxes." Martine sniffed. "It is not my fault if they wish to be rid of an infant."

Martine had made a valid point. Yet, when the conversation turned to the topic of a dead infant, everything about Martine seemed to relax as if she were expecting different questions. Should she mention the scene at the docks with the men loading the wagon with her boxes?

The customer that just left the shop—what if that box held absinthe bottles instead of a silly hat?

"Do you have children of your own?" Even as Inez asked this, she knew this hunch was wrong. Martine was gaunt. Frail. Sickly. Her body did not suggest having recently given birth, nor could Inez picture Martine mustering the strength to dig a grave on the side of A steep hill.

"Of course not. They smell dreadful, and they make appalling noises. Anyway, that is not my life here. I am a milliner." Martine reminded Inez of Circe, the beautiful bored sorceress that turned men into swine. Her named meant falcon.

"You said some women 'wish to be rid of an infant.' So you think the infant we found was murdered?" David had informed Inez that the victim in the hatbox was female. There was not a ligature around her neck as with the river baby. There were no obvious wounds. The neck bones were intact. No one could say one way or the other if the baby was murdered. At first, she wondered if this was the missing baby Madeline that Annah cried over at the station, but the hair on the corpse was dark, and Annah had described her daughter as very fair.

Martine scowled and said, "What other reason for putting a *bébé* in a hatbox?"

"The pregnancies may have been concealed, and the child died at birth. There are families that cannot afford a traditional burial." Inez thought of Mrs. Chormansky as she said this. "Some babies are not wanted. Poor families can't feed or clothe another child."

"Then they should contact my apprentice, Ella. She takes in unwanted babies."

"Ella works for you?"

"Yes, I was trying to teach her my art. She had some sewing skills and made deliveries for me from time to time. You know her then?"

"I have spoken with her. Did you fire her?"

"Ah, such a long story. One problem is that she has the ridiculous notion she can sell les infants. They have been here in the shop several times! Euuw, if I did not pity her so much I would have made them leave immediately. They are not good for business." Martine's mouth flattened to a narrow line, and she dramatically held her nose.

"So Ella has access to your supply of boxes, and she has babies in her care. Do you think she would cause a baby harm? Is it in her nature?"

"Oh no—she loves them despite their looks. One had a face like dried fruit."

"You think she has feelings for them?"

"I don't understand it either," Martine shrugged.

"You have not seen anything to make you think she is violent or unbalanced?"

Martine considered this question. "She cries a lot. She doesn't think I know, but I hear her when she is working in the back room. She told me her young husband died in the winter. She is poor—that much is obvious. I leave little biscuits for her." Martine dropped her voice to a whisper. "Sometimes I hear her talking to herself, or maybe it's to the dead husband." Her eyes widened.

"Ella did tell me her husband died."

Inez counted the things she had learned. Ella worked here. Martine knew of Ella's care of unwanted babies and confirmed the scope of Ella's grief. Clearly, Martine didn't like babies, especially the ones cared for by Ella, but it didn't seem likely she'd commit murder. Inez pulled out her notebook as the shop bell clanged.

A man opened the door, and as Inez turned to look, she saw Martine shake her head and raise her hand to halt his entrance.

"Pardon me, mademoiselle." He tipped his hat. "Wrong shop!"

"Men, they are always lost." Martine shrugged again.

"Is it customary for men to shop here?"

"Some buy beautiful hats for their wives. They like pretty things on their arms. Perhaps you could send your husband here to pick something for you?" Martine's eyes flicked to Inez's hands.

"I don't have a spouse." Inez steeled for a hostile remark.

"Then you are smarter than I first assumed. I am not troubled by a man either." Martine clicked her tongue and raised her dark brows. "So, I have answered your police questions, no? Can I ask you to leave now, by the back way?" She gestured to the curtained area. "It is not good for business to have the police here—especially a woman asking about a *bébé morts*! My customers, they are the nervous types."

Inez had been dismissed. There would be no more information. There were questions for Martine she had not yet formulated. She tucked her notebook and pencil away. "Perhaps if I have additional questions later?"

"Of course!" Martine was already out from behind the counter, her small hand at Inez's back pushing her toward the curtained area.

Inez pulled back the curtain and stepped into the cluttered room. Dim light filtered through a dirty window, and Inez saw a table stacked with crumpled swatches of fabric, hat forms, and boxes. A bottle of absinthe and a dirty glass were nearly hidden in the mess. Inez wrapped her fingers around her night stick. Was there a way she could jam it in the door and then return later to look around?

"Next time you return, I'll show you my ideas for a hat that would be perfect for you. I have in mind a particular shade of blue." Martine used her cane to toss a length of fabric over the table. She moved to the door but struggled with the sliding bolt. Her face crimped with effort. "Stubborn thing."

Inez moved the pin easily, and the door creaked open to a narrow, muddy alley. A roof drain splattered a stream of water over the cobblestones.

"Au revoir!"

"Thank you for speaking with me," Inez said as the door slammed shut. She heard the bolt slide into place. Such an unusual woman. Her fingers itched to illustrate today's exchange in the Book of Crime. She longed for the moment when the brush and the image told a part of the story without words. She wondered what questions David would have asked. Would he think Martine to be somehow involved?

Behind her, something thudded against the metal drainpipe, and a crate tipped over. As Inez turned to see the cause of the disturbance, a blurry image swiped the edge of her vision, and then she felt a sharp pain and the cobbles rushed up to meet her face.

Chapter 55

Inez woke up alone in the alley, her blouse wet and stained with dirt and grease. She rolled over and watched the stripe of bright-blue sky above her as she moved her arms, legs, ankles and neck. Satisfied that nothing was broken, Inez stood, pinned her hair and went down the alley and back around to the front of the shop where she had left her bike. What else to do? If she told Chief Murphy, he might remove her from the department since this was evidence she couldn't take care of herself. No, best to quietly push on. But why would someone hit her? She had no valuables. Her clothes had not been torn or removed to suggest an encounter of a sexual nature. Was this incident related to the case? As the breeze cooled her face, she smiled. Perhaps her questions had made someone uncomfortable. Someone was worried enough to try and scare her off.

She got on her bike and maneuvered around a horse and cart. The driver tipped his hat and then stiffened in alarm as he stared.

Oh, this turn of events will set Louise to worry. Inez could predict the way Louise would grimace as she scrubbed the grime of the alley assault from her blouse. "Inez, I gave you a gun," she would admonish. Not that a weapon would have helped her with any aspect of today's work.

The bicycle tires rumbled over the wooden slats of the Wabasha Bridge, and her head throbbed. The thick heat of the day simmered and squeezed her chest; the back of her blouse was drenched with sweat.

What would she say to Ella? The most compelling facts were the matching dressing gowns both dead babies wore, identical to the one in Ella's laundry basket, and the fact that she had access to a supply of hatboxes. If she told Ella about the discovery of the buried infant, did she really expect a confession? She thought of her father's handcuffs and gun and the possibility of a false arrest. How likely was it that she could talk Ella into coming to the station?

A black cocker spaniel nipped at her heels and barked as she pedaled the muddy streets. After a few blocks, he lost interest and slunk back the way he had come. Should she see if she could find the embroidered dressing gown in the house that matched the ones the dead infants wore? Would removing it and taking it to the station weaken or strengthen her case against Ella?

Inez swung her leg from the bicycle and propped it against the porch rail of Ella's house. She knew she looked disheveled, but maybe it lent her an air of toughness. She heard someone crying and strained her ears to follow the sound. Inez walked along the side of the house and past the pale pink climbing roses slumped on the trellis until she reached the back yard. Ella was sitting on the back steps sobbing into her hands. Her stockings and shoes lay in a heap. An orange male cat rubbed back and forth against her shins. When Ella looked up to see Inez, she cried harder.

"Miss, why are you in distress?" Inez's job was dense with crying women. She knew to wait for an answer. Inez noted a discolored abrasion on her temple. Did both of their professions put them in danger?

"I was looking for Mrs. Pavlak—me neighbor—the one that came to see you. She's not at her house—I can't find her anywhere." Ella's eyes were red-rimmed, and her hair was snarled and matted.

"What's the trouble?"

Ella's face was raw with misery and secrets. She chewed on her bottom lip and finally replied, "She's minding a baby for me."

"You are caring for a new child?"

"Umm, for a couple of days."

"Your face... has someone hurt you?"

Ella reached a distracted hand to her temple, prodding it as if she were a blind person. "Oh, I fell. Last night when it rained." She looked up at Inez. "What happened to you?"

"It seems we are both clumsy." Inez tucked her blouse into her skirt.

"I probably made that," Ella sniffed. "Your shirt-waist. I sewed so many at Seeger's, I can't count." She tipped her head to stare at the sky as fresh tears flowed. "Sometimes I sit here and pray for me heart's last beat." Her voice cracked. "I count them off, you see, and ask, is this the last one?"

"Your sorrow is hard to bear."

"I miss me husband. I miss me old life. I wake every day, and it's just like the morning he died. I hate that I go to that worn-out place all over again."

"You seek nepenthe then."

"Who is that?"

"It is not a person. Nepenthe is derived from the Greek language to mean *no sorrow*. It was also a drink that the wife of Thonis gave to Helen to induce forgetfulness and ease sorrow."

Ella gave a bitter chuckle. "This is the second time I've been offered a drink of forgetfulness."

"What were you offered?"

"It's not important." She looked at Inez and licked her dry lips. "I don't want to forget Connor, but my heart feels like it's full of broken glass. Maybe if I could just take a little dose of it. Can a doctor give me this medicine?"

"No. It's a mythical thing spoken of in books. Edgar Allen Poe talks about taking it to forget his love, Lenore."

"What help does it do to tell me about a medicine I cannot have?" Ella looked at Inez with misery.

Inez's back and shoulder muscles cramped. Now her elbow throbbed. She was tired of standing, thirsty, and mad at herself. Why on earth would she talk of mythical drugs and characters to someone who would not share her fascination? Inez moved an empty crate from the steps and sat down next to Ella.

"I'm sorry. I didn't mean to add to your discomfort."

"You say discomfort as if I'm hungry or me shoes are too tight."

"I don't always have a good sense of what to say to people." The tomcat jumped into Inez's lap. His oily tail flicked across her face.

241

"What do you want of me?"

"A letter was sent to me at the police station. The information led us to a grave of a female infant. She was found in a hatbox from your employer, Martine."

When Ella wailed a high plaintive cry, the tomcat sprang from Inez's lap, his claws gouging her thigh through her skirt. "Oh Janna!" Ella sobbed. "She was so sick you see, the weakest of the babies. She had runny bowels, and I couldn't make her well. I held her, I fed her, but she was too ill."

"I thought you just had the twin boys." Inez's leg stung. The cat slunk away.

"I told you that, but it wasn't the whole truth. She was their sister. I called her Janna." She rubbed her runny nose with the back of her hand.

"So she died, and you committed her to the grave on the side of the hill."

Ella bent over again. Her teary words were muffled. "Her body was stolen." There was something else uttered that Inez couldn't decipher.

"Stolen?"

"I was trying to bring her to the cathedral, to the Sisters for proper burial in blessed ground. When I wasn't paying attention, someone took the hatbox. At first, I thought a thief might have believed it contained something to sell, like silver."

Inez measured her next words carefully. She waited. "So you said you believe a thief stole the box. Who buried the box? Why would this person write to me and direct me to the grave?"

Ella shot up from the steps and paced on the worn dirt path.

"Do you know who this person is?"

"I can't say." Ella clenched her palms, and her knuckles became white shiny knobs.

"Can't say? Or won't say?"

"You don't understand. Bad things will happen if I tell."

Inez saw a rivulet of blood snake around Ella's anklebone. Did she have her monthly?

"What bad things? Tell me. I can help!"

"I have never been so alone in my life! It's all my fault. You can't help me."

"Your fault? Did one of the boys die by natural causes too?" Inez baited her, knowing if the baby died by disease there was no reason for the strip of linen to be cinched at the neck. "Last time we spoke, you said they were living with a family in Wisconsin."

Ella's voice went flat. "The boys were to go to a farm. Together. That was agreed upon."

"I discovered the body of a male infant in the river. He was wearing one of the embroidered gowns—"

"A bartender at Bucket of Blood told me yesterday."

"I believe this was one of the infants in your care."

"Can I ask? Did you only find the one?" Ella stared at the ground.

"Yes. Only one body was discovered."

"Then maybe the other boy is safe. He is at the farm. Someone is holding him at night when he cries." She nodded and rocked as if she were holding an infant.

"Is the woman involved... the one Mrs. Pavlak talked about when she came to the station? She said a person named Lettie was taking advantage of you. There is reason to believe she was involved in a theft accusation at Jueneman's."

Ella crouched on her haunches. Her fists beat against her temples, and a woven sound of pain and anguish burst from her. The dust grayed the blood on her foot.

"Let me help you," Inez pleaded.

Ella gathered her stockings and shoes, pulled them close to her chest, and shook her head. Tears made trails in the grime on her cheeks. Inez thought Ella's face held the collective sadness of all the women she had seen since she started her police work. Ella suddenly ran away from Inez, heading toward the gate in the backyard. Before Inez could call out, the gate swung shut behind her, and she was gone.

It was futile to call after Ella. She had failed to win her confidence.

Inez walked up the back steps and into the kitchen and observed the scene. Broken glass and blood splatters, a damaged chair. Who had been injured? Was this Ella's blood? The baby's?

She searched the bedroom and saw the knives and the feathers released from the slice in the pillow. She smoothed the crumpled paper on the bed and started to read: "I know you talked to the White Ghost…"

Inez headed home to get her gun.

Chapter 56

The gun bumped against Ella's leg as she followed the path near the river. The sweet smells of clover and ripening grasses filled her nose, and these comforting fragrances called Connor to mind but did nothing to soothe her wild thoughts.

The police officer knew of Janna's grave and the murder of at least one of the boys. The hatbox-coffin made her look guilty. A judge would easily order her hanged by the neck for her part in these crimes. No one would believe she had been duped by Lettie, who would probably disappear before Officer Inez could find her... Lettie, who planned all along to make everyone think a girl in a green cape had murdered babies. All she had was Beata to defend her actions, but when Beata found out about the murdered baby boy she loved so much, would she blame Ella for ignoring her warnings? And what had become of Beata? Had Lettie murdered Ella's only witness? The images of broken glass and blood splatters made her throat swell to think of Beata, pale and unmoving, as the life seeped from her. Ella had looked everywhere in the neighborhood for her, even at Ambrozy's meat market, but no one had seen her or the baby.

The last heat of the day baked the ground under her feet into cracked furrows. Ella stumbled, no longer finding sure footing as if the absinthe had forever altered the way her legs moved. At the horizon, cool purple ribbons of sky wrapped the orange sun. She longed for the feeling of buoyant flight, soaring away from this river. Oh, to fly directly to the sun to become nothing more than wisps of ash that would float back to the river!

The sturdy bones of the bridge came into view. She remembered the morning Janna died, when she had stood here on the bridge and thought of jumping into the currents. Then she heard Milo's voice last night at Bucket of Blood telling of a caped figure flinging a bundle off the bridge.

Her darling boys.

All of her good intentions had rotted. Finding homes for babies. Supporting herself without charity. Now, the babies were dead, Beata was hurt or worse, and all because of her. She had carelessly taken a lover and stopped now for the first time, to wonder if she might be pregnant. Another unwanted baby. She shook her head. Life without Connor was sour, and she was as guilty as Lettie.

She had to prevent Lettie from doing more evil acts.

She sat down and leaned against the wood supports, wishing she had brought a knife to relieve the feelings billowed in her chest like steam threatening to split her skin. Instead, she dragged her thumbnail over the freshest cuts until the pain flared deep and bright. She held the gun in her lap, realizing vaguely that she had never shot one before. Then she closed her eyes and listened to the stinging song in her quivering muscles. It came to her as colors, orange and fiery as the last of the sky.

* * *

Ella woke as her hand stung with pain. She opened her eyes to see Lettie looming above her, hands on her hips. She had kicked the gun out of Ella's lap—it was spinning across the slats. When Ella cupped her hand, she felt blood and a piece of bone poking through her skin.

"You kicked me!"

"Before ya fuckin' shot me!"

"I wouldn't shoot anyone. You broke me bleedin' hand, Lettie."

"Looks like you had a plan. You and that Polish cunt should be in the madhouse together. Look at my neck!" Lettie turned her head to reveal a wound that started at her earlobe and curved toward her collar-bone.

Ella scrambled to stand. "I'll defend meself, I'm warnin' yus. Seems you borrowed me cape *again*."

Ella inched across the bridge away from Lettie. A wind kicked up, swirling grit and the aroma of a nearby campfire.

Lettie shouted, "That old cape's pretty. It suits my needs and is wasted on you." Her hand emerged from under the cape holding the longest and sharpest of Connor's knives.

"You wear it to get me in trouble. Where is Beata?"

"I had enough of her poison mouth. She got what she deserved."

"You killed her then? Just like the boys?" Ella moaned. "She was so good to me after Connor died." Ella bent over with the pain and sadness. "It was all lies, wasn't it? There's no family in Wisconsin." Ella walked backward, her hand on the splintered rail. The gun lay across the deck. Could she dart over and pick it up? Lettie locked eyes with her, and she advanced with each of Ella's retreating steps.

"I didn't kill the *both* of 'em! Ya put up such a fuss about keepin' them as a pair."

Ella's anger pounded in her head.

"Nobody wanted the one that looked like a circus freak. God, I hate you. You ruined it! We could have made so much money if only you'd listened to me." Lettie wagged the knife back and forth. "I could have been done with the men and the stealin'. Done with Bucket of Blood. But no! You kept draggin' home those broken babies."

"Why'd you bury Janna behind the pub? What an unholy place!"

"A favor for you, more like. Saved you the time of diggin' a hole."

"I was bringing her to the church—to the Sisters." High overhead, bats swooped through the dimming sky.

Lettie laughed. "Yeah, that's why you were standin' in front of Bucket of Blood. Church. I've heard some of the fellas call it that."

"I was on my way. I got distracted." She flashed to Richard's first appearance.

"Ya know, I would see your Conner there, at Bucket of Blood. I didn't know his name at the time. Oh, he loved the workin' girls there. I mean *loved*." Lettie licked her lips.

"Lies."

"Reddish sort of hair, 'bout this tall." Lettie held the knife up over her head. "Wouldn't ever keep his yap shut."

"I don't believe a word. Anyway, you're the one that wrote the letter to the police."

"Because you talked to the Ghost." Ella felt a spray of spittle land on her cheek.

"Officer Inez *knew* things. She's the one that found Gerick's body in the river. I told you I didn't breathe a word." Ella's heart butted against her ribs. "We were partners. I trusted you."

"See what that got ya? People always whine, *I trust you, do you trust me?* Ugh, it's worthless. I don't trust anyone."

"You mean to kill me then?" Ella shouted. Her hand throbbed. A full moon had risen, casting a creamy light over the bridge.

Lettie untied the bow to the cape and shrugged it off. As the cape fell to the decking, Lettie held out a burlap sack. Ella watched it writhe and twist.

"Oh God, give him to me!"

Lettie dangled the sack over the rails. They were near the middle of the bridge now, and Ella could see tiny winks of campfires burning along the beaches.

Ella moved toward Lettie and screamed, "Don't, Lettie! Please! I'll take care of him." She reached out with her good hand for the bag. "I won't tell anyone about Gerick!"

"Both of you—move away from the railing." Ella turned to see Inez standing on the bridge, holding a pistol in both hands and pointing it at them. Her blouse, hair, and skin glowed in the moonlight.

Lettie shook her head, and smirking, said, "Isn't this rich? The White Ghost is here to save you."

Ella shouted, "She means to drown the baby!"

"Aren't you the little helper." Lettie waved the knife.

"Put the sack and the knife down. Now!" Inez said calmly.

Lettie popped up on her toes and leaned farther over the rail, swinging the bag back and forth. "If you really want me to, I will."

"Stop!" Ella screamed as she moved to the rail and reached for the bag.

"Ella, walk over to me," Inez called.

"If you do, I'll let go, and your little broken brat will make a nice big splash down there," Lettie hissed.

"I'm here to take you in for your crimes." Inez held a pair of handcuffs over her head.

"Will we be sharin' the cuffs, then?" Lettie snorted. "And what crimes are ya speakin' of?"

"I hid under the bridge. I heard you admit to murdering the baby I found in the river. Let's take a walk to the police station and sort this out." Inez started walking toward them.

"Just like a troll, you are, skulking under the bridge. Sounds like you'll just throw me into a jail cell. Not much to sort out, is there?"

"I want to hear both of your stories. I write them down, you see. I've drawn pictures of the both of you."

"What sort of pictures?" Lettie asked.

Inez inched closer. "Pictures that tell the story of what happened. The *why* of the story."

"The why..."

"The grave behind Bucket of Blood? Why drown the boy?"

"The girl, Janna, was in my care, but she was so sick—she died." Ella pushed the hair from her face. "It wasn't Lettie's fault! I should have had the doctor." Ella's heart pinched with the telling.

"See, that's the story," Inez said. "Come and tell it all to me."

"Isn't that a crime to leave a dead baby at a church?" Lettie asked. She moved the tip of the blade so that it scratched Ella's neck.

"Hand me the sack. Let's walk back together," Inez' said. Her glasses glinted.

"Please, Lettie." Ella's sobs choked her. Lettie's response was to furiously shake the sack. When Ella heard the faint cries, her knees sagged.

"If I give you the baby, you have to let me go. I'll disappear. You won't see me again."

Inez shook her head and said, "I can't allow that."

"Let Lettie leave town! I'll gladly hang for her crimes. Save the baby." Ella's vision blurred with tears and misery. Anger and sorrow burst from her like a live lashing thing. Birth. Loss was the only child she would have.

"Just like all the fucking men, you are."

"If a man is interested in justice, then yes, I am like a man." Inez now stood just a few feet from them. Lettie twisted the bag around her wrist, grabbed Ella roughly and put the knife to her throat.

"You really expect to arrest me?"

"I expect you to comply with the law. Put down that knife. Give me the baby." Inez aimed her gun directly at Lettie's heart.

Lettie laughed. "The police at Bucket of Blood told me you're not allowed a gun. They won't let you. They all laugh at you, you know. The Ghost Police Girl."

"Well, I have a gun, and there are no men here."

"I wonder what you'll write about this night? What pictures you'll draw?" Lettie raised an eyebrow, then released her grip on Ella and threw the burlap sack into the river.

Ella jumped over the rail after the baby. As she flew into the darkness, she heard two gunshots. She hit the water all too soon.

Chapter 57

The gun handle was slick in Inez's hand, and her arm fell heavily to her side. She blinked hard. In an instant, Ella had lunged over the rail. Gone. Lettie crumpled to the deck, moaning and cursing as she clutched her knee.

Inez had failed to save the baby. Would Ella survive the fall and the currents?

Footsteps pounded behind her on the bridge deck. David appeared, breathing hard. "I heard gunfire. Are you all right?"

Inez nodded. "A woman jumped into the river. She was trying to save an infant."

"Christ on a bike." David turned around and ran back to the path that led down to the riverbank. Inez heard branches thrashing and then nothing but the sounds of the waves hitting the shore. Lettie pushed herself to a sitting position, held her thigh with shaking hands and rocked back and forth.

Moments later, Tim Gorman raced up, gun raised. His eyes darted between Lettie and Inez. "Gabes?"

Inez pointed to path. "He's gone after a woman in the river." What had she done? Winds churned around them.

Gorman leaned over the rail and peered into the twilight, then aimed his gun at Lettie. "It's the goddamn famous Lettie Kokinos. Now whatcha been up to? No good as usual, I expect." Lettie scowled. Gorman picked up the knife and gun and handed them to Inez. "I'm glad you alerted the station, but you should've waited for us."

"As you can see, I couldn't."

"Well, yes. We came as fast as we could."

As she watched Lettie writhe in pain, she said, "Arrest her for the murder of an infant. I heard her confession," Inez said.

"Yes, officer."

She felt numb. There was no exhilaration like the night she caught the Tombstone Thief. She adjusted her glasses and looked into the sky. The first constellation she saw was Ursa Major. Any other time that significance would have made her smile, but not tonight.

"You do the honors," Gorman said. "It's your arrest. I'm going to help Gabes."

"You know, it's not allowed. I'm not a proper officer."

"Gabes told me about your work, and I say it's fine by me. It was right to tell us you were comin' here tonight." Gorman offered her a set of handcuffs,

She said, "I have my own." She laid all the weapons on the planks well out of Lettie's reach and pulled out her father's set.

"Do it. Stick her in the van. It's parked on the street."

As he turned to follow David's path, Inez longed to call after him… *Find him. Help him. Keep him safe.*

Lettie kicked and spat as Inez approached her. Her eyes were like a wild horse's, and there was blood from her hands smeared on her pale face, but she was alert. When Inez opened the cuffs, Lettie scooted backward. Inez, remembering her experiences with the drunks, bent over and squeezed Lettie's injured knee, causing her to scream and go limp. She adjusted the cuffs around Lettie's slim wrists and clicked them shut.

Chapter 58

The last customer of the day opened the shop door and tucked her chin, bracing for the November winds that stirred snowflakes across the slate skies. At the final clang of the bell, Ella turned the key in the door, drew the shade and flipped the closed sign. Since she had taken over Martine's shop in the fall, business had been good, better than Ella had hoped for. She was making hats of her own creation. Not the fussy varieties favored by Martine, but practical hats for working girls. Hats that kept off the sun and rain but also looked smart and fashionable. She also made bonnets for babies and girls and wool caps for boys. Ella untied her apron and hung it on the peg behind the register. She squeezed the roll of bills in her pocket and smiled.

One of the babies gave her an open-mouthed greeting showing two bottom teeth as drool wet her chin. She sat up straight in the new stroller, and her legs pumped back and forth. Her brother rubbed his eyes and stuck out his lower lip. "The door is locked," she cooed to them. "Let's go home."

Ella parted the curtain and pushed the stroller into the workroom. She handed them a biscuit to stave off the hunger and tucked blankets around them. As she tugged the wool hats low over their ears, she kissed each nose. Ella pulled on her woolen cape and marveled in the comfort of heavy warmth on her shoulders.

There was a knock at the back door. Ella slid open the bolt allowing a blast of frigid air to fill the workroom.

"Is my family ready to walk home?" Connor blew into his cupped hands and danced up and down before he leaned in to kiss Ella. His cheeks were cool, and he tasted of ale. The babies both craned their necks to look at him. Connor cupped Janna's and Gerick's heads and then pressed his lips to the crown of each hat.

"You've snuck a pint without me," Ella scolded but then smiled. Snowflakes clung to his red hair.

"I've delivered a wagon full o' hats all over the town. I say it's well-deserved. Anyway, let's have another together! Come on, just one pint, will ya, please?" He folded his hands in prayer and winked.

"There's no such thing as just one pint. I'm tired. I want to go home. I'll take you up on your fine offer another time," Ella said and leaned into the rough wool of his coat. Even though fatigue buzzed through her arms and legs and numbers and hats and boxes jumped around in her head, the pure peace of this moment swelled in her chest.

Connor grinned and moved to cup her cheeks with both hands. "And home is the best place to be, *mo mhuirmin dilis*."

"Yes," she sighed. "You are me own true love."

Chapter 59

Inez stroked the charcoal stick across the paper and then smudged the line with her thumb to soften the line of the man's jaw. His head was tilted back, and his dark eyes were open in surprise. His throat had been cut, an incision that spanned ear-to-ear, nearly severing his head. She made sure to capture the wide arc of blood spray across the snow in relation to the body's position. The cold drilled through her knees, but this position, crouching close to the dead man, allowed her to see there were no wounds on his hands even though they were dark with blood. This led Inez to surmise that the man had been attacked from behind with a swift and single stroke of a sharp blade. He had clutched his neck, fallen to his knees, and then slumped forward into the fresh snow. The man who discovered the body on the frozen shores of Lake Phalen had turned him on his back, causing the neck wound to yawn open. Inez's fingers were numb on the charcoal stick, but she continued at a deliberate pace to capture all the details before the last light of the December afternoon seeped away.

The officers surrounded her as she sketched; plumes of frosty breath bloomed around their heads, but they left her to her duties. She could feel their eyes flicker over her and detected when they moderated their language in her presence. Tim Gorman often peered over her shoulder to watch the images appear.

Inez was now writing the Book of Crime for the entire city of Saint Paul. The officers called her to scenes, mostly murders or assaults, where she rendered all the details and then was often asked to offer opinions about manners of death or theories about the nature of the misconduct. Sometimes she was asked to draw, based on a victim's description, a portrait of a suspect that was then published in the *Saint Paul Pioneer Press* to alert watchful eyes in the city.

This shift in her duties began during the trial of Lettie Kokinos, who was charged with the murder of a male infant. David had offered Inez's Book of Crime to a writer who worked for the paper, and every day the front page featured scenes and portraits she had drawn related to the story: the body of Gerick found in the river; Ella Byrne wearing her green cape; and Lettie Kokinos, her head cocked at an angle, lips pursed, the medallion resting between her breasts. Sales for the paper surged, and it was generally believed that the Book of Crime had helped convict Lettie, who received a life sentence to the newly opened Minnesota Correction Facility in Stillwater, despite the citizen demands to bring back public hanging.

The second news story, accompanied by more of Inez's portrayals, described how the police, led by Officer David Gabrielli, had dismantled the absinthe smuggling ring. David had staked out the warehouse Inez had discovered and arrested Richard Gale as the last bottle of absinthe was packed for deliveries throughout Saint Paul. Richard immediately pointed a finger at Martine Burreau Carpentier, the local French hat maker, as the mastermind. However, Martine disappeared quietly back to Paris, many suspected, before she could be questioned. While Inez's drawing depicted a man of Richard's stature and dress standing near the wagon full of absinthe, the evidence against him was weak, and he was later released.

The two stories of women committing heinous crimes ran for weeks in the paper, commanding the top and bottom folds. This caused tongues to wag and hundreds of candles to be lit at the cathedral, mourning the loss of purity of the city's young women.

Inez thought of Ella daily. She admired Ella's need to stand alone and her battle to support herself. She remembered Ella's claim that her grief-filled heart was full of broken glass. She had begun to realize, only now, since she was engaged to marry David in the spring, the forever-nature of Ella's love for Connor. Ella's story made Inez see all the weary love of struggling women in her city. Her newly tender heart broke for those who had to feed and clothe children they could not afford. And for the few, brave women who let Inez render portraits depicting the beatings they endured at the hands of their employers, or worse, their husbands, she vowed to help them in some way.

And it always came back to Ella.

She pondered the unnecessary loss of Ella's life, her selfless dive to save the last baby in her care. The day after Ella's body was recovered and the story of the confrontation on the bridge was reported in the press, a tugboat captain spotted the burlap bag where it had gotten hung up on some dock pilings. He managed to snag it with a gaffing hook. Instead of recovering the body of a drowned infant, he discovered the sack held a tomcat.

Lettie had won her final bluff with Ella.

Inez, broken by this news, cried in front of David for the first time. David pointed out that if Inez had not been at the bridge it would have been said that Ella lost her mind and decided to end her own life. There would have been no live witness to Lettie's murder confession of the River Baby.

The same morning the captain opened the burlap sack, Beata and the baby were found safe, hiding in the same cellar where she had exiled her husband. Despite her age and mounting aches and pains, she was determined to raise the baby she'd named Bartek, in honor of Ella's work and life.

As for Inez, she relaxed into her feelings about her different ways and started to see these distinctions as gifts, finally fully appreciating both the intellect and body she was given and able to use. The work at crime scenes, her upcoming marriage, all of it seemed full of coiled power, as old as the Greeks she revered. It was an unnamed promise deep within her, something she began to touch and taste.

Inez revisited the scene on the bridge over and over in her mind. As the winter nights settled in and sleep eluded her, she drew Ella's portrait. Sometimes Ella was holding babies, like the Madonna with children playing at her feet. Other nights, Inez advanced Ella's age, crimping lines at the corners of her eyes, threading gray streaks through her red hair, so that at least on the page, she had experienced the life she deserved. Every time she captured Ella's image in a way that seemed true, she fed the page into the fire and watched the edges smoke and curl.

Acknowledgments

Thanks to Kevin who pushed me to write this novel, and for all the times you said, "Please go write while I make dinner." You were my first reader and I remember how you would shake your head and chuckle even though this manuscript was not comedic. I'm sorry you were not here to see the completion of the first draft but I suspect you had something to do with that despite your death.

I appreciate all my early readers: John, Janet, Ann, Karen, Robin and Wendy. It's always a good idea to hand your new baby to someone who knows how to tenderly support an infant's head.

My deep gratitude to Ian Graham Leask, my cheeky editor at Calumet. You sharpened everything about this novel and wisely informed me that a book with a pus-soaked bandaged hand was not really "beach-read" material. Thanks also to Rick Polad for his eagle-eyed copyediting of my manuscript.

I'm grateful to John Doyle who proposed the book's title, and like a good muse urges me to keep writing.

About the Author

Mary DesJarlais accomplished it all in the Midwest. Born, educated, twice married, twice widowed, she raised two lively daughters, survived a breast cancer siege, and launched a career as a fiction writer with her first novel *Dorie LaValle* in 2011. Calumet Editions of Minneapolis re-released *Dorie LaValle* in 2017 and her second novel, *The Cutter's Widow*, in 2018. Set in Saint Paul in 1916, this second novel is a story of survival, grief and an adoption business gone awry. Mary DesJarlais currently lives in St. Paul, Minnesota.

www.ingramcontent.com/pod-product-compliance
Lightning Source LLC
Chambersburg PA
CBHW031054020726
47495CB00007B/1876